TIME TRIALS: H333

John Allyn

NEWMAN SPRINGS PUBLISHING
320 Broad Street
Red Bank, NJ 07701

First originally published by Newman Springs Publishing 2019

ISBN 978-1-64096-687-1 (Paperback)
ISBN 978-1-64096-688-8 (Digital)

Printed in the United States of America

In Memoriam
Frank H. Lindsey Sr.
Always loved, never forgotten

To my wife
The love of my life
Without her, life would not be possible

To my son
The most intelligent and talented person I know
The son all men would wish for

To my daughter
The loveliest child God ever created
The voice of an angel and a face to match

To my parents
Simply the best

As a joke
God helped me or I'm possessed
I could never have done this by myself

In reality
God gave me a multitude of talents
Fortunately, I had the opportunity and luck
To wise up and use this one

1

"*WHY* AM I HERE?" BRAD Kelly asked, pacing the plush office. "I have too much work to do to sit here all day and wait on a guy who's not showing up. I can't leave the Fieldman story. Someone else may break it first."

His frustration grew at a steady rate, as he had little choice but to continue waiting. Phil, head of the newspaper Kelly worked for, told him that upper management sent word for Kelly to be there until told to leave, if either of them wanted their jobs. It had come down from the head of the corporation that not only owned the newspaper, but a vast number of other interests in the U.S. The parent company, *TNT*, had holdings of close to a billion dollars, which gave Kelly a large expense account with few rules to follow. Kelly had gained a reputation among his peers as a "*get-the-story-guy*" in the few years he had worked as a reporter.

A striking woman in a dark pinstriped suit with a matching short skirt that accented her long, shapely legs entered the room. Her dark hair was pulled back in a small bun, and her blue eyes sparkled from behind a pair of black-framed glasses. Her eyes seemed to flash at his as he stared. It looked like sunlight glinting off a car's windshield, and for that reason, Kelly dismissed the odd sight as glare from her glasses. It was easy to ignore, as awestruck as he was. Kelly could not tear his eyes from her. There was just something special about her that captivated him.

She moved to the desk at the center of the room and pulled a TV remote from one of its drawers. After moving back in front of the desk, she turned on a small wall-mounted set and adjusted the sound to a level audible across the room without being too loud. She turned to Kelly, who had the appearance of a man in shock. She was perfect, in Kelly's opinion; she seemed to draw him to her.

"I was told you might enjoy some entertainment. This should suffice. We apologize for the delay." Her soft, deep, sultry voice seemed to flow through to his soul.

He shook off the blank stare and quickly asked, "When will I be able to see the boss? I have a story that can't wait. I can't wait too long or months of work will be out the window. Could you see if I could come back? Is there anyone else I could see? I need to go! *Now*!" Excitement steadily raced back into his voice.

"The paper stands to lose millions in sales if I don't break this story first," he continued, trying to persuade her.

"The… *boss*," she said sharply, "will see you as soon as possible. Please make yourself comfortable." With that, she left the room.

Kelly was checking his watch for the thousandth time when a newsflash on the television caught his ear. He turned his full attention to it and could not believe what he was seeing.

It was his story. HIS STORY! It was on the news. He was sitting in a room, waiting on some anonymous executive, and *his* ground-breaking story was running on TV. He could do nothing but stare in shock. All the months of crawling through the gutters and putting his life at risk was now for nothing, and he felt certain that if he wasn't under orders to be here, it would be *him* breaking the story.

A shorter, chubby woman in the same dark pinstriped suit entered the room. She was the polar opposite of the other; round face and body with what seemed like massive legs. The only similarity was the suit and the eyes. Oddly enough, she seemed to be pulling him toward her just like the previous woman had, even though she was everything Kelly did not like. Her eyes seemed to twinkle exactly like the other woman's. She moved to the desk, laid a folder down, and opened it.

"This is for you, Mr. Kelly," she said in a high-pitched, nasal voice.

Still numb and growing angry now, he moved over and looked at the papers on the desk. It caught his attention. He grabbed the papers and rapidly soaked up the information.

"This is wrong, all wrong. I followed up on all of this. This is not the way it *was* or *is*. The *real* story is on the TV right now. I can't believe this. I lost this story to sit here and wait for this load of crap. Where is this guy I'm supposed to see? It's time we had a talk. Where *is* he?" Kelly was almost screaming now. "I don't care about this job anymore! Where is this *guy*?"

The woman looked up at him with a stare that sent a chill up his spine. Her eyes seemed to drill directly into his soul, the same way the other woman's had done before, just unpleasant this time.

"I'm sorry to inform you that your appointment has been rescheduled for tomorrow at 10 AM. I am to tell you that your job is forfeit if you fail to comply, whether you care or not. Also, a story has been sent to the paper in your name based on *this* information." She tapped the open folder on the desk. "It will run in tomorrow's *The Echo*." She turned and left the room.

Shocked beyond words, he all but stumbled when he moved. Who was this guy and what kind of nightmare had he stumbled into? His life had just turned upside down and was spinning out of control, and he had no idea why.

He stood looking at the reporter, Ms. Terry Carson, a blonde-haired, blue-eyed beauty, giving juicy details about a corrupt senator as if she was reading from his notes. A totally opposite story would run, in his name, and at this point there was nothing he could do about it.

He left the building.

All cell phones had to be turned off inside the building, so as he left he turned his on, it rang instantly.

"Hello," he answered.

The voice on the other end said only, "The story Ms. Carson ran is incorrect. She will be disgraced before you return here," and hung up.

He stood for a long moment and stared at his phone. There was no name or number on the ID. He could not believe that his world had spun out of control so quickly. Who or what was behind this attack on his whole future? The reporter in him started to come back to life.

He called Phil Jansen, his boss, to see if he could stop the print on his story.

"Been trying to get you, Bub," Jansen answered, without saying hello.

"Been sitting in an office all day waiting on the '*big boss*,'" Kelly replied sarcastically.

"Some kind of story, Kelly," Jansen rubbed.

"It's not *mine*, Phil," Kelly snapped. "Can we cut it from print?"

"Not this time, big boy. This one came straight from the top. Word is that the entire management staff at the national level was put on notice. If this story doesn't run, we all go to the unemployment office in the morning. You either have a friend somewhere *or* you have made a very powerful enemy. I would bet on the last one. What did you *do*? More importantly, *who* did you do it to?"

"The only thing I can figure is the head of the corporation must be in the senator's pocket and is trying to clean up the mess I planned. It must be a cover to limit the damage done to the paper when the full impact of the charges hit home. I can't believe the paper would do this to me after funding the investigation the way they did," Kelly stated.

"Hate to disagree, old friend, but if they were worried about the paper they would just have killed the story. This work of fiction that showed up has to be a shot straight at you. It couldn't be any more different than night and day from what we discussed. You are in it deep," Jansen replied sarcastically.

"You've read it then?" Kelly barked.

"Not all of it. There was a guy from corporate that jumped down my throat for looking. He stayed till print was over, and still has guys down there watching the copies. I'm telling you, this is big."

"It has to be the senator. He's the only one I can think of with the power to pull this off," Kelly added. He found a bench and sat down to talk. Feeling calmer, his thoughts were becoming more rational.

"I don't know if you've been watching or not, but every TV station in the world has picked up on Carson's story. It's the biggest story to hit the wires in years. Sorry they shot you down, pal. Carson is the hottest thing in the media. It's gonna make the rest of her life *real* easy."

Kelly had known Phillip Jansen since they were in high school. They met at a newspaper convention honoring outstanding students. They were instantly friends and stayed in touch over the years. When an opening came up at the paper in San Francisco, Phil offered it to Kelly. He jumped at the opportunity and proved his worth in his short time there.

"It's hot out here, and there's not a lot more I can do. Whoever *our* boss is wants me here. So I guess I'll just finish my career here in a motel room. At least it's a good one," Kelly said, starting to feel a bit depressed.

"He wants you close, so you're easy to find for the firing squad in the morning," Jansen said with a laugh.

"Yeah, thanks a lot, buddy. I hope all your kids are born naked." They hung up, both chuckling.

Kelly was sitting on a bench in a small park-like setting in front of the office building. He had spent most of the day doing nothing. The sun was setting and the humid Houston air had become unbearable. In reality, it hit him like a fast moving truck as he came out the door. It took time for it to soak in with all he had on his mind.

The small area, floored with red brick, a few benches, and freshly trimmed trees seemed out of place. The building was old and only five stories but well-kept. It seemed the property was overly cared for, too well-groomed. Kelly was soaking up all of this when a limo pulled up at the curb a short distance away.

"Mr. Kelly," the driver called, his thick accent showing.

Kelly looked his way.

"The office said you needed a ride to your hotel," he said, as he opened a rear door.

Kelly stood, flapped his arms in frustration, and fell into the seat after the short walk to the car. The air conditioner felt fantastic. It took what seemed like a ton of water out of the air, which made Kelly sweat in buckets, temporarily. The air only felt better after the door was closed. Without a word, the driver drove onto the 610

Loop, then headed east toward downtown. Kelly lost track of his surroundings, then fell deep in thought.

Jolted back to reality by the driver, Kelly exited the limo and was once again blasted by the heat. It was staggering. He hurried into the hotel without looking around, trying to escape the inferno. He went directly to the desk and asked for his messages.

"There were several calls, Mr. Kelly. Here you go." The clerk handed a large stack of message cards across the counter with a practiced smile.

"How do people survive down here in this heat?" Kelly asked, wiping sweat from his brow.

"Oh, it's not hot yet, wait until next month. It'll be *hot* then," came the reply, but the smile this time was a little wider.

Kelly left the desk, not sure if the clerk was joking or not. He had spent most of his life in milder climates, and was still shocked at what he had found. When he had been outside on arrival, it had been night at the airport and early in the morning at the office. The afternoon heat took him by surprise.

After ordering a salad, steak, lobster, and a pitcher of iced tea, Kelly started a long, cool shower in a feeble attempt to wash his troubles away and the memory of the heat. He had told the desk to enter and leave the meal inside the room because he would be occupied. There had been no hint of reluctance to comply with any of his requests since his arrival. He was told that everything had been taken care of and the paper would pick up the tab. Everything was first-class.

After what seemed like a week in the shower, he toweled off, put on the thick robe provided by the hotel, and sat down to eat.

"A fine last meal for the condemned man," he said out loud, only half joking.

The meal was one of the finest he had ever eaten. The steak was cooked to perfection, and the lobster was fresh, large, and full of flavor. His mind was spinning so fast that he lost track of time. The meal was gone before he realized it, but not an ounce of the quality of the flavor was lost.

He sat in silence for a long time, sipping the tea. Suddenly, he noticed that the tea was exquisite. He sipped a bit more, and it seemed that the entire meal made a second impression as one of the best he ever had. A bit more relaxed, he started to dress for bed. Looking in the full-length mirror as he did, he took stock of himself. He was never very pleased with the fate he was handed. He was too plain. Not big, not small, and not very handsome. He was fit, not fat. Hours in the gym and jogging kept him that way. *Not a chance in this heat. Jogging would be inside only around here*, he thought. No matter how hard he tried, he could not put on a lot of muscle, just stay trim.

His hair was brown, and so were his eyes, which made him like most of the world, and even his face was just... plain. He consoled himself by saying that by being just another face in the crowd, it made his life as a reporter easier. He could fade into the background and go unnoticed. It was easier that way. No one took notice of him at all.

Enough of that, he thought. *I've got enough troubles now without worrying about that stuff. I've got to get a handle on this thing before I'm digging ditches for a living.*

He turned on the TV and started watching, wanting to see if he could find out something new.

2

KELLY WOKE UP EARLY THE next morning, laying on the edge of the bed. He had fallen asleep watching various channels, but there was nothing new to be said. Terry Carson's story ran on every channel, making news all around the world, blasting the senator for ties to organized crime and murder. She had proof from fingerprints to DNA, all tied up with tapes and photos. All commentary said that there was no way out for the career politician. She had it all sewn up, an airtight case. His support had already started to crumble, despite his steadfast claim of innocence.

There was a knock at the door. He wiped the cobwebs from his mind and answered it. It was room service with breakfast and a newspaper. Still too sleepy to refuse and grasp the fact that he had not ordered anything, he graciously accepted the hospitality. The attendant left with hardly a word, and Kelly moved the cart to his spot on the bed. Starting with toast, he nibbled away at two buttered slices and read the paper. It was the paper he worked for. The one with his supposed article. After reading it he could not believe it. It was good. In fact, it was great. It was all garbage, but it was a great article. He wished it was true and that he had written it.

The TV stations started to pick up on the article after a while and were having a field day with it. It was almost a bigger story than the first, but this was a direct attack on Kelly. Even Terry Carson had a spot laughing at her friend and colleague. The most common comment was, "How could anyone write something so far from the truth?"

Resigned to his fate, he finished breakfast and started to get ready for his meeting. He had to have a paycheck, and after this unexplained disaster it looked like this was the only place he was going to get one. He turned off the news and sat in silence, once more running over every fact about the story he could think of. Not expecting to be here this long, he did not bring any notes, just his two laptops. The first one wasn't Internet-capable, so this was the one he put all of his important information on. Even then, he was afraid of hackers, so he only put enough information on it to jog his memory in case his notes disappeared. He turned the computer on and after a considerable amount of scrutiny, decided that no one had accessed his files. The other computer was for correspondence. He flipped it open and connected to the hotel's network. A quick check of his e-mail showed over 300 new messages about the story. He just sighed and closed the computer. They could wait.

This trip was supposed to be a quick visit and then back to Frisco to finish up the story for release. It was still a mystery how all of his detailed information, notes, and files had fallen into Ms. Carson's hands. It was not likely that she could have found all the same people to question or happen upon so many of the facts. It was apparent that he had been betrayed. Someone had sold him out and given all his work to the competition or sold it, most likely. It still made no sense that after his dogged pursuit of the story, his would be the only voice that supported his conclusions. Not even Phil was backing him up.

The same limo driver showed up at the door, but today he seemed huge. There was no doubt that it was the same man and that he was a body builder. His uniform looked a size too small, and he bulged out everywhere. His voice was deep and clear. The accent was the only thing that seemed the same.

"Ready, Mr. Kelly?" he asked.

"As I'll ever be. What can you tell me about our boss?" Kelly returned.

"He pays well, and all I have to do is mostly drive, maybe some security when he calls me. It leaves me plenty of time for other things and money to do pretty much what I want. Can't ask for much more than that," the giant said with a smile.

"Do you know anything about him?" Kelly asked.

"Nothing. I was hired by the office we're headed to by the babe in the pinstriped suit, and for what they pay I don't ask questions. Before you ask, no, I don't have to do anything illegal or even questionable. If it were like that, I never would have taken the job. They have been good to me and I would get into trouble for them if I thought it was the right thing to do."

There was very little conversation on the way to the car. The massive driver cleared the way of all awestruck passersby quickly leading Kelly to the lobby. They stepped out onto the sidewalk on Louisiana Street and into the morning heat. It was not as intense as the evening before. It felt more like stepping into a sauna instead of a forge. Kelly stopped for a second and looked around. There was not much to see, just a long row of buildings with a lot of one-way traffic. Unimpressed, he entered the open door into the welcome coolness of the air-conditioned back seat.

The trip was a little longer this time. There was construction on I-45 downtown and the backup was pretty bad. It added about twenty minutes. Finally, they made it to the speed limit and shortly thereafter, arrived at the office on the loop.

Not waiting for the car to stop, Kelly said thanks to the driver and bolted out the door to the large double doors at the entrance to the building. As he entered, a couple of people rushed to meet him.

"Mr. Kelly, we would like a statement about your story in this morning's *The Echo*," a balding man in a bad blue suit said, sticking a mike in his face.

Kelly stopped and looked around. The other reporter was a short, plump older lady with graying hair. Both looked at him with intensity, waiting for any word.

"No comment. Excuse me," was all he could think of after a long pause. It was the first time he had been put on the spot like that, and he probably would not have said anything, even if he had had anything to say. He had nothing. He was kind of lost. Still. He rushed to the elevator while the two reporters remained there looking stunned.

He reached the top floor and stepped out cautiously, afraid of more people waiting for him.

"So that's what it feels like," he said out loud, thinking about all the times he had been on the other side of the story. "Must have talked to Jackson when they called the paper. He never has the sense to lie about where anybody is. Just glad everybody doesn't know. Yet."

The chubby woman in the pinstriped suit opened a door into the hall and motioned Kelly to come in her direction. It was in the opposite direction from the office he was in the day before.

"My name is Sophia. Please come this way," she said, and shuffled her way into the outer office. It was almost empty. No personal touches or extras, a desk and that was all.

"Please wait here," Sophia said, and entered the door to the inner office.

Kelly looked around the room, and there was nothing but the bare essentials. It was odd, like it was never used. A store display of what to have to start your office, and nothing more.

Before he could finish his inspection, the door reopened, and Sophia invited him through the door with a wave. He entered without a word. Inside was worse than the outer office. There was a smoked glass wall to the rear of the room with a sliding door. In front of the door was a cheap metal desk with a simulated wood top. On the desk was a small speaker. There wasn't even a chair at the desk. In either corner there was a grassy, weedy artificial plant, and that was all. There were no personal effects, no pictures, nothing, not even any supplies. He was becoming concerned. It was just too odd.

Sophia switched on the speaker and left the room. Kelly stood a bit on edge as he watched her leave.

The voice from the speaker was spooky. It seemed to echo several times before the words formed, and sounded like it came from the bottom of a well.

"G-G-Good morning, Mr. Kelly," the voice shattered the silence.

"Hello," Kelly choked out.

"I-I-I suppose you would like a few answers. Given the events of the last few days, I can't really blame you," came another haunting statement.

"Who are you, and what's the deal with your voice? Where are you? Why use the speaker?" Kelly shot out, trying to look through the glass partition.

"Y-Y-You will find that the story in *The Echo* is indeed the truth. It will bring you all the fame and employment offers you have ever dreamed of. The story is breaking as we speak. You will even win a Pulitzer," the disembodied voice replied, without regard to the questions.

"That load of *bull* couldn't be true even in somebody's wildest dream. What's going on here?" Kelly's frustration started to boil into anger. He grabbed the handle on the glass door and yanked at it. It seemed to sting him. It was like a slow lingering static shock from the carpet on a cool day.

A massive hand grabbed his arm and pulled it away from the handle. He looked up to see the bodybuilding driver at the other end of his arm. His face was grim, and even the muscles in his face bulged as he moved Kelly back. His massive blue eyes almost seemed to glow in the low light.

"Where did you come from? You weren't in here a second ago!" Kelly screeched.

"C-C-Carl! Do not hurt him. It is all right," the speaker blared.

The vise-like grip loosened, and Carl took a few steps back, still on the alert.

"I want answers now," Kelly shouted at the glass. "Tell me what's going on, or I'm out of here! I have had enough of this crap! Who are you and what... is... going... on?" He shot a glance at Carl, but did not seem to be concerned anymore. He turned and started for the door to the outer office. A TV came on as he did and it caught his attention. He had missed it earlier.

"This is a special report," the reporter started. "There is break-ing news regarding the Senator Wallace Fieldman story."

Kelly froze in his tracks.

"This story first broke in the San Francisco *The Echo* and has led to an arrest that has cleared the senator."

Kelly's jaw fell open.

"The senator has a twin brother, Mark Jamison, who was taken at birth and sold to a family in Washington State. The adopted parents were killed in a suspicious accident when the twins were only ten years old. He inherited a large sum of money, and grew up in the care of his adopted father's brother who reportedly did not care for the boy at all. While spending most of the inheritance and even selling off other assets, the uncle, John Palmer, introduced Mark to a life of crime.

"At some point, the pair realized that the resemblance between Mark and the senator was more than coincidence, and set out to use this to their advantage. For several years now, they have watched and mimicked the senator's movements and even his appearance. Using threats of government retaliation for revealing any information about the illegal transactions, they were successful and made millions. They may never have been caught if the story had not been broken in the news."

"Can't be," Kelly muttered. "I've got the fingerprints to prove it."

He had hope that he could still pull his real story out of the fire. Almost as if the TV was listening to him, the young woman continued, "The story broken by this station's own Terry Carson has now been proven false. Claims of the senator's involvement have been shown to be impossible. While she was very thorough with her investigation, and even had DNA and fingerprint information gathered, there was no consideration for a twin being involved. A report sent to the FBI by a newspaper reporter from the San Francisco *The Echo*, Brad Kelly, confirms a match to the DNA. The FBI also reports that fingerprints on the right hands of both men appear to match, until more stringent tests are used. With the standard check by most law enforcement, they would come back as a match. According to FBI spokesman, this is a first and could change their test procedure.

"The entire scope of the charges and criminal activity could take years to completely uncover. On the surface it seems to be extensive, and is estimated to be in the millions, possibly even a billion dollars.

"Mr. Kelly could not be reached for comment. *The Echo* said he was on assignment, but the senator has sent a message of thanks to him."

The station cut to a film clip of the senator. "I don't know Mr. Kelly, but he has the heartfelt thanks of the senate, my friends and family, and of course myself. If there is anything I can do for you, do not hesitate to ask. This investigation and subsequent report has taken a toll on my family and myself. It is a great relief to us all to finally have the proof of my innocence. Thank you, Mr. Kelly, wherever you are, and thanks, *The Echo* and their staff."

The senator was visibly shaken and haggard from the ordeal. It had indeed taken a toll on him and his family. There had been calls for his removal from the senate, and warrants were in the process of being filed, until the story in *The Echo* broke. The FBI stepped in and quickly made arrests on the information in the report that was sent to them. There would be a landslide of arrests and convictions, and the courts and jails would soon be brimming with new business. There was a special effort, for publicity's sake, to make public the arrests of Mark and his uncle. They were dragged out of their million-dollar homes in the middle of the night with plenty of fanfare. The cameras paid special attention to the lavish surroundings and the large number of almost nude women in both houses.

The anchor on the TV continued after the clip.

"The sales of *The Echo* have reached incredible levels. The editor has said that they will be running twenty-four hours a day until they fill orders that are coming in worldwide. Now back to your local programming already in progress."

The TV went blank, then off. Kelly just stood there, staring at the black screen and blinking his eyes, his mouth hanging open.

"M-M-Mr. Kelly. Mr. Kelly." the voice came from the speaker with the same spooky effect. Kelly did not respond. He had spent more than a year of his life putting together a story that someone had broken ahead of him, then the company he worked for had released a story in his name that was the exact opposite of his own. The senator, who he was so determined to put behind bars, now seemed to be in his debt. He had the credit he wanted. The only problem was that his story was all wrong and he had not written a word of the story that was the truth. After the events of the last few days, and now this on top of it, he felt as if he was going to pass out.

"M-M-Mr. Kelly," came the disembodied voice once more.

Kelly did not move. He was still frozen looking at the blank TV screen.

"C...-C-C-Carl," the voice prompted.

Carl moved his huge frame closer to Kelly and grabbed his arm just above the elbow. The vice-like grip jarred Kelly back to life. He turned to the desk and stammered out a question.

"Who wrote *that*?" he asked quietly.

"M-M-Mr. Kelly. I know that you are tenacious in aspects of reporting, but how open are you to abnormal abstract concepts?" was the only response.

Kelly squirmed in his clothes, as if flexing his whole body, and seemed to gain some composure.

"I'm as open as the next guy, I guess. Look, in the last twenty-four hours I feel like I've jumped into another dimension or something. Nothing makes sense anymore, and you, whoever you are, didn't answer my question. Who wrote that story? 'Cause it *really* sounds like my work."

"O-O-Odd that you should make a reference to dimensions. To answer your question, you did... in another dimension, if you like."

"Now that's just *nuts*. Do you really think that you can sell me that? After all, I was just joking before. You can't possibly think I was serious," Kelly shot back, his frustration showing in his voice.

"You should be. It is possible. I can see into other realities, and I would like your help. I think it is possible for you to visit some of them."

"*My help*," Kelly interrupted. "Me... visit?"

"Y-Y-Yes. I must move to my new facility, and I must have your help to do it. I have searched for years to find a proper DNA match. You are the closest so far."

"Count me out. I don't need a ticket to the funny farm. The help you need, you'll find it there. Job or not, see you later." Kelly turned to leave.

"Before you leave I will ask you to reconsider, and offer you this. You are a reporter and I have the story of a lifetime. I offer it freely and will give you total credit should you decide to publish it. There are a few conditions, but no restrictions. We can begin as soon as you are ready, if you decide to accept the offer."

Kelly had turned slightly, showing at least some interest, but did not seem to accept.

"M-M-Mr. Kelly, think of the flash you saw in Sophia's eyes. Try to remember all the times that you have noticed it before."

"I'm outta here." Kelly threw over his shoulder.

"You… *will*… see it again."

Kelly left the room and then the building. The limo was waiting at the curb, the door open, with the driver waiting patiently. They arrived at the hotel in what seemed like seconds. Kelly said thanks as they rolled up to the curb, and almost jumped out onto the sidewalk. At a walk just below a trot, he quickly made his way to the elevator, planning to gather his few belongings and go back home.

He exited the elevator at the proper floor and ran into a maid making her rounds, knocking both of them down. As they struggled to free themselves from each other, Kelly started apologizing.

"I'm sorry. I'm *so* sorry," he said, trying to get to his feet.

The maid made it to her feet too, looking down at her clothes and trying to straighten them. When she looked up, Kelly stepped back, startled. Her eyes twinkled at him.

"I'm sorry, sir. Are you all right?" she asked, as if her job was in jeopardy.

"I'm fine. Are you okay?"

"Yes, sir. I was just startled," she returned.

"I'll be on my way if you're sure that you're not hurt," he said, still a bit wary.

The small woman just nodded her head, looked down at herself, and then backed up. As she did, her eyes flashed again, and Kelly shot down the hallway toward his room. Once inside, he closed the door and leaned against it, as if trying to hold out an unseen intruder. He felt almost in a panic.

"I must have been drugged or something, *but how?*" he said, breathing heavily.

He wiped the sweat from his forehead and took in a long deep breath. Letting it out slowly, he crossed the deep plush carpet to the bed, falling on it as if wounded. Turning over, looking at the ceiling, the room started to spin.

I was drugged, he thought.

Somehow, in the midst of his panic, he fell into a deep sleep.

3

"WHAT HAPPENED?" KELLY STUMBLED OUT. "How long have I been out, and what did they give me? Oh, my head hurts." He tried to roll over but stopped because of the pain.

"You have been out for eighteen hours, Mr. Kelly. I found no trace of any drugs in your system. The pain will soon pass. You're not the first case I have treated with these exact symptoms. It is quite strange," the tall, frail man said. He continued to examine Kelly, peering through a pair of large glasses. He was an older man with a proper haircut, graying at the temples.

"*Symptoms? What symptoms?* All I did was pass out on my bed back at the—" As he looked around, he realized that he was still in the same room. He had thought that he was in a hospital, understandably.

"What am I still doing *here*? I thought I was—" Kelly said, still groggy.

The doctor interrupted, "I am on staff here at the hotel. I recognized the symptoms, saw where you had been, and knew the proper treatment. Hydrate and monitor. As a precaution, I sent out blood samples for analysis. As I suspected, everything was fine. You should recover rapidly. You will be up and about in a bit, and free to be on your way."

"Now that you mention it, I feel better already, just tired still," Kelly said as he sat up on the bed.

"Yes, typical. You'll be right as rain in half an hour. But—"

"Wait a minute, don't I know you? Yeah, you're Doc Taylor. We used to see you when I was a kid."

"Yes, Mr. Kelly. My dad and I saw your whole family for some time. I can see the resemblance to your father," Dr. Taylor replied.

"So what happened to me? You said you knew what it was," Kelly asked.

"You were exposed to some form of radiation. We could never find an exact cause or type. We do know that it has no lasting effects. Every once and a while, someone who visits that building ends up like you. I have treated four cases myself and consulted on several more. The first one I found we rushed to the hospital and ran every conceivable test. Besides the trace readings of residual energy, there was nothing. What kind of energy, we haven't figured out yet, but it's not so strange that it would cause us undue concern. After all the panic and tests, the patient just sat up in bed and said she wanted to leave. We ran everything again and there was nothing, so we let her go. I have monitored her health through her doctor, a friend of mine, and she has no ill effects so far." He paused to rub his chin and continued. "You couldn't tell me what goes on up there, could you?"

"Well, if there was anything to tell, I would, but all I did was talk to the owner of the company on a poor quality speaker box. I think the guy is *nuts* or something. He started talking about other planes of existence and stuff like that. I left. Things have been too weird for the last couple of days for me to sit and listen to that kinda stuff. He wanted to send me on some story hunt. I'm a reporter. Sounded like a load of bunk to me. I got out, came back here, and passed out. That's it. No energy or radiation that I could see or feel. The carpet gave me a real pop when I touched the door, but other than that, just a madman rattling on," Kelly reported.

"That is close to what the others said as well. There are fifteen to twenty people who work at that building every day. None have had this problem that I am aware of. There are visitors periodically, and only a select few are affected. I've been keeping track on my own time, when I can. I tried to get in there and was denied admittance. I find it... *perplexing*, but not worth reporting to the authorities. Besides, it's really nothing more than a bad hangover of sorts. Can't report what you can't prove," the doctor stated.

"Yeah, well, you don't have to worry about me coming back. I may have to go to work *flippin' burgers*, but I'm done with this outfit. I'll be going back home as soon as you will release me," Kelly said, as he got up and started moving around.

I tried to tell you before, it's about 3:00 AM, Brad. If you can sleep, it would be best, and you can leave in a few hours. I gave you a mild sedative in the IV that you had earlier, so travel is ill-advised. I know it sounds backward, giving a sedative to someone who is unconscious, but that particular drug helps with the symptoms. I'll leave you alone now, but I stay here in the hotel when I'm on call. Just call the desk if you have any problems. I'll be back by in a few hours to check on you. I have a master key and will use it with your permission."

"I do feel a little tired, and use the key if you want. I would rather be safe than sorry," Kelly replied with a smile.

"See you in the morning, then." Taylor returned the smile and disappeared out the door.

Kelly walked to the large window in his room and looked out at the Houston skyline. It was impressive, but small in comparison to Los Angeles or New York.

Sleep, he thought. *I've been out for nearly eighteen hours. Why would I want to* sleep?

With that, he returned to the bed and soon found himself nodding off, falling into a half-asleep, half-awake state. It was like watching a TV in his mind. He was looking at the world at the height of a child. He was in a hospital, wandering down the hall. Going somewhere. He walked up to two white coats and looked up. It was Dr. Taylor and his dad. The older looked like the man who had just left and the other was a young man.

The elder bent down and said, "There you are, Brad. Are you all right? You can see your mom now. She will be just fine," then stood back up. Both the men looked down at the boy and their eyes *flashed*. Kelly was instantly awake.

4

HE LOOKED AT THE CLOCK. It was 8:00 AM. He quickly gathered his belongings and fled the room. He stopped for only a second to make sure the company was picking up the tab, and all but ran out the door. The limo was sitting at the exit. He turned up the street to get away from it, and what it meant. He looked for a cab but saw none.

In his haste, he bumped into an elderly woman, and as he turned to apologize, her eyes lit up like the others he had seen. In shock now, he turned to get away and almost ran into a mountain of a man. He looked up, and the giant's eyes flashed as well. He stepped away, looking insanely at the man, not saying anything. He began to notice that all the people on the crowded street had started to stare at him, and as his eyes moved from one to the other, most flashed at him.

He fell to the sidewalk. The world started to swirl around him. It was like being very drunk. Then everything started to become exaggerated as a crowd gathered to see what was wrong. Their eyes started to glow and the light consumed their eyes, and then their faces. Their heads soon became glowing balls of light. Kelly heard a voice, and everything snapped back to normal. He could feel the heat of the concrete on his backside as he sat on the sidewalk. He looked for the voice. It was Carl.

"Mr. Kelly, would you like a ride to the airport?" the mound of muscles asked in his deep voice.

"Yes… I would," Kelly returned quietly.

Carl offered a massive hand, and Kelly took it. He flew to his feet as Carl misjudged his pull. They recovered and quickly moved to the waiting limo.

"You work there. Have you ever had anything like that happen to you?" Kelly blurted out as the limo started away, as if expecting Carl to know what he was talking about.

Carl sat in the rear seat on the left behind the driver. He looked Kelly up and down and stared directly in his eyes for a long moment. He leaned forward and told the driver to take him to the office.

"I cannot be sure what it is you are talking about, Mr. Kelly. I am too far from a match to be affected. If you are still having residual effects from such limited exposure, then you are who we have been looking for. It is important to a lot of people that you take the job you have been offered. I dare say that I would jump at the opportunity if I were able. From what I am told, it would be an incredible journey."

"I don't want a *journey*," Kelly barked. "None of this makes sense. I just want to leave and go back to being *just* a reporter!"

"It is your choice," Carl said calmly. "It will take a few years to find someone else."

"Now wait a minute. What is all this '*I'm the one*' crap? What is all this?"

"It would be to your advantage to find out. All you have to lose is a bit of attitude and some time. We will be back at the office shortly. Talk less and listen more. Calm down and *listen*. I think you will like what you hear if you give it a chance," Carl said and fell silent.

Kelly looked long and hard at the man in the seat beside him. He seemed to give off a radiance of friendship and trust. Kelly calmed down and started to think like a reporter again. He decided that he liked Carl. Granted that he was twice his size and looked to be able to rip him limb from limb, that's not what he saw when he looked at Carl. After some careful thought, he had decided to hear out the *nut job* that was his boss. Besides, like *Godzilla* Carl had said, what did he have to lose? It could turn into an exposé about a rich and powerful man's insanity.

When the limo pulled up to the front of the office, both men in the rear seat exited. Carl was all smiles.

The atmosphere was relaxed as Kelly became more comfortable with his choice. He told himself that it could be, like the boss had said, the story of a lifetime, just not the story the voice had referred to.

"So you think this could be a good deal, do you?" Kelly asked Carl as they entered the building.

"I think it would be as exciting as life could get. My DNA does not meet the requirements. If it did, you would not be here," Carl replied.

"So how did you land this job?"

"My family was assisted, helped to survive. I was offered a job after the fact and took it gladly. With the money I make here, my parents and I live quite well. My brothers work for the company and both have good jobs. We are fortunate. I am thankful and feel lucky to have what I have."

"That's a bit vague," Kelly stated.

Carl just looked sternly at Kelly and offered nothing more.

"Have you met the boss? By the way, who is he, and what is his name?" Kelly asked.

"No, I haven't met him, at least face to face. As far as his name, he likes to introduce himself," Carl said as they entered the elevator.

Neither spoke during the short five-story ride up. The building was old, and the smell of hydraulic oil was strong in the elevator. The thought crossed Kelly's mind about failure, but was not really a concern.

They walked into the outer office and then to the inner one.

"We will wait until we are called," Carl said, and then he sat down.

Kelly stood for a short while, then started to pace, slowly slinging his arms in long arches back and forth and clapping in the front, almost goose-stepping as he went. The speaker finally crackled.

"I... I... I am glad you have returned, Mr. Kelly. I hope that this time, things will turn out better for both of us." The voice still had its strange distortion.

"I don't really know why I'm here. What was the deal with the radiation or whatever it was?" Kelly asked.

"An... an... an unfortunate side effect. It will not be as severe this time. I will not have to increase the power level as high. You must understand that if you do not meet with me, you will have to sleep off the effect again," the box said.

Carl sprang to his feet. "He will actually be able to meet you, in *person*?"

"Y-y-yes, Carl. If everything works as planned, Mr. Kelly will be able to interact with me in person."

"This is getting weird again. Are you here in the building?" Kelly asked.

"D-d-do you want to be a part of this project or not, Mr. Kelly? You must make up your mind... *now*. I must move and there is little time. You will have to commit yourself to keep my secrets and agree to hold any story for at least a short period of time. I will have to recover from the move before I can do any damage control."

Kelly thought for a second, running possibilities through his mind. It was intriguing and puzzling. He was almost excited, on the hunt, and what did he have to lose. It was like Carl said, what was a little time. There was always the exposé.

"Yeah. I'll agree to whatever you want. What's the worst that could happen? I could end up looking like Carl," Kelly said with a chuckle.

Carl did not seem amused.

"If you are certain, we will proceed."

There was a long silence.

"Carl, please escort Mr. Kelly into my office."

Carl moved to the wall and slid back a panel, then opened a door that led into another office. It was barren. There was no furniture, no decorations, nothing. The room was cavernous. It took up the rest of the building's floor. The ceiling must have been twelve feet high. They stepped around the corner and out of the nook that led to the rest of the room, and Kelly jumped back as he saw what filled the space.

Kelly was half-frightened and half-amazed. There was another set of doors just outside of this office. It seemed to be filled with a boiling mass of smoke. The smoke was a swirling mixture of colors, from black to white. It looked like a storm cloud trapped inside the room. There were small bright flashes of blue light occurring randomly across the surface. It was a staggering sight beyond explanation.

Kelly looked at Carl with fear in his eyes and a huge smile on his face.

"I can go no closer without being affected. You may approach the vortex, but do not touch it. It will hurt you. Prolonged contact will kill you," Carl said.

Kelly looked hard at Carl, taking in what he had said. He looked at the cloud, and then back at Carl, who motioned him on. Carl pulled a chair from the other room and sat down, with his chest to the back of the chair and his arms resting on top. He gave one more wave to urge Kelly on.

"Come closer, Mr. Kelly. I have a device that will allow you to remain in the room without too many ill effects." The voice had become louder and lost its echoing effect.

Filled with curiosity, tainted with fear, Kelly slowly walked the short distance to the first set of doors. He had not noticed that there were two sets at first.

"You will have to pass through the foyer. The device is inside, to the right, on a shelf," the disembodied voice boomed.

Kelly felt the same static tingle as he had before when he touched the long U-shaped door handle with his right hand. He stopped for a second to reassure himself, and then entered quickly. It was a small entryway to the other doors. A small box of glass was all it was. It seemed odd that there was glass on the ceiling and tile on the floor. It was a drastic change from the deep carpet in the rest of the offices. He passed through into the next room, feeling a larger jolt from the door handle this time.

Inside, for some reason, he expected noise, probably from all the motion of the cloud, but it seemed to be beyond quiet. The edge of the cloud receded as he entered, but stayed within a few feet of him. There was only the feeling of a slight breeze and a sensation of static electricity dancing across his body. As he looked down, there were small blue streaks of energy passing over his clothes. He reached out and put his hand close to the vapor. It shot out small charges of what looked like lightning bolts to his palm. He turned, looked toward Carl, and smiled. As he did, he let his arm fall into the vortex unintentionally. He turned immediately from the pain. He pulled his arm back and watched it wither to a dried stalk of flesh wrapped around bones. He screamed, passed out, and fell stiffly on his back.

The spinning clouds gathered into the shape of a tornado, extending from the side of the torrent, then the large end pounced on Kelly, covering him completely. It stayed only for a few seconds, then lifted slowly back into its original shape. It seemed to be disturbed for a time, swirling out of control. Slowly it calmed down to resume its former look.

Kelly sprang to his feet, looking at his arm. It was back to *normal!* He moved his arm and shoulder and flexed his hand. He backed to the wall as if something was chasing him, without taking his eyes from the cloud. The jolt of contact with the wall made him look at the apparition in front of him, then to Carl.

"I felt that it was necessary to show you that what Carl said was true. We must proceed. On the shelf to your right, there is a headset. If you do not put it on soon, you will pass out from contact with me," the voice stated even louder.

Kelly squinted his eyes and looked at the cloud, stunned.

"You are this *thing*?" Kelly shouted.

"Put on the headset, Mr. Kelly, or we will not be able to continue."

Kelly started to feel woozy. He stumbled to the shelf and picked up what looked like a set of small headphones. They had a metal band extending from the foam speakers to make a circle, and another making a half circle perpendicular from the full circle. It was easy to see that it was meant to be like a hat, with the speakers resting on the temples. Kelly slipped it onto his head. There was a prick of pain on both sides of his head, and the sick feeling was gone instantly.

"It will take a few moments for it to reach full power, so I will start to explain if you are ready," the voice said, becoming clearer.

"Okay… I'll repeat the question. This is *you*?" Kelly asked, feeling better now.

"Yes, at least a part of me."

Kelly shook his head and looked at the floor.

"What have I stuck my foot in now? Okay, so what happened to me just now?"

"You came in contact with an energy field that a device in my possession generates. The headset that you have on protects you from the effects it causes. I had to increase power when we were talking the other day, and you suffered the consequences. Oh, and by the way, it took five tries to get the headset in the proper configuration for you to put it on correctly. You kept trying to put the generators on your ears."

Kelly lifted his arm and twiddled his fingers in front of his face.

"So how did you fix this?" Kelly asked with a bit of irritation in his voice.

"I reached out and absorbed the energy back into the field."

"If this energy is so destructive, how do you survive it? And what do you mean it took five times to get it right? I've never been in here before."

"The field is a part of me. It cannot harm me because I generate it myself."

Kelly suddenly realized that the voice was much clearer. It also seemed that all his senses were more acute. He could see cracks in the wall from across the room. It felt invigorating. He moved closer to the swirling mass and ran his finger along the outside edge. Once again a small lightning bolt came out, touched his finger, and played in the air between the two.

To Kelly's surprise, a woman appeared in front of him. She was lovely and looked as if she was underwater. She stared straight into Kelly's eyes for a second, smiled, then seemed to flake away into small pieces flowing to Kelly's left. Shortly, she was gone.

"What was *that*?" Kelly reeled back from the sight.

"It was a bleed over from another time stream. It will not be long before you will be able to enter the vortex, and we will be able to talk face to face."

"I'm not so sure I want to do this. This is a bit far out in left field for me. For all I know, you could be looking for lunch! What do you need me for? I just don't understand."

"You are feeling a temporary effect of the adaptation device. In order for someone to enter the vortex, they must have a certain DNA signature. I need an assistant, for lack of a better word. I have to move to another location soon. I need more power to survive. They will soon find me, and I cannot let that happen. I need you to enter and interact with me for a short period of time. This will allow me to power down if there are no complications. With the help of Carl and yourself, we will be able to move to the new facility, and it will take years for them to locate us."

"Still a little cryptic here. Who are they? What is all this about? And what is this thing?" Kelly demanded.

"I assure you, Mr. Kelly, you will not be harmed and may leave if you like, but if you want to know what this is all about, walk into the vortex when you are ready."

It took only a second. Kelly was convinced that he was onto something and was tired of the evasive way his questions were answered. He walked closer, reached out his arm, and touched the cloud. I did not seem to affect him. He paused, closed his eyes, and stepped forward. Nothing happened. He opened his eyes and seemed to be in a fog bank. It changed in density from what it looked like from the outside. He walked for what seemed a hundred yards, which was impossible. The room wasn't half that long. All at once, he stepped out into a garden. He could hear the twigs snapping underfoot. The air seemed to smell sweet, like the room was full of flowers. He looked around him again, and it looked like he was in a forest, an endless forest. He reached out and pulled a leaf from a small oak tree and tore it in two. It was real. It smelled real and felt real too. He was beginning to feel that *in-over-his-head* feeling again.

Kelly heard a voice calling him. It was the same voice he had been talking to through the speakerphone, but he could not find where it was coming from.

A man stepped from out of the brush a few yards down from where Kelly was standing. He was tall, and as he approached it became clear that he was impossibly tall. Kelly stood looking up at someone whose height reached at least ten feet. Kelly could not take it all in.

"I'm sorry. Let me adjust myself," the giant *boomed*.

The oversized man shrank down to a normal height, about five foot eleven. He was thin, pale, and wearing a white lab coat. He was a poster child for a geek. He adjusted his pocket protector and reached out his hand.

"Hello, Mr. Kelly, my name is Terrance Newton Tupnic. I'm glad to finally meet you in person."

There was a pause as Kelly slowly shook Tupnic's hand. While he grasped it, he examined it as if to see if it were real.

"TNT. That's why TNT, the parent corporation to the newspaper. I looked into the background of the company a little. Records were sketchy. Seems like a group of young people from Texas started some rather basic companies that turned a profit. From there the company grew exponentially. The identities of the original six members were easy to establish, but details were vague. Facts were impossible to verify. The more successful the company became the less personal information became available. Everyone just seemed to almost disappear. Is this what happened?"

"Care to sit down?" Tupnic asked.

A pair of chairs was suddenly there. Kelly reacted slowly. He was starting to believe that he was drugged again.

"I think I would rather stand, if you don't mind, and I would like the whole story. Now, if you don't mind."

"Fair enough. Are you happy with the surroundings? I could change them." Suddenly they were on a beach. The waves were gently lapping at the shore and the sun was warm on Kelly's face. He freaked out. He ran a few steps away from Tupnic, then turned to look back at him.

"Tell me now, or I'm going to leave!" Kelly reached up to pull the headset off of his head.

"Do not remove it here or the energy field will kill you. You must exit first."

Their surroundings changed back to the forest. The birds singing and the rustle of the wind in the trees replaced the sound of the surf.

"I am sorry. I have thrown too much at you at one time. I do not think that I would be in as good shape as you given the circumstances. If you are still willing, I will explain everything and answer all your questions. If not, I will show you the way out," Tupnic said.

Kelly stood still, almost frozen. He was beginning to believe that he had been drugged again or was still caught in the same nightmare. Finally, he let out a long breath and looked at the grass under his feet.

"This is still *unbelievable*. How is it that you can do this to me?" Kelly asked meekly.

"Then you will stay?" Tupnic replied.

Kelly looked up and said, "Yes, but start telling me now."

"Good."

They were instantly standing in what seemed to be a room in an English castle. The ceiling looked twenty feet high, and was made of stone, as were the walls. It was dark in the room. The only light was a huge roaring fire in the fireplace. There were two oversized, high-backed chairs in front of it, with a small table separating the pair. The chairs were angled together in the front, which made them ideal for casual conversation. The firelight gave the chairs an orange glow on their brown leather surface, and strange shadows danced over the entire room, in time with the flickering flames.

"Have a seat, Mr. Kelly. Would you like something to eat or drink? Is this room suitable? It is from a book you read at some point," Tupnic said, motioning toward the chairs.

"No, I'm fine. Let's get to this," Kelly shot back, taking a seat in the chair on the left. Tupnic took the other chair.

"As to how I can do this to you, I believe that was the question," Tupnic stated.

Kelly nodded.

"We are inside a field that I generate using a device that I have. When inside this field, I can manipulate the environment as you have seen. It is not as large as it seems, but because it is under my control, I can make it seem as I wish. As large or as small even hot or cold. You are able to survive the energy it generates because of the headset."

"You are in control of this? You actually do this yourself?" Kelly asked.

"Yes. The device that I have allows me to do so," Tupnic returned.

"Is it hypnosis, or is this real?"

"While inside this field, everything is as real as in the outside world. If you were to put your hand into the fire, it would burn, hurt, and still be there when you left the field, unless I intervene. I have personally experienced its effect," Tupnic said.

"What kind of device do you have that can do all this?" Kelly asked.

"If you will allow me, I will start at the beginning and tell the complete story."

Kelly nodded again.

5

"I WAS A PRODIGY AS a child. I finished high school at fourteen and went on to college. I graduated in a little over two years with a degree in physics. From there I landed a job with the government doing research. One thing led to another, and I ended up at a government lab called ARGO. No one would say, but the joke that we told was that it stood for Alien Research Government Organization. Yes, it is true. There was a UFO at Roswell. One damaged ship and one intact ship was captured and moved to ARGO quickly. The entire ARGO complex was updated with hangars to facilitate the crafts and construction was started on the facility I worked in. An army base was added to the construction for security reasons. Tents were used until barracks were completed, and all materials were transferred to the new buildings. Work accelerated.

"We were trying to reverse-engineer the technology. It was compelling work. I got a bit of a promotion and a device to research, basically to figure out what it did. One morning, I checked the device out and had it in my briefcase to take it to my lab. On the way there, I was called to the colonel's office for a debriefing or a chewing out for not making enough progress. I could not stand that guy. His one mission in life was to yell and scream at everybody in the world.

"At the time I had a small addiction to jelly beans and a huge crush on Colonel Vic's secretary, Jan. She was out of my league, but that's not saying much, all women were. At the time I had never been out on a date. Vic was a bandy rooster of a guy, short and all GI. I was always a bit nervous around him, so I sat at a desk in the outer office, looking at Jan and grabbing a jellybean from time to time out of my briefcase.

"Jan was tall with flaming red hair and bright green eyes, and had a body that sent shivers up my spine. She got up and was moving back and forth between her desk and the file cabinet. I could not take my eyes off of her. I was mesmerized. I did not know what my hand lying on the device in my briefcase was about to do.

"It turned out that I was given the wrong item out of lock up. It was the device that I have with me now, along with others. With my eyes focused on the beauty in front of me, I failed to notice that the lights blinked and a small ball was spit out. I picked it up, thinking it was a jellybean, and put it in my mouth.

"At about that time, Vic came out of his office and started yelling at Jan. I started to feel angry with him but was unable to remain that way. Without thinking I continued to put the candy in my mouth one after the other only biting each once then swallowing it. What I thought was a piece candy melted instantly when it hit my tongue. I gagged, chocked, and started to spit, from the rancid, metallic, putrid taste. All eyes turned my way, and Vic turned his wrath to me.

'What is wrong with you, you *freak*?' he shouted and then just stopped. Everything just stopped. The room seemed to tilt one way and then the other. It even seemed to change shapes, twisting at the corners.

"I don't know how long I sat there, but I was stiff all over when I finally moved. It seemed like days. No one else was moving, and I couldn't get them to."

6

"I PUSHED, SHOVED, AND GRABBED everyone in the room. It was just like they had turned to nicely colored stone. I was sort of dazed. Much like I would think you are now. I started to wander through the complex and I couldn't get any response from anyone.

"It was like the old story of the geek that turned invisible. I went to the female quarters and took a peek. After a few moments looking around, I felt like I had been hit in the gut. It was wrong, and I could not stay there anymore. As I left, I had a thought. The shower was in the next room. As I peeked in the door, there was a female airman in the shower. The scientist had taken back over. While she was a very attractive young woman, it was the water that I was interested in. It too was not moving. I put my hand in the water stream and the drops of water stayed on my hand, but the rest were still frozen in place. I licked some water from my hand and looked back. There was a handprint missing from the flow.

"I had an idea. I went back into the women's quarters, rummaged through the girls' dressers for a moment, and started back for my briefcase. On the way, it hit me that I needed to look at a few other things. I started looking in all the labs and gathering up anything that I thought might prove interesting. I had read some of the reports from other projects, and some had potential.

"I was in one of the labs at the far end of the complex, reading notes from a guy named Ned Perkins. He was an honest young man and had good instincts. We had lunch once or twice at ARGO and visited each other at home a time or two. I think if none of my misfortunes had happened, he would have done very well.

"As I gathered up the equipment and Ned's notes, the room seemed to shift. The ceiling seemed to shift over to one side, and the walls seemed to move with it, making the room seem slanted at the top. I felt nauseous. The walls seemed to bulge in places and then started to spin. It was difficult to move, but I struggled toward the door. As I got closer to the door, the effect started to lessen, and by the time I was out in the hall, it was gone.

"The unit I was connected to had a range limit. I am still uncertain as to what would have happened to me had I not moved back into range. It was a mistake that I did not care to repeat."

"Now, wait a minute. I've been sitting here listening to this load of crap, and it's just hard to swallow. I mean, you seem to just to go with this like it happens every day, and yes, I am overwhelmed. You seem to be able to control all I see and feel at your whim. I can't take this thing off without dying, and really don't, as of yet, have any real explanation. I'm way past stressed, I think I'm about to have a *stroke!*" Kelly started out calm and got more excited as he went. He ended up standing, shouting, and waving his arms.

"Calm down, Mr. Kelly. As I told you, it may take a bit, but all your questions will be answered in time. As for my nonchalant attitude, I had lived with the fact that alien life had visited our planet, and had been for some time before this happened to me. I dealt with extraterrestrial life and its technology for most of my adult life. It was a bit more overwhelming than I have led you to believe, but I didn't think that a trip to the latrine or throwing up in the hallway was necessary to report," Tupnic replied calmly, looking up at the still irate Kelly.

Kelly turned and began to stare at the fireplace. He put his arms behind his back, grabbed one wrist, and took a few deep breaths.

"Okay, go ahead. I'll give it a go," Kelly said finally.

"I am attempting to adjust the headset at this time. It will help calm your fears if I can get it properly aligned. It seems to be over-compensating. The energy field usually emits a calming effect on those exposed; at least the ones who survive long enough. Allow me to continue." With no response from Kelly, Tupnic continued.

JOHN ALLYN

"I made my way back to the colonel's, office, poking around as I went and picking up whatever I fancied. I had to borrow another briefcase on the way to hold all I had collected. It was a cheap one anyway. The last thing I needed was a pair of scissors, and I picked them up in the last office I was in.

"As I said, the thought of nudity without permission had kind of put me off earlier, but I had to make an exception. I went back in the office, put all my ill-gotten gains into my briefcase, and started the dastardly deed. With a stolen kiss from Jan for luck, I proceeded to cut off the colonel's uniform. I took the undergarments that the ladies had so generously donated and installed them in the proper places. They were all tie-together, so I really didn't have to move or touch him. With the job finished, complete with eye makeup and frilly lace women's underthings, I finished the final piece of my plan. I filled out a leave of absence request, stamped it in all the proper places, and scribbled (as best as I could) the colonel's signature. I found the file it was supposed to be in, filed it away, took my stuff, walked out of the building, and left the site."

"So what happened to the colonel, and what was it you did exactly?" Kelly asked with a chuckle.

Tupnic smiled. "Well, the lady who provided the special attire was about the right size for the colonel and had a part in a play in town. Everyone knew it was, shall I say, not for children. Like I said, all the clothing had ties for easy removal. Red lace panties and bra, and a red leather bustier, along with a heavy dose of makeup. It was the best I could do, anyway.

"I got a call from Ned Perkins the next day, and he said that the colonel had been replaced. It seems that he came out of his office screaming at the top of his lungs, as usual, and when everybody looked up there he stood in women's underwear, make up, and all. The whole office busted out laughing, and at first he didn't know why. Before it was over, the MPs had to take him away. He kind of lost it. From what I hear, he went on to have a good career, just not in a top-secret facility. In my opinion, he deserved whatever he got. There was no need for him to treat us the way he did. We were not military, and did our best to comply. I guess that was the last really

44

bad thing I did just for spite. There are some things that I have done that have been for survival that are worse, but that's survival."

Kelly seemed to be more calm and almost at peace with his situation. He smiled in the lingering silence as he thought of the tough GI finding himself in a crowd out of uniform, as it were. It sounded like the classic nightmare of being in high school in your underwear, just much worse.

Kelly broke the silence, and asked as he took his seat, "So what happened next? How did you end up being so rich, and like this?"

"Well," Tupnic said slowly, considering all of the questions, then he answered.

7

"AFTER THE MAKEUP JOB, I went up to ground level and took one of the janitors' cars. He was always talking about how fast it was and I just had to find out. It was a '65 Mustang Fastback, blue with a white top. I couldn't really drive a stick."

The mantle above the fireplace blurred, and a screen replaced it. The image of Tupnic and the hot rod filled it, and sound soon followed.

Tupnic entered the driver's door as the screen became clear. Knowing that the keys were kept in the ashtray, it was not long before the engine roared to life. The sound was a symphony only a true car buff could truly appreciate. At an idle, the engine loped roughly with the power that only a full race cam could produce. The throttle response was instant and extreme. The small block Ford's classic sound was unmistakable, loud from the straight exhaust pipes.

The car lurched from the parking spot, tires squealing in reverse, then burst forward with a lurch. It jumped, jerked, then erupted in a cloud of smoke, screeching tires, and roaring horsepower. Everything stopped except for forward motion, then there was a crunching and grinding of gears and the tires lit up again. The speed increased and the gear grinding repeated. It looked as though Tupnic was beginning to get the hang of it now.

There was not much notice paid to the commotion. It was a tradition at shift change to drag race out of the facility, one of the few rules they permitted to be broken. Little attention was paid to the fact that Tupnic was leaving in Charlie's car. It was early and only one car on its way out. Tupnic weaved all over the road. The tires squealed with every movement, due to his inability to drive. He stopped once

46

and tried to start over from a stop. The second time was not much better than the first. The roar of the engine and smoke from the tires was still impressive, but it was a little disappointing when the gear change went wrong. It was very clear from the smile on Tupnic's face, then and now, that he was overjoyed at the experience, and did not mind his mistakes one bit.

The Mustang finally glided into a parking space near the guard shack. Tupnic dropped the keys back in the ashtray and got out with a smile as broad as he could muster.

The images faded, and the two men were sitting in the dimly lit room once again.

"I felt powerful," Tupnic started again. "The exhilaration from the ride and from being in control of what seemed like the entire universe. It was a unique state of mind. Until then, I had felt like I had been riding a rail and ended up at the lab.

"It was a bit of a shock when I found that everything seemed to be normal, until I walked up to the gate. Everything was elongated there. It seemed like I was looking into a tunnel. The guard shack looked like it was a mile away, but I could hear what was said as if I was inside it. I tried to keep my cool and act as if there was nothing wrong. I walked in the direction I needed to go, trying to get a grip on what was happening. After a few steps, the guard greeted me as usual. I stumbled and stammered. I was talking to a man that seemed to be standing in the next county as if he was right in front of me. As the guard handed me the clipboard to sign out, my arms seemed to stretch for the mile it took to get to where the shack was. I took the clipboard, signed it, and gave it back."

Kelly had a puzzled look on his face, as if he didn't understand. That was all it took. His chair started to move away from Tupnic. When it stopped, Tupnic said, "It was sort of like this." His voice was as clear as it had been, but he looked like a spot on the wall. Tupnic reached out and patted Kelly on the shoulder with a hand that looked normal, but was connected to an arm that looked like a string reaching into the distance.

"Okay! Enough! I've got it," Kelly shot at Tupnic. He moved back into the comfort of room with the fire.

47

"I stumbled my way through getting out the gate. To this day, I still don't have any idea how long I ran around in the complex before I left. It could have been days. I know I felt hungry enough for it to have been that long. I checked out as normal, with only a bit of flack about the car. I finally told the guards that I wanted to get one and was going to have the man that owned that one build me one. I had to have a test drive. That seemed to satisfy the guards who had built their own cars to compete with.

"I boarded the bus back to town. Since the ARGO Lab was the main source of income for the town, the bus dropped us off at the nearest corner. It was a sort of perk, a service for those of us who chose to avoid the expense of a car. It also kept us a bit more dependent on the lab. Those of us who worked in the lab were discouraged from having cars, and really, property. Most of us had little family and were not the most social group. It was considered better for the lab to keep contact with the outside world limited, and social misfits are a good place to start."

*****

8

Tupnic

I RENTED A ROOM WITH my subsidy. It was more like a small apartment. When the base expanded years before, a lot of the people added a couple of rooms to their houses to supplement their income. I had the good fortune to find a good one. The woman who owned the house was a widow. She and her husband had moved there with a past expansion of the base. Harvey Baker drove a truck for the army for most of his life, retired, and died in the only house he had ever owned. He had worked on his family's farm until going into the army working mule teams, and graduated to trucks. His expertise had solidified his army career during World War I. He saw no action in World War II, but was deployed overseas. He and his wife had married and lived on base until the move to this part of the state. They decided to buy a house and were fortunate enough to stay in it until retirement.

Mrs. Beatrice Baker was seventy-eight years old and was a template for her generation. The house stayed virtually spotless, meals were always on time and hot. There were no shortcuts where food was concerned. If you ate at her table, it was an official event, and always worth any effort. She made sure that you were up on time for work, and for a little extra kept the room clean and your clothes too. It was kind of like having the grandmother I never had as a part of my life. We lived halfway across the country from all of our relatives, so I only saw a few of them a few times in my life.

Bea insisted on calling me Newton. She had an uncle named Newton and liked using the name. He had been a judge in Texas. It made her happy, so I did not mind.

After I explained to her that I would be working at home for a few days, everything worked rather smoothly. She didn't wake me up anymore, and I spent most of my time shut in my room. I was trying to find a way to make the device work, with no luck whatsoever. After a wonderful meal and about an hour of delightful conversation with Mrs. Baker, I felt better, but still was shocked about what had happened. The thought occurred to me that it might have been some type of experiment the lab had tried on me without my knowing. I was in a particularly dark mood when all this started, very thoughtful, sort of a daze, with my mind adrift.

With a more relaxed attitude, I found that three of the bobbles I had found in the other labs fit on the one I had been assigned. They simply snapped into slots in the side of the bigger unit. It still had no effect on making things work. That part came a little later. I finally sat back and started to eat some jellybeans, and that's what set things in motion. It had something to do with the composition of the jellybeans and their being in the proper position, combined with me being there and in the proper frame of mind, or so it seemed.

It spit out a small silver ball. It just came out of the thing, not through an opening, just out of it. It hit the table and made a bit of a click, and that caught my attention. After handling it for a little while and wiping my mouth, I recognized the taste and put it in my mouth. The effect was not as intense, but just as fast. Everything stopped again. There was nothing to explore this time except the town. It was not very interesting in real time. I milled around a little, and soon was back looking at the inside of my room. I started trying to mentally make something happen. It seemed for a while that I was having luck getting the clock to move back and forth. I was trying to get time to move, then the effect just stopped and everything was back to normal.

In another section of the ARGO Lab, a startled worker jumped from his seat and called a guard. He told the guard to wake everybody that even looked like they had rank and get them in there. The MP didn't question the order, just ran down the ramp leading out of the ship and started rousing both military and non-military personnel alike. The order was too vague, so he woke everybody.

The first few to arrive stumbled into the lab office shocked at what they saw. The console that had been acquired at the crash site was now active. This particular console had been removed complete while most of the others were disassembled for study. It had been decided that the undamaged one would remain intact while the damaged one would be dismantled for study in hopes of making the other ship work.

This was the first glimmer of hope that their plan might be possible. As the other personnel slowly filtered in, they saw and quickly moved to the unbelievable scene. The technician who had sent for everybody was seated at the console with a projected image in front of him. It was in midair. You could see through it. There was no tube there to contain the images being broadcast; it was just there suspended in the air. One man was brave enough to pass his hand through it. The image waved like it was water, then refocused, as clear as before.

They were looking at a young man walking around town, and then it would show an image from above. All along the sides were strange markings, or some form of writing. They were flowing in several different directions. Twice, there was a beam of blue light that seemed to reach out from the console and feel around the man sitting at the console, but then retreated, as if not finding what it was looking for. It lasted for only three minutes. Most of the others missed the show, but the commotion it caused would last almost twenty-four hours.

Those watching the display nailed down the location displayed, and agents were dispatched to observe. Cameras, lights, and extra personnel were put inside the ship. Conferences and interviews were conducted over and over again. They knew who they were looking at and where he was. The next thing was to find out why and how he had made this happen. Hopes were high that this was the key to unlock all the years of study. Plans were made. "Leave him alone for now and let's see what happens. Maybe we can figure out what he did to make it work," someone in authority had said.

It was very frustrating for the next few days. Nothing I did after that short trip made it work. I did everything from burying it in jellybeans to making patterns around the device. I put it back in my briefcase, filled it up with jellybeans, and left it overnight. I slept with it next to me that night, still in the briefcase and still covered. No kind of response at all. I started to think it was on some kind of odd time schedule, and I had no influence on it at all.

Finally, I gave up, temporarily anyway. I spent two days away from everything. Mrs. Baker and I went shopping for groceries, talked to Mr. Hooper the local grocer, and she took me to a small museum in the middle of town. It was really a joke. It had some mining photos and a few old tools, but with good company, it was enjoyable. I found that Mrs. Baker was a wonderful woman, quite intelligent and well-informed about most everything. I was very surprised. I was always under the impression that most housewives of that era were not well-read. Not stupid by any means, but just cut off or shielded from most of the world. Part of it was leaving home at an early age and not having a social life at all. I was surprised and extremely happy to find out I was wrong. It was a welcome change to have someone to have a proper conversation with, especially one with a unique point of view. She had an older perspective on most things and a well-informed point of view on the rest. I found it very refreshing. It was like having a grandmother who was your best friend. Given different circumstances, and born at a different time, I think that she would have had quite a different life if she chose to.

On the second night, after a superb meal, I decided to ignore my oath to the military and discuss what I was doing with her. At first, she seemed not to believe me, but after a while she came around. I, after a long question-and-answer session, showed her the device.

"It doesn't look like much," she said, looking at it as if it would bite her.

"No, it doesn't, but it is very powerful when it works," I said.

"So this thing can stop time," she stated, but it was more of a question.

"Well, when it was on, time seemed to stand still. Everything stopped but me. I was free to do as I pleased, and the rest of the world didn't seem to notice. I don't know if they stopped, or I was going really fast. I guess it really doesn't matter, the effect was the same. I have no idea how to control it or even turn it on. Of all things, it seems to have something to do with jellybeans."

"I know I didn't notice anything here the day you said you turned it on. If it truly is some sort of alien contraption, then there is no telling what it has to do with anything. As far as we know, the whole thing could be powered by cotton candy."

It was one of those things that just hits you the right way. We laughed until we cried, and when we would get our composure and look at each other and we would start again. Our ribs, chests, and stomachs hurt beyond belief when we finally gathered ourselves. We breathed heavily and chuckled for a few more minutes, then fell silent. She pondered something for a few seconds clearly becoming emotional.

"I love my husband more than any one person should be allowed love another. He was my entire world. I thought I would die myself when he passed on. Life was just not worth living anymore, but somehow I held on. Then you rented our room, and the responsibility of looking after you gave me enough purpose to live, to hold on just long enough to realize I need to live the rest of my life. To give up would be a disgrace to him and the first part of my life. You know that Ned fellow that comes around here to see you? He seems nothing at all like my Harvey, but I really like him. He seems like a good friend to you."

For a moment, she seemed to be lost in the past. Her eyes became moist, and I could tell that she was thinking of her beloved Harvey. She thought for a moment more and added, "How many jellybeans had you eaten that day? Maybe it had more to do with how many you had in your system than how many you had in your briefcase."

I thanked her for her input and a wonderful evening with a deep bow and a lot of overacting. I called her my lady and she called me Sir Newton. We laughed and both retired early to our respective rooms.

I mulled over the suggestion of jellybeans in my system. It seemed ridiculous, but I had pursued less likely possibilities. I started eating jellybeans, and did not stop until I had all but made myself sick. I ate all I had and was debating on going out to the store to get more, when I realized that it was too late, the store was closed. I fell asleep in the chair, looking at the device in my briefcase.

9

I WOKE UP THE NEXT morning to the sound of Mrs. Baker' clattering pots around in the kitchen and humming some old tune while fixing breakfast. The thought of eating made me feel worse. I had a stomachache that must have set a world record, and there was still no change in the time machine or in me. I spent about twenty minutes trying to shake the pain in my middle and the rotten feeling that went with it. Hearing the sounds from the kitchen was comforting. It felt like being back at home more every day. I just relaxed, held my aching stomach, and soaked it all in.

"Who are you?" Mrs. Baker said, startled and almost shouting. "Get out!" she added, then there was the sound of a crash, and she let out a muffled scream.

I jumped up and grabbed the device. I don't know why, but I pressed it to my chest with my left hand and hurried toward the kitchen. I suppose I wanted to try to protect my newfound friend. It was a joke. I had lived a very sheltered life. The closest thing to a physical altercation I ever had was a few short words with a student in college. It was cut short by the professor of the class when he entered the classroom. That was it, but now I was on the warpath. I had someone and something to protect.

When I entered the kitchen there were two men in GI uniforms in the room. One was standing over Mrs. Baker, who was half lying and half sitting in front of the stove.

"LEAVE HER ALONE!" I shouted and started her way, when the soldier on my side of the room must have been startled. He was like a mountain of flesh. A huge man who seemed to be all muscle, but in my rage it did not matter. He had his pistol in his hand, whirled and fired at me. Everything started to slow down again. In that instant I could see the bullet leave the barrel headed straight at me. It, and everything, came to a stop. I simply stepped to the side, out of the path of the bullet, and closed in on the goliath soldier. Just before I got close enough to touch him, things seemed to go back to normal. I reached out with my right hand and shoved. He was not concerned about me at all and stood there with a small crooked smile on his face. It may have been that he thought that he had shot me or that I was too small to be a threat, but he did not react.

When I touched him, he *dissolved* instantly into particles and fell to the floor in a loose pile with the sound of small gravel falling to the wooden floor. I was petrified for a second, and then it didn't seem to bother me. I turned to the other man in the room. He had not seen what had happened to the other man. His attention was still on Mrs. Baker, who had started to try to get up. The soldier put his foot on her stomach, and I exploded with anger. Another GI and two men in black suits rushed in through the other door just as I screamed. There was a small *thud* in the air. My ears popped like I was diving deep in water. I felt a burning in my chest, and there seemed to be a ripple in the air like a wave in the water. All of the men in the room fell like the first. They were just *gone*. All that was left was the same kind of particles on the floor.

I tried to go to see about Mrs. Baker, but fell before I made a couple of steps. My chest seemed to be on fire, and the thought of a heart attack was the first thing that crossed my mind. That thought passed when I saw smoke coming from it, and I wondered if I had really been shot. *No!* It was the device. It burned and burrowed its way down to my ribs. It seemed to connect to them. The pain was unbearable. I'm not sure how long I was like that, but fortunately I passed out.

10

At the ARGO Lab, twenty-five floors underground, one of the many stations activated on the bridge of the complete ship. Unlike before, this time, when it came to life there were plenty of witnesses. After observing the previous results from the individual unit, shifts were set up immediately to cover any contingencies twenty-four hours a day.

Console after console came to life, as did hordes of personnel assigned just for this event. The display screen, if you could call it a screen, popped up above the first console that activated and expanded to sit above a total of five consoles. On the display was a scene of chaos. The images split up into different angles and levels of view. Soldiers started to disappear, and waves of blue energy shot out in waves in different directions.

The entire screen transformed into an aerial view of the house that was filled with activity. A blue wave exploded from all sides, and the ARGO personnel and soldiers outside crumpled into piles of what looked like black sand. The view that followed looked as if the camera was aboard a rocket that had been launched. It was to facilitate the tracking of the beam of blue energy that, in an instant, was too far from the house to see how far it extended. The image continued to enlarge in scope, and the wave of blue simply faded before a destination could be determined. If there had been one at all, there was just no way to know.

It was clear now that there was more to this mission than simple observation and a broader plan had to be made. There had been loss of life due to activation of alien technology. Superiors would excuse the lives lost as collateral damage, but the loss of active alien equipment would never be accepted. Government officials and military advisers would now have to meet to determine a plan of action before anything else could happen. Until then all they could do is wait for orders.

11

I WOKE UP TO A *lovely young* woman patting my cheek. The added pain helped to bring me around. I gritted my teeth and screamed through them. The smell of burning flesh filled my nose. I retched slightly and turned to my right side away from the young lady. The smell and pain lessened, and I turned to see who it was that had come to our rescue. I looked at her and looked around the room for Mrs. Baker. She was *gone!* I turned back to the other woman. Something was *wrong!* Really *wrong!* The woman was familiar somehow. She was about my age, with blond hair and brilliantly blue eyes. Quite lovely, and still it seemed I knew her. My mind was still reeling from the last few minutes, at least the ones that I could remember. I realized then what it was. Her clothes hung off of her to the point of almost exposing her breasts, because she was on her hands and knees, still trying to comfort me. It hit me like a ton of bricks. She was wearing Mrs. Baker's clothes. Then I heard what she was saying.

"Newton. Did they hurt you, dear boy? Are you all right? Say something."

I felt better. I scooted on my behind away from her and stood up.

"*Mrs. Baker!* Is that you?" I half shouted.

"Yes it is. Are you okay?"

"I'm not sure about me, but you're *not!* What happened to you?"

"I don't know, but I sure do feel funny. I think I passed out when that soldier kicked me in the belly. I may be hurt inside. I don't feel hurt, but I really don't feel well," she said, progressively slower, looking at her arms.

"What's wrong with *me*!" she shrieked. Her hands began to shake wildly, and she ran her trembling hands across her face. Tears welled up in her eyes and began to stream down her cheeks. She pulled at her clothes, trying to make them fit. All of the sudden, she stopped and looked at my horrified face.

"What happened to me?" she whispered. "And to those men? Are you hurt? I heard a gunshot." She was on her knees now, looking straight at me.

"You're young," I stumbled out.

"What?" she whispered back.

"You're my age... now... again. You're young again. I don't know how, but you are," I said slowly, and reached out and touched her face.

"You've hit your head, son, and I'm just in shock from that brute walking on my middle. Did they shoot you?" Mrs. Baker asked more calmly, and she started to stand.

"No. I dodged the bullet. It stopped in the air in front of me. Go look in the mirror, Mrs. Baker. You look... *lovely*," I said, urging her to her room.

Bea sprang to her feet. A funny look came over her face, and she stood there in silence for a few seconds. She pulled at the collar of her dress and slowly looked down. She ran her hands down her sides and then across her face again. With a quick glance at me, she half-ran into the bedroom, and then there was a loud thump from her falling to the floor.

This time it was her turn to wake up. She came to a strange room. As she began to move, I rushed to the side of the bed and told her to take it easy. I refreshed the wet cloth on her forehead and sat down on the bed beside her.

"Is this some sort of *dream*?" she asked quietly.

"I only wish it was," I replied.

"It's true, then. I'm young again. I'm not going crazy?"

"No, ma'am, I think I have it all figured out. Things are spinning out of control. I think it's *me* that's going nuts." I choked on those words and walked to the window. It was completely covered, shades and curtains pulled shut, and I peeked out a corner, looking outside for split second. I could not see anything anymore. It was dark, but I still stood there as if the curtains were wide open. I sniffed a few times, as if I was on the verge of crying.

"Where are we?" Bea asked, rising up on her elbows.

"At the motel on the edge of town. I know it's poor cover since there are only two in town, but it was all I could think of. I brought what I thought you might need. They will be looking for us, or at least for me. They won't know who you are if you distance yourself from me before they tie us together."

"You said you knew what happened. Tell me please."

"The *thing* we talked about last night is the cause of all of this. Well, I am, for taking it from the lab." There was a pause. "I *killed* them," I choked out. "I killed them *all*." I choked again and fell silent.

Bea started to get up and slowed to note the difference in how she felt. It was amazing how much stronger she felt, and the ease of movement and lack of pain when she did.

She was still wearing the dress she put on that morning, but it did not fit anymore. It swallowed her up. Now she was slim, trim, and a bit taller. She pulled her collar out again, looked down inside her dress, and chuckled.

"That's what made me realize that something wasn't right. My boobs stand up by themselves again, and my back didn't hurt when I was trying to help you up. When I saw myself in the mirror, it was like looking at a picture from sixty years ago. I just looked and then I woke up here."

She moved close behind me. She wanted to comfort me as before. Like I was her grandson. That was still the way she felt, but she was unsure how to behave now that she seemed to be my age.

"What did you mean when you said you killed them all?" she asked, reaching out and putting a hand on my shoulder.

I turned and looked down at her. She truly was a lovely woman, but I had already known that from looking at the photos scattered around her house. I was taken aback for a bit at the sheer shock of what had happened. I slowly unbuttoned my shirt and opened it. I pointed to the almost square lump that was on top of my breastbone.

"At first, it was just sitting there on top. Somehow, in the middle of what happened at your house, it burned down and attached itself to my breastbone and ribs. Now the flesh has grown back over it. I don't think I'll ever be able to get it off, and I'm not sure if it's going to kill me or what.

"When the first guard shot at me, the bullet seemed to stop before it got to me. I just walked around it. The guy was a monster. I had no chance of moving him at all. When I touched him he just turned to dust. When the other one kicked you, I felt the burning on my chest, my ears popped, and I got a bit nauseous. There was a funny-looking wave that seemed to come from me and go out in all directions. All the other men in the room turned to dust too.

"After you passed out, I got you into your car and gathered up some clothes for the both of us, some food and some sewing things I had seen you use, thinking that you could alter something to fit you better. I found five other piles on the outside of your house. It must have gotten them all at the same time. They must have found out that I had taken these things from ARGO and came to get them. They wanted their property and me back. Since the device has reacted to me before, I think that it was in the process, but this time I had it pressed to my chest, I was trying to get away with it or protect it or something. I just don't know. Somehow, it attached itself directly to me, all the way down to the bone. If it doesn't kill me, my *friends* at ARGO will. They will cut me up in little pieces trying to find out how this thing works. It is inside me, and I couldn't tell them anything if I wanted to. I still can't believe I killed those men," I said, shaking my head at the last statement.

"Oh Lord, Newton. You don't think that thing killed everyone close by, do you?" Mrs. Baker asked, afraid to hear the answer.

"No." I chuckled. "I talked to Mr. Decker on the way out. I told him that you were my date and I had to get you back home. You were supposed to still be drunk from last night and needed a change of clothes. I asked for permission to use your car and Bea's dress. He didn't believe a word of it, but he smiled like he thought that I was lying to cover up mischief, not real trouble. He seemed to be okay, and I saw Mrs. Miller hanging out her clothes. No one seemed to notice anything at all. It won't be long before someone comes looking for me, and I'm not going to be able to hide for long. I just don't know how. They will be able to find me without much effort."

Bea patted my shoulder again and said, "Maybe not. I have a piece of property that dear ole Uncle Newton bought near here. It is still in his name, and it would be pretty hard to connect us together. He was really a great uncle and lived most of his life in Texas. I can call Edna and tell her that my car has quit again. I'll see if she'll let me borrow her car, and see if she will let you pick it up."

"Who's Edna, and will she let me pick it up? I don't know her."

"I've known Edna since we moved here. Floyd and my Harvey trained together for the war. They went to different places after they left Fort Sam. Floyd went to Europe. Harvey went to the Pacific and ended up in China. Because of his age Harvey stayed back where it was safer, but he still saw some terrible things. Never did have to fight though. It was great for them to see each other again. Talked all the time.

"Edna has a new car. A fancy one. I'll just tell her that mine broke down and you are helping me out. She knows who you are. We talk about you all the time, dear boy. She knows that Harvey's sister is in poor health, so I'll tell her that I need to go to see her. That's in the opposite direction that we'll be going. We can leave my old car at the grocery store. Mr. Hooper knows it and will watch after it."

"You have a sneaky streak that you have been hiding, don't you?" I said, a bit amazed by the plan.

"Well, since Harvey died, there's not much to do but read and watch that blooming TV. That thing can give a body of ideas," she said with a smile.

She picked up the phone and dialed Edna's number. I jumped to her side and hung up the phone. Before Bea could react, I explained.

"Your voice has changed with the rest of you. Try to sound older if you can."

She tried several old people impressions, got close enough to please us both, and made the call. The conversation was short.

"She said yes, but I'm afraid she suspects something. She acted kinda funny," Bea said thoughtfully.

12

WE ARRIVED AT THE CABIN late that night. It was a bit cool, but there was a fireplace, and Harvey had brought wood in on the last trip they made before he passed away. It didn't take very long for Bea to have a roaring fire after I had tried and failed to be able to start one.

"I never thought that there was an *art* to fire building. I thought that you put wood there and lit a match and it burned," I said, standing with my back to the fire.

"Harvey and I had kin who fired boilers on trains and stationary steam engines. There is an art to most things that you are good at. As we progress, the simple things are forgotten. Someday soon, people will forget how to build a fire altogether. I could not grasp the things that you do every day. The first thread of it, but there are simple things like the fire that you could learn and use for years if need be. I learned things from the necessity of life that I had to know growing up in the first part of my life. I was born in 1889. Things were very different then."

"I never thought of it, but you're right. We get lost in how hard our lives are, without thinking how easy it is compared to our parents'. I left home at sixteen to go to college. It may have been different if I had stayed home longer."

"You were in college at *sixteen*?" she asked.

"Yes. I have an IQ of 227. It's what got me into the lab. My physics professor got me the job, really. He introduced me to the people that brought me here. It looks like that may have been a rather large mistake."

The small room had started to warm. I opened my shirt and tapped on the square on his chest.

"A really *big* mistake."

We could not sleep, so for most of the night we sat near the fire to stay warm and just talked about everything. It was the most time I had ever spent with a woman in my life. We talked about our families and some history that Bea had really lived. She now insisted that I call her by her first name. The turn of the century and how things were when she was a child. Her memory was extraordinary. The way she told it, you would think you really were there.

One story she told caught my attention. I was, up to that point in my life, fascinated with treasure hunts. I had it in my head that I would someday go out into the desert and come out with a fortune in my pockets. I guess I was right in a way, just not the kind of treasure I had in mind. She said that dear old Uncle Newt was an outlaw of sorts, and had accumulated some wealth through less than honest endeavors. Some of that loot he had buried on this property, and no one really knew where. Rumor had it that it was a large stash from his outlaw days, and it was still there. Harvey and Bea had entertained themselves during their long marriage by using what clues they had looking for it, more as a joke than anything else. She told of a few digs that were filled with laughter and fantasies of riches. It was a grand time I could tell, and the tales were a delight to relive with her.

The night wore on and fatigue finally took its toll on both of us. About noon the next day, we woke up, stiff from sleeping in chairs. We moaned, groaned, and stretched our way into the kitchen to look and see what we could eat. There was little, but we did the best we could. Bea had not been here for two years. Harvey had not been up to roughing it for a few years before he had passed away, and she had not had the heart to come by herself.

Bea had somewhat adjusted to her new age. Her logic was that she was now twenty or so, and there was really nothing she could do about it, so she should make the best of it. It was the same logic she had used all her life, really. She had said many times that she was seventy-eight, widowed, and had to live with it and make the best of it. She may have been young now, but she could still cook like before.

There was nothing in the house that was still good, so Bea sent me up to the small local store just a few miles away. She made a small shopping list because of our shortage of cash. I filled the list easily. After a meal of what she called white flour biscuits and postolic gravy with bacon, we set out to make life a bit more comfortable. She quickly altered a few dresses to fit, and I gathered what wood that already chopped outside. I finished first and started looking at the electrical circuits to find out why we had no lights. There was little in the house that required electricity, but it was far better lighting than a candle or just the fireplace. It would make me, at least, feel more at home. Bea said it was okay with her either way.

We were finally working on the problem together, and she guessed that it was a fuse in meter box outside. We gathered up a few fuses and made our way out to it. On the way, she was talking about the times that this had happened before when she and her husband had repaired it. The conversation turned to a trip where they had spent a week there looking for their buried treasure. The two were very much in love and did not really want the money that was allegedly there, it was the shared adventure.

After looking for wasps and turning off the power to the fuse box, I started removing the fuses one by one. There were only three. They were about the size of a wiener, with a brass band on each end. They fit into a two-sided clasp on each end, and took considerable effort to get free.

"There is no real way to tell if they are bad, so we always just replace them all with new ones. We were always going to spend the time to check out the old ones but never got around to it. The last time we blew one out here, we had spent all day digging in the back of the house. We had blisters all over our hands. We found some odds and ends, spoons and the like, but, alas, no money. We had a ball. You can turn the power back on when you get the last one in," Bea rattled on as I replaced the fuses.

We looked at each other to confirm that we were ready, and I pushed the arm up to connect the power. As I did, there was a flash. A stream of light came from the panel and touched my chest at the box that was buried there. It was a stream of electricity. It grew. There were soon three fuzzy lightning bolts, and they grew until they connected to one large jagged bolt lapping into me. The single line

66

began to dance around the outline of the device. The lines to the fuse box started to hum and shake. The paint began to peel off of it. There was the smell of overheating insulation, and the bolt moved from the box to the wires above it. The surge grew stronger, and then, in the distance, a transformer exploded. The power surge died, and I fell backward to the ground, a cloud of smoke erupting from every inch of me. Unlike before, Bea was close enough to see and smell the results of the transfer. The smell was unbearable. She felt the bile rise in her throat but was able to push it back. She watched as the severe burns and even openings into my chest started to glow blue and repair themselves. Within a few moments all traces of the wounds were gone. Only the damages to my clothing remained.

13

IT ALL HAPPENED IN AN instant, but to me it seemed to take hours. Bea had little time to react, but was at my side when I hit the ground. In my mind, there was a kaleidoscope of visions. That would be the best way to describe what I saw. It was like watching bits of thousands of memories all at once, and being able to keep them all in perspective, but still just pieces. Bea said that I was hot to the touch, like I had a fever, and I turned pale and then a grayish color. Slowly I came to and returned to my normal, less than tanned color.

"Newton! Are you all right?!" Bea almost shouted.

I sat up, really feeling no ill effects from the experience, even though the front of my shirt was burned away, my face was a bit charred, and my hair stood on end with sparks dancing through it. I felt different, but not at all bad in any way, even though I could see streaks of electricity pulsing across my lower body. It was like the feeling you get when you win something big. You know, excited, frightened, and happy all at once.

"I know where the money is," I said, slowly getting to my feet.

"What?" Bea asked, slowly making efforts to touch me without making contact.

"I'm fine. It's this thing that's in me. It pulled in power. Don't ask me how I know it did, but the money is here. I watched him bury it. He said that the money was his nest egg when he was done. You and Harvey dug in the right spot once, but didn't go deep enough. Let's go ahead and get it. We will need the cash," I said in a very serious tone.

"You feel like you are on fire. You can't be all right. Let's at least get you in the house and let you sit for a while," Bea said with authentic concern. "You need a shirt."

"No, really, I'm fine. You can look at yourself and see what this thing is capable of. My mind seems to be opening up. I can see things that seem to be impossible. It is like I can look across time. They will be here in a few days and we have to be gone. I have a shirt in my bag."

It seemed that I had a purpose now. All of the insecurity that was there before seemed to be gone. What I had to do was clear, and, all of the sudden, nothing was in the way.

Bea and I made our way to the house after we made sure our part of the electrical problem was solved. It would take major repairs to the lines now, but we had done our part. I was very steady on my feet. My mind was very clear, and I kept having visions of things that made little sense. It was like watching ten minutes in the middle of a movie. I understood what I saw, but what it meant escaped me. We sat in the living room and talked. I explained to Bea what happened and what I had seen in my mind. We had almost become numb to the fact that this was too strange to believe.

"Money will be very important to us both soon. We should get the money and leave here. They will find us shortly."

"How do you know?" Bea asked.

"This thing is telling me," I said, tapping the lump in my chest.

"Does it talk to you?" she asked.

"It seemed to for a while after the power surge, but now it's like reading a single line in a book. It just gives me information, then stops."

Bea insisted on wrapping me in a blanket and having me drink a couple of cups of hot tea. Both were comforting, but did not feel or taste the same as they did the day before. I knew that they were there, but it was as if both were at a distance. The flavor of the tea was weak, not usually a problem, and the blanket felt like it was not making contact with me. It was there, but it didn't feel like it touched me.

14

"Feel better now?" Bea asked out of the blue.

"Yes. Thanks."

"I thought you might after your nap."

"*Nap! What nap?*" I blurted out.

"You've been asleep for almost thirty-six hours," Bea replied slowly.

I looked around, and it was growing late in the afternoon. I was astounded. I felt none of the usual pangs that were associated with sleep. I was alert and had not had the sensation of waking up. I was sitting there thinking, oblivious to everything, for what seemed to be a few brief moments, and an entire day was gone. I felt fine before. I was energized, excited, and fell fast asleep.

"Did I do anything strange or say anything while I was asleep?"

"You had your eyes open for a while. I got the feeling that you were blinking your eyes very slowly. They looked like they moved a little every time I came to check on you. Other than that, you never moved or made a sound. I was worried that you were dead, but you stayed warm. I've made some soup if you would like some. The lights came on a few hours ago," she said.

"I don't remember sleeping, and don't feel hungry."

"Nonsense. You have to eat, it's been a stressful couple of days for us both, and it would not be the first time a long nap snuck up on somebody. Go sit at the table. I'll get us both a bowl and some bread."

The meal seemed to have little taste. I knew it was good, but that was about all. Despite feeling no hunger, and with Bea's urging, I finished off almost three bowls of her soup and a large portion of her homemade bread. I had both before, but never so much as today.

"There is plenty more if you like. Who knows what that electricity did to you yesterday. You probably should be dead. You need to keep your strength up. Have a bit more," she stated.

She sat another bowl in front of me, and the aroma hit me like a brick. It was overwhelming, almost more than I could take. I had been sitting there eating the same food for a half an hour, and in an instant it was the most fantastic thing I had ever smelled. When the liquid touched my tongue, it almost choked me it was so intense. It was incredible.

"Too hot?" Bea asked.

"No, it's fantastic. My taste buds seemed to be on holiday, and they just got back," I said with a smile and went for another spoonful.

When the spoon hit my mouth, it was all I could do not to spit it out. It was cold as ice. The lights were dim and it was dark outside. I looked for Bea and heard her moving in another room. As I turned to look, a blanket slipped from my shoulders to the back of the chair. Bea was suddenly there, almost crying, and threw her arms around me, holding on tightly. She released her grip and sat down at the table around the corner from me.

"I thought you were *dead.*" She choked out. "I didn't know what to do."

"What happened? I was eating and then it was... *now!*"

"We were eating and chatting and then you just stopped. Your eyes started to glow like there was a flashlight behind them then they turned... *gray.* Your eyes. It was *awful!* The entire area around your eyes lit up not just your eyes this time. The light was stronger from inside. Then slowly all of you turned gray. I tried to wake you after I gathered myself, but you were just... *out!* You wouldn't turn loose of the spoon or anything. I shook you once, but couldn't bring myself to touch you again. You were as cold as ice. I got a blanket and put it on you, and cleaned everything up and then... well... *they* came," she said with a slight sob.

"*Who?* Did *they* find us already?" I asked, looking around with fear.

"No... no," she said quietly, putting her hand on my arm. "They were... they looked like... well," she continued to stumble and stopped for a moment, looking down at the table. When she raised her head, her eyes were moist, and disbelief filled them.

"They looked like… *ghosts*," she continued finally.

"Ghosts?"

"I really don't know how else to explain them. You were frozen and gray all over for about an hour. I was about to panic. You are the only one who knows what is going on and what has happened to me. You are the only one who knows me now. If I showed up back at home, the neighbors would call the police. I didn't know what to do with you or myself if you didn't come back," she said with distress in her voice.

"I had cleaned and put everything up, and when there was nothing left to do I just started to get more and more afraid of what would happen to me. I got a blanket from the closet and took it outside and beat it over the clothesline to get the bugs out. Just as I covered you up… you looked like you *iced up*. A thin layer of *frost* started in your hair and moved down until it was all over you. Then the *fog* came. It started to show up around your head. Soon it was all around you. I couldn't see you. It stayed around you for at least an hour, and then the fog started to pour out of where your eyes should have been. It covered the floor and started to rise to about waist high. Then the *ghosts* started coming. People in different kinds of clothes from different times. Some looked like they belonged with George Washington, and others were definitely from the Civil War. Soldiers, not in battle, just going about their business in a normal way, but in uniform. At times they seemed to be able to see me, but it was only for a second. There was no sound. They talked. It was clear that they were talking to someone. They just didn't make any noise when they did. I was frightened out of my *wits*. I wanted to run away, but I had no place to go. I'm not even sure I can drive that car of Edna, and I couldn't bring myself to leave you until I was sure you weren't coming back. There were more people in clothes I didn't recognize, and some things that looked like people but I guess weren't… I don't know how long it went on. A few hours, I suppose, then they just vanished, and the fog slowly went away too. After that you just sat there. I decided to wait till morning and make up my mind what to do then. I couldn't sleep, and was just sitting in the chair trying starting to doze off when I heard you move. I was so relieved and happy you were all right. You are okay, aren't you?"

"I seem to be. I sure don't feel like I've been sitting here for hours," I said, stirring in my chair. I looked around to get my bearings. The clock said that it was three in the morning. I was out for almost eight hours. One thing was clear; something had to be done about Bea. She had been through so much because of me, and it was time I did something for her. I had to make up for all this somehow.

"I think that I'll be okay at least for now. You try to get some sleep. Things are going to change in the morning," I said.

"But what about the *ghosts*?" Bea insisted. "What if they come back? I'm still scared. It was *horrifying!*"

"They were not ghosts. They were *real* people. Just take my word for it right now. They will not hurt you. I think it's like looking through a window into the past. It's true. It's all tied to this thing in my chest. Please, don't be afraid. I won't let it hurt you. Just get some sleep if you can. You'll need it in the morning."

We sat in the living room for the rest of the night; both in oversized chairs with stale smelling blankets over us. I acted like I slept, and am fairly sure that Bea did the same. The night was almost cold, and again I knew it was, but could not really feel it. Under the blankets I was comfortable, and being at ease my mind started to drift. I saw things from history that I knew were real. Sometimes it was just a flash of something, and others were several minutes long. In some strange way, I knew that what I was seeing was the real thing. It was like being a fly on the wall or another person in the room. I could clearly hear conversation and at times feel the emotion of the situation. It was incredible. The strangest part of all was I was not afraid. Whatever happened, it just did not frighten me.

15

I WAITED TO STIR BEA until it was close to eight o'clock. She was up in a flash and still ruffled from the night before. She went to the kitchen and I went outside to check over the car and get some shovels from the shed behind the house. It was neatly organized. What little there was in it was all in its proper place. I grabbed a pickaxe and a couple of shovels and headed back to the house.

"Newton!" Bea shouted and shook me roughly.

I jumped slightly at her sudden appearance.

"*What?*" I shot back.

"You froze up again. Are you okay? Come on, I've got breakfast ready."

"How long have I been out here?"

"I finished in the bathroom and fixed breakfast, not sure what you were up to. When it was ready, I came looking for you and I've been out here for at least twenty minutes or so. You weren't gray this time, just not moving at all. I couldn't even push you down. You didn't come to with me trying to shake you, so I tried to shove you over, thinking it would jar you awake. It was like pushing on the side of the house. I even ran into you like a football player. I just bounced off. Whatever happens to you *is* more than just you being stopped. It's much more," she said.

"Like before, I never knew that I had stopped. It was just like you appeared out of nowhere. This thing, as we know, has some link to time. It must be locking me out of this timeline somehow, but we can't worry about me right now, we have things to do."

"Come on, breakfast is getting colder."

"Not hungry."

"You have to eat, feel like it or not. I used to have to spoon-feed Harvey when he was sick. You have to eat to *do*. My mother used to tell me that when I was sick, and it's true. Let's eat. If you have a plan, it'll help make it happen," she said, tugging at my arm again.

After a hurried and lukewarm meal, I gathered the tools I had left by the back door. Bea followed. Equipment in hand, I started out into the field, stopping occasionally to get my bearings.

"You really think you can find it?" Bea asked at a stop.

"You and Harvey were digging on top of a few years back, the time you found the lead soldiers. Uncle Newton sprinkled them in the hole as a sign so he would know when he came looking. It was a common tactic used at the time. It was like a beacon, in case the area had changed when you came back for whatever you buried. He never thought it would be this long," I said.

"How do you know what he thought? I mean, you never even saw him outside the picture I have of him at home."

I stopped about fifty yards from the north side of a stock pond. I gauged my spot to be just about dead center. The tank was twice as long as it was wide, and the north and south sides were the short ones. Once I picked the place I wanted, I stopped and opened my mind to what I was doing. It worked poorly, but well enough.

"It was late in the afternoon when you and Harvey were here. You laughed a lot and kept telling him what you would do with all the money he was digging up. He said it would make retirement a bit more comfortable."

Bea was a bit surprised. "How?" she said slowly.

I simply tapped the proper spot in my chest and started digging.

"It started to rain on Uncle Newton and Bill Wilson before they finished covering it up. Bill said it was a lot of money just to leave buried for long, and Uncle Newton said it would only be there long enough for things to cool off. It was mostly stolen money. Uncle Newton was not the most ethical man there ever was. He was a criminal for several years, and narrowly escaped death on more than one occasion. By chance, he started making a more honest living and stuck to it. He planned more than once to dig this stuff up, but would put it off in fear of it linking him to some of the crimes. He really never needed it, so it's still here. We'll have to thank him for it some time," I said, throwing a smile at Bea between shovels full of dirt.

"Start looking for the soldiers and gather them up as we go. They are toys made before the Civil War and are very valuable by themselves," I said without stopping. "When they expanded the stock tank they buried everything deeper. This could take a while. There was a huge oak tree here when Uncle Newton buried this here. The stock tank was only a small pond."

I stopped talking and just dug intensely. I did not sweat or run out of breath. I just kept digging.

"Here! I see a soldier!" Bea shrieked.

I stopped long enough to watch her pick them out of the pile. With her on that pile of dirt, I turned and started spreading out the shovels of dirt around the growing hole that had enlarged to three feet in diameter and almost four feet deep. It didn't take much longer till I hit something hard. I fell to my knees and felt around in the bottom to see if I could find the outline of a pot. Once I had found the entire edge, I dug out around it about six inches all the way around. It was about eighteen inches in diameter and would be too heavy to lift by hand from a hole that deep. It was another common practice of the period to take a cast iron wash pot, fill it with your valuables, cover them in a thick layer of beeswax, and then bury them. That was what we found. It was about eighteen inches around and seemed to be still intact. We struggled to clear it and had to build a makeshift lift to get it out. Lucky for us, Harvey had a small rope and pulley in the shed.

It took a few hours to plan and build the lift. It was not my field of expertise, so Bea did most of the design work. She had seen her dad build a few in her day, she said. We took three old fence posts that they had in a pile of spares at the house, dug a small hole to anchor them in their respective places, leaned them against each other, and tied them together at the top. The rope used to tie the top had enough slack for a small loop for the hook on the pulley to go through. We made a loop around the pot, threaded the other end through the pulley, and we were ready to lift. It would work well when finished.

"I hope it's not Confederate money," Bea said. "That would make it worthless, wouldn't it?"

"If it was Confederate paper money, it will have some historic value, but very little real worth. Most of it's federal. Double eagles and the like, all coin. Unless I miss my guess, it's worth a small fortune. It will be enough to set you up for the better part of your new life," I said, looking deep into her eyes.

"You have a chance for happiness now. We need to get it back to your house and clean it up. There is a place in town that Ned knows about where we can sell some of this to get things moving our way. It will be important later, but you have to make up your mind now whether you can trust me with your life. Things are going to get worse for a while, even compared to now, and it will be critical when the time comes for you to follow blindly if you have to. It *will* come to that if you stay with me long. Think about that. We will be all right for the next day or so."

We worked in relative silence from then on. Bea was pondering what I had said. It was kind of out of character for me to be so bold, but it had to be done. She was trying to get a handle on her new life, and I had thrown more fuel on the fire. It was tough to imagine what was going on inside her head, but it could not have been easy. I know I was having a tough time getting a grip myself, but both of us seemed somehow to handle it well.

I had her go and get the car. She had been unsure if she could drive it earlier, and it was time she took an aggressive stance for her future. The 390cid engine roared to life when she started it. It was clear that she was still used to the '46 Ford she and Harvey had had since it was new. The engine roared several times, then I heard clearly the sound of the automatic transmission being engaged with the engine at too high an rpm. The tires spun in the grass and caught, pushing the car on its way. She had a little trouble with the power steering and the power brakes, but made it back out to our site without any real problems.

We got everything ready and tied the rope to the pot and to the bumper of the car. I eased up until the pot was close to the top of the rope. We took a couple of the extra posts, put them across the hole, backed the car up, and let the pot set down on the posts. After that, we moved our lifting stand and tied off directly to the bumper and pulled. The posts allowed the pot to slide across them and clear of the hole. We retied the stand in position away from the hole. We lifted the pot then tied the rope off to the posts to hold it in place, backed the car close, and lowered it into the trunk. Bea pushed the pot forward so it was over the cavernous trunk, and I strained to lower it with some control. We looked at each other and smiled. It was almost as unreal as the other things we had seen over the last few days. I never thought we would have been able to do it, but it was Bea's older mentality and experience that made it possible.

After a short break, we loaded everything, tools and all, into the trunk then drove to the house trunk lid still open. Bea insisted on a snack, and then we closed up the house and headed back to town. The trip was uneventful. The large automobile was smooth, powerful, and quiet. We stopped once to get gas and sodas. I had Bea drive for a while on the open road. She was starting to get the hang of being young again. It was hard to get her to give up the wheel. We arrived, as planned, in the middle of the night and backed the car into the garage after clearing a few items. I closed the door and Bea fell into her bed and was soon fast asleep. I did not sleep.

16

I NOTICED THAT BEA'S CAR was in the drive at the neighbor's house. I thought it a little strange that Edna's husband, Floyd, had insisted we leave Bea's car in the grocery store parking lot once it was repaired, saying that he would not need it until later. He had left his keys in the ignition and said to just take his car, it was full of gas. Well, maybe something had come up and he had needed it anyway. It still felt odd for some reason.

After being fairly sure Bea was asleep, I left my room and went to the garage. I opened the trunk and simply lifted the pot out and placed on the workbench nearby. It would have been a real advantage to have known that I had that much extra strength the day before. The construction of the lift would have been unnecessary. After thinking about it, I probably hadn't acquired it at that time because it wouldn't have been so difficult to lower it into the trunk. Now I lifted it with ease.

There was a propane torch with a full bottle on a shelf, and soon I had heated and scraped off most of the wax. The gold coins underneath had corroded only a little bit. It was a good way to store things, at least this time it had worked well. I took the coins and the soldiers and sorted them in groups on the workbench. The collection was impressive. Some of the coins dated back to revolutionary times. Others were twenty-dollar gold pieces, and there were other various denominations of coins. I had flashes while sorting the money of the people that Newton had taken them from. I also saw flashes of the exchanges when he sold things. In some cases, it was a little disturbing to witness a robbery firsthand, then a barter and sale. Newton was not a nice man, for the most part, but now he was going to make Bea's new life very comfortable.

Ned came to visit me at the house a few times. He was young too, and we had a few things in common. The restrictions placed on us at work had prevented us from being too social. Neither of us was very good at it anyway. He had spoken more than once about a love of coins, and had a friend in town that was in the business. It was my hope that he could help us sell at least a few of the coins for some much needed cash. Bea had said that she had some money put up at home, but it was not enough for what we would eventually need.

With the pot empty and the car cleaned, I sat down to see if I could make sense of a few more things. My mind was full of different streams of memories. Very few made sense. It was like watching two minutes of someone's life and trying to figure it all out. It became too annoying to sit still, so I went to my room and started writing down the events of the last few days. It took my mind off the intrusions into my mind for the most part. After a while, I looked at the paper and I had been doing calculus problems way above my understanding. It was like an annoying neighbor shouting in my head. I just couldn't get away from it. I wasn't sure I wanted to anymore. I tried the television. The movie that was on the only all-night channel kept being replaced with flashes of things from my head until I couldn't watch anymore, so I just quit fighting and relaxed. Things became more ordered, but still random. The visions, for lack of a better term, came at regular intervals like pulses. I started to time them. And I would get a two-minute stream every seventeen minutes. I still made no sense what I was seeing, but I became more and more comfortable with them.

In the morning, I waited for Bea to wake, informed her of what I intended to do, and went to the station to fill the car with gas. It was full when we left, so I filled it so I could return it that way. There was a slight coat of road spray on the car, so I went by the car wash and scrubbed it clean too. It was a kind gesture to allow Bea and myself to use their new car without a second thought. The least I could do was return it as pristine as possible.

There was something that seemed to worry me. It struck me as odd when I picked up the car. Edna said that the keys would be in the ignition and not to bother to come to the door. Bea had even commented that it was a bit strange for Floyd to just let me take the car without even meeting me. We took it in stride and did not ask questions because of our situation. Things were not much better now, but it seemed to trouble me more and more. I had seen Floyd Bales on more than one occasion in his yard as I came home. He enjoyed it outside, Bea told me. He just couldn't sit inside all the time, retired or not. The problem was I had not seen him since all this started. He should have at least tried to find out from Bea if she was all right, or what was going on. Edna had gotten off the phone quickly, and neither made any contact with me when I picked up their new car. It just bothered me.

Floyd Bales was born about 1906 in West Texas. He was born at home on the family farm like a large portion of his generation. While he knew the day he was born, the year was somewhat unclear. He had simply accepted 1906 as close enough.

He was too young so not drafted in World War I and remained working as a farmer for the first part of his life. Edna Parker lived on the next farm and married Floyd at sixteen. They worked the fields together until Floyd was drafted in late 1942.

While designated a truck driver he had seen action in Europe because of the shifting battle lines. While fighting furiously and with gallantry, he was always returned to his unit. The excuse used was his age, and he reluctantly accepted his assignment. He was a bit bitter over the decision each time but was never afraid to return to the front lines. It was his duty. He thought he was well able to serve in a combat unit, and he was right. He would think of Edna and the safety of the rear areas seemed more acceptable. He had remained in good physical shape all his life even into his old age.

I parked in the drive beside Bea's '46 and went to the door. I knocked several times and was about to leave, when Floyd told me through the door that the keys to the old Ford were in the ashtray. I thanked him and offered their keys. He told me to just drop them in the driver's floor and be on my way. He said that he would collect them later. I complied, but the entire time it was like bells were going off in my head. Something was just not right. I hurried back next door with the thought that the Bales were under duress of some kind, most likely people from the lab looking for me. If so, I had no chance, but needed to explain to Bea before they entered the house again. After thinking about it, I went back and moved the '46 to Bea's drive and backed it in.

I found her in the kitchen, sitting at the table drinking coffee. As I started to tell her, I saw someone coming to the back door in a large coat with a hood pulled up over their head. Whoever was there was not very big. I was still thinking of the giant from the time before. There was no time for explanations anymore, I had to run.

"I think ARGO have the Bales and they are here for me now. I have to go," I said to Bea and started to run to the waiting car, knowing it was a futile effort, but taking the confrontation outside.

Suddenly, the fear was gone. I stopped. There was a slight knock at the door. I waited for the crashing sound of it being kicked in. It didn't come, only a frail voice calling to Bea. I listened and reentered the kitchen to see Bea headed for the door.

"It's me, Bea, Edna. Please let me in. Hurry! Quick! I don't want Floyd to see me," she pleaded.

I motioned Bea to move behind the door out of sight so I could let Edna in. It would be a scene at the door if they met there. She shot in as soon as I slid back the bolt and stood just out of the doorway, sobbing softly, still hidden completely in Floyd's huge coat. In my mind, it must have been an ordeal, military police holding them prisoner, waiting for my return.

Bea could not help herself at the sound of the sobs. She rushed out to comfort her long-time friend. Peeling back the hood, both fell into a state of shock. Edna was not Edna, at least not what we expected. She was young too. After a moment of shock then recognition, both women grabbed each other and started crying. There were no soft sobs anymore, it was full open weeping. I was not sure if it was fear or relief, but it was loud and vigorous. I moved closer to try to get some information about the police next door, and they just stopped crying. Both looked at me almost calmly, then back to each other.

"You look *amazing*!" Bea choked out, looking at Edna. She still could not speak and kept looking from Bea to me.

"F-F-Floyd will be over soon. He didn't want anyone to see us yet. We just can't understand what is happening. H-H-He is like this too. W-W-We locked ourselves in the house. We were afraid to go out. Bea, it's really you. It happened to you too," Edna stumbled out.

"Yes, dear. Me too. Here, sit down and have some coffee. It'll be just fine," Bea said calmly, removing Edna's coat and ushering her to a chair at the table.

"Newton, would you please go next door and get Floyd? I think they need to hear what we know," she added.

I did not get to the door before Floyd barged in, looking ready to kill. In an instant, he lost the intensity in his face. He just stood there as if he had been given a large dose of sedative. He just relaxed.

"Have a seat," I almost demanded. He complied and became stunned again when he finally saw Bea. He slid slowly in a chair next to Edna.

"*What?*" was all he could manage.

Bea turned her gaze to me. The other two followed suit. It looked like I was on.

"As you all know, I work at the ARGO Lab outside of town. Without permission, I brought home some equipment that we had for research. In the process, that equipment activated. It happened twice, and I'm not sure that after the second time it has turned itself off. The second activation happened in this house. It caused the death of nine federal agents and military policemen. It is also responsible for what has happened to the three of you." I paused to sit down at the end of the table and pour a cup of coffee for myself.

"We were doing classified research on instruments recovered from an alien spacecraft. I can only assume that what I have is a time distortion device, we think it's from their drive system." I stopped and opened my shirt to display the square lump on my chest. "It is either malfunctioning or maybe doing what it's supposed to do. Maybe it's lacking a component in its control. Whatever the case, I'm... well... stuck with it, and sooner or later the ARGO Lab will most likely find me and take it back, one way or another. You seem to have been given a new lease on life. It happened to Bea when the MPs attacked us. I assume that the two of you were affected at the same time."

"Yes," Floyd finally spoke. "It was during the commotion over here. It was like a small electrical shock, and we passed out. Once we woke up, we were just scared and shocked. At first we were a bit panicked, but rather calm, like now. After about an hour or so, we almost went berserk. It was pure bliss and terror all in one."

I thought for a second or two and said, "It would seem that those affected... this thing must generate some kind of field that calms fear or just calms... us. I just don't know. If it hadn't switched itself on at the lab, none of this would have happened. For now, that is unimportant. We have to try to get you three situated so I can get away. They won't bother you if I'm not around, provided we prepare you properly."

Everything seemed to slow down, like a movie running in slow motion. When anyone spoke, it was slow too. It was that way for what seemed to be a short while. It was actually over an hour, but when it stopped, I had some answers.

We all settled in at Floyd and Edna's to delay any detection, hopefully. They seemed to adjust, and with each other's company and an explanation, as weak as it was, started to accept what had happened. I ate little and still did not sleep.

Edna had a cousin. There had been some sort of rift in the relationship that no one ever speaks of. She had three children who had died in a flu epidemic in 1949. Many in the area had died from the flu at almost the same time. They all died at home, and while the families were devastated each time, it would be the thing that would work now to secure their future. In the mid to late forties, the issuance of death certificates was lax. It would be easy to get my three fledglings an identity. I could see that in the future it would more important than it seemed now. I watched parts of the past and future all through the night.

I knew who to send requests to for birth certificates in that particular county. The next morning, I had everyone write out their statements for each child's name we would need. We mailed them and hoped that it would work. I knew it would. I added a return address to the bottom of each request unknown to the others because they did not know where we would be that far in the future bit *I* did.

Later that morning, I had Bea call Ned. He went to work late on most days, so he had some time in the morning. She asked him to come by her house because she had heard from me that he knew something about coins, and she had one she needed help with. He expressed his concern for my safety, but said that the word was that they thought I had left town. The search was going in that direction. His interest peaked when she told him about one of the double eagles. She also said that her granddaughter would meet with him. She had an appointment and would be gone for most of the morning. He never suspected what he was walking into.

We had moved most of the coins into Bea's bedroom and planned to show Ned only the few we selected. We hoped he would have an idea of the value. We needed to get an estimate of what we had before we sprung the surprise on him. I had already seen that we had a small fortune on our hands, but was still unsure of what the facts really were. If what I had seen was true, we were on our way.

Ned arrived, and we were waiting in the living room.

"Do you think we can pull this off? I mean, will Ned believe all this?" Bea asked nervously.

"We're not going to be in any danger, are we?" Floyd asked.

I felt a wave of some kind slip over me.

"I asked Bea the other day if she could trust me without question. You must decide to do that, or go home and leave here as soon as possible. I've laid out what you will have to do. At this point, that's all I can do for you. To answer your question, they are watching Ned and will get here soon after he does. We will be able to get by with this if we all do our part."

They looked at each other, then back at me.

"We have a whole new life ahead of us thanks to you and that... *thing*. Provided we live and don't get old again by in the morning. If there is anything that we can do to help you, we will, as long as the girls will be safe," Floyd said with authority.

"You must assume your new names, soon, then and act like you are your new age when they arrive. They must not suspect that we are not what they see."

They only nodded. They were seeing it already.

85

"I… will… be… Floyd… for… now," I forced out as I aged. The other three in the room could not believe what they were seeing. I now looked to be about sixty.

"*How?*" Floyd stuttered out.

"Not sure," I replied. "Thought it was a good idea and it *just happened.*"

17

WHEN NED ARRIVED, I MET him at the door. He was wearing his lab coat over his usual suit and tie. He was a bit surprised to see me. He was expecting a young woman. I explained that Bea had asked me to come over, since she could not be here, and watch out for her granddaughter. She was not as well-acquainted with him as she would like. He took it in stride and quickly went for the coins. After a long inspection of all five coins, he took a small can out of his jacket pocket and polished a small spot on one. He was amazed.

"Aside from a small amount of tarnish, these coins are in *mint* condition! They will be worth a *fortune*! Where did you get them?" Ned asked with excitement in his voice.

"My grandmother got them as a child and just found them again. She said that your friend Newton always talked about you and your love of coins. Not knowing anything about them, we thought you might be able to help us. Grandmother was hoping that they might help her pay some bills or something," Bea said, playing her part well.

"Well, I think that will not—" He did not finish, because two men in black suits entered the room. The front door was unlocked, so they had just eased their way in and listened. Bea and Edna jumped at the sight of them. One of them made a slight gasping sound.

"Can I help you, gentlemen?" I asked quietly.

The real Floyd jumped to his feet and almost shouted, "What is this, *man*! What are you doin' in here?" Doing a good job acting his new age.

They did not speak; they just pulled government issue 45 automatics from their jackets. What the pair saw was an older man standing beside a young man in a white lab coat flanked by two young women and a young man all looking like typical *"hippies"* of the time, long straight hair and cloths that fit the stereotype.

One proceeded past us to the rest of the house and looked around. The other stood there with an icy glare fixed on us. The second suit returned, and they just left.

"They were looking for Terry... Terrance. I'm sure of it. They must have followed me here," Ned said slowly, as if ashamed of the fact.

"It's okay, son," I said.

He looked at me, half smiled, then looked back at the coin in his hand. I walked to the door and watched them leave. I knew they would not be back today. I returned to the living room.

"Ned, we haven't been completely honest with you," I said, getting his attention.

"What do you mean?" he asked, unsure of what was to come next.

He stared in disbelief as I returned to my real age. He almost ran out of the room when he recognized me. Then the calming effect took hold of him. It still took him some time to catch his breath.

He started to babble, but I stopped him and had him sit down.

"I'm getting real tired of explaining all this, so I'll give you the short version. You're a bright boy. You should pick it up fast," I said, twisting my head to pop my neck.

I gave him a quick overview, and when I had finished, he looked around at the others.

"You're Mrs. Baker. You're *Bea*! I recognize you from the picture on the shelf by the dining room. You are... were... are... *beautiful*," he caught himself and blushed, squirming in his chair.

I broke in to get him out of trouble and to move things along. I had had an idea that he felt that way because of all the attention he gave to the photo of Bea as a teenager when he was visiting.

"Do you know anything about the device that I took?" I asked, to save him.

He snapped back to himself and answered.

"Yeah. They made us take an inventory after the alarm went off. Well, there really wasn't an alarm but"—he looked around sheepishly and continued—"I had parts of the dash components from the first ship, the one that crashed. Everybody on our floor had separate parts from the same area in that section what they called the console section *H 333*. There were five parts unaccounted for. They said you took them all. A large portion of my research notes were also gone. They thought I was in on it for a while, but they cleared me later."

"Do you know how they can track me?" I asked.

"There are other parts that activate at the same time the parts you have are on. The closer you are to them, the easier it is for them to triangulate your location. They left to go somewhere upstate yesterday. That's probably why we only had two visitors just now. They think you are not too close. They just were watching me, hoping to find you."

"It must be all part of the same system, and when power enters this section, it powers all of them. That's fantastic! Power transfer over that much distance, it's just *unbelievable*! If I could only get my hands on the rest of it!"

"Not likely. They have guards at every door now, and you have to check in with you research material every two hours. It has really slowed what small progress we were making to nothing," Ned said with disgust.

"If you can identify what you need specifically, I will get them," I said slyly. "I just need to learn a little more first."

"Their presence today proves that they are still watching me. They want you *bad*! It seems a little strange that they would want that stuff that much. No one but you have made anything work," Ned continued.

"If they only knew." I laughed. "I don't know how I made it work. I think it has something to do with *jellybeans*." I laughed again.

"*Jellybeans*!" Ned laughed out loud.

"What about us and the coins?" Bea brought the subject back to business.

I looked at Ned with all the seriousness I could muster. "We are in *real* trouble here, Ned, and I will understand if you don't want to help us. We need some cash. Do you think that you could sell a few of Bea's coins? There are more to sell, we just showed you a few."

"We could go to see Mr. Schwartz. He has always been real helpful to me in the past. I think that we are friends. I believe that he would help me, even if he knew all the facts. When do you want to go?" Ned replied.

"As soon as possible. Remember that we cannot afford to trust anyone, no matter how trustworthy you think they are. You and the others can go now." I looked at the other three and said with a smile, "That is, if you children are ready."

There was a round of laughter, and everyone started gathering the coins and themselves. I went to my room to try to rest and to try to make some sense of it all. There was a question of control. There had to be a way, some way to make this thing in me to do what I wanted it to, some way to use it to my advantage when I wanted to, not as it saw fit. On my timetable, not on the one it had. Maybe it would just take time. I could only hope.

It seemed like only a second before they reentered the house. They were laughing and talking loudly. It was good to hear Bea and Ned having a good time. Neither had a lot to be happy about since I had known them. I had only seen Edna and Floyd a few times in passing, so I was not sure about them, but they were joining in the good time as well.

"Quite a haul we made there," Bea almost shouted.

I walked back into the living room. Everyone calmed down a little when they saw me.

"What's wrong with you, dear boy?" Bea gasped, rushing in my direction.

I had no idea what she was talking about, but it had to be apparent that something was wrong by the look on everyone's faces.

"You're gray again!" Bea said, more annoyed than frightened.

I jumped slightly and looked down at myself. My hands and arms were gray. They looked the same shade as a battleship. I just froze looking at myself. Bea touched me and recoiled at the touch.

"You're as cold as death, boy. What's that thing done to you now? Even your face has turned. At least you're moving this time," Bea said.

The others seemed shocked at the sight of me, but more amazed at Bea's lack of surprise.

"How long were you gone?" I asked suddenly.

"Just a few hours." Ned shook himself loose and spoke. "Mr. Schwartz cleaned everything up and did real research for us. It took a while, but it was worth it. We cleaned up, and Bea said there was more where that came from! What is wrong with you? Did she say that this has happened before?"

"Yes. It is different every time though. It is a side effect of activation of the device. I really can't tell you more than that. It seemed to me that you walked out the door and came right back in. I must have frozen up again. This time I had no dreams or whatever they are. It was like when I was eating at the cabin. I just lost that amount of time," I said, still staring at my arms, when the gray color seemed to flow back up my arms, leaving me flesh-colored, fingers first.

There was a slight bustle in the room as everyone, in one way or another, showed their surprise at what had happened. All four crowded around me and looked intently at my skin. Ned took my arm, poked at it, and made a few grumbling sounds.

"The beings that they found were a lighter shade of gray than you, but they were gray. Maybe it has something to do with that," Ned said studiously.

"I don't like it," Floyd stated flatly. "That just ain't right."

"It may not be right, but there is little we can do about it at the moment," I said, and became dizzy. It was hard to stand. My mind reeled. There were more flashes of people and places. Finally, it was more than I could take. The room spun and then went black.

I came to on the couch. My head felt like it had been split in half. It pounded with each heartbeat. It was dark once again, and I was under a blanket again also. I could not move, and the pain in my head was almost sickening. I started to see stars. It felt this time like I was going to die. Then suddenly, the stars turned to some kind of letters or symbols. It was like looking at a typewriter putting a line on a piece of paper. The pain eased. The odd lines of figures started to stream along, slowly increasing in speed. Soon it was almost a blur. Then it just stopped. The pain in my head was gone and it was breaking day. I could move again, and I seemed to have the energy to do so and do so quite well. It was like waking from a long slumber, refreshed and ready for a spring day. I all but leaped from the couch and started to look for my friends. My friends. It soaked in that now I had friends. It made me feel even better. No one was at home, and that puzzled me a little, but since I did not know how long I had been out, it would be wrong to give it too much thought.

I realized that I had not eaten in several days, so I thought it would be a good idea to try. I fumbled around in the cabinets and found some bread, and in the refrigerator found leftover meatloaf. After making the sandwich, I poured a glass of milk, sat down at the table, and started to eat. Nothing had flavor. It was like chewing solid air, and the milk was the same. It had less flavor than water. I lost the willingness to try any more of the flavorless meal. I was not hungry anyway. It was clear that either I was getting some kind of nutrition from the box or that I would just soon die of starvation. I had no real option.

I felt fine, so I went to see what I could do to pass the time. I had an idea. From memory I tried to document time and duration of each "episode" that had occurred. It had no pattern when I had finished. Then I remembered what Ned had said about the other devices becoming active when power was fed to mine. I surmised that if I could activate theirs, then in theory at least they could activate mine. Possibly without knowing it, someone at the lab could be turning this thing on as they tried to determine what the other did. If this was the case, then I was at their mercy and had no hope of gaining control or being free at some time in the future. The only variable I could add was the acquisition of power at the farm. It drew it into me on its own, like it needed it, or knew what to do and how get it. If it could react to its surroundings, then it may have a mind of its own, at least of some kind. If some of the parts were linked over this much distance, then it was at least a possibility that more than our floor at the ARGO Lab was linked and active at the same time.

I went back to the one thing that I did know, and that was adding power to the unit, but I had to be able to control it. There had to be someone on hand to shut it down in case things went haywire again. There had to be a way.

The chattering foursome came in, clamoring as usual. I returned to the front of the house to greet them and to find out how long I had been on the couch.

"Well, he is alive," Edna joked with a smile.

"How long this time?" I asked flatly.

"Two days," Ned replied, sort of looking me over. "We knew that you were at least sort of alive. You would make some noises from time to time. For a few hours, you sounded like you were speaking gibberish. We didn't know what else to do but watch and try to keep you comfortable. It would be a death sentence, so to speak, to take you anywhere. They would just notify ARGO, and that would be the end of all this, probably of all of us too. I shudder to think of what they would do to all of you once they found out what happened. They would have parts of you guys in different rooms of the lab with everybody trying to find out how and what happened. They would just shoot me to make sure I didn't talk."

"Where did you go?" I asked directly to Ned.

"We went back to see Mr. Schwartz. He picked up some money from the bank to pay us. He'll have more in a few days when he has his buyer in. We still have only sold about twenty percent of the coins, and Mr. Schwartz says that he has a few thousand dollars' worth. He's given us a thousand so far. The description of the older coins we gave him made his day. He was like a kid in a candy store. If it is what he thinks it is, it's one of the rarest coins ever produced in America. He says that we could get ten thousand for just one if we wait and put it in an auction," Ned filled me in proudly.

"It will pay off for us all if we are smart about it. Do you have, or can you get, a large heavy-duty rheostat? It will have to graduate slowly."

"What's that?" Floyd asked.

"It is a device similar to the dimmer on dash lights on your car. It regulates electrical current flow to a device from a power source," I explained then continued speaking to Ned again. "We also need to have a dead man's switch to shut down everything at a second's notice. I think I have a way to make this thing work and also give us some control too."

"It would be a little difficult to find one here, but if we went to Gunny's he should have one there. You know, that surplus store on the north road," Ned replied.

"If that is the closest, then that is what we need to do. I have a feeling that if I can make this thing work, our world will change forever. See if you can get the others to go and get the rheostat, if you can make them understand what we need. Floyd is pretty sharp. I think he won't have a problem with it, and since you're now rich… cash should not be a problem. We need to talk for a while."

Ned had Floyd lined out quickly. He seemed very intelligent and picked it up the first time he was told. He, Edna, and Bea were on their way within half an hour, and Ned and I sat at the dining room table and started to explore the possibilities before us.

"I'm seeing bits and pieces of the past, and somehow I know that it is real when I do. I think it may be possible to see more than bits. With the proper amount of power fed into this thing, it feels like it will tell me secrets that we cannot even imagine," I stated.

"You keep saying that you *feel* and *think*. Do you really *know*?"

"Not really. It seems to be telling me things subtly. It's like it is trying to communicate with me. It's possible that the gibberish I was speaking is actually the language the aliens speak. I was watching a line of figures in my mind. I think that it was feeding a written line of instructions into my mind. The only thing is, I could not read what was written. The things that I do gain at those times are like an impression. It would be like opening the door first thing the morning and smelling the scent of rain before daylight. You would all but know that it had rained, but never saw the moisture on the ground. Something like that. I can't be positive, but I'm still pretty sure."

"You are talking about changing the world. How do you mean?"

"Only *our* world, and only that the five of us will have a very interesting time for the rest of our lives if we don't get caught, or this thing doesn't kill me. The money in Bea's coins is nothing compared to what I saw the last time I had visions of the past. There are untold numbers of just such buried items, with no one to claim them but us. Everyone connected to them has passed away, and they are just sitting there waiting for someone just to happen upon them. If we can gain the control we need, it will all be ours. We will be able to live and stay hidden long enough to get this thing out of me."

"And if we can't get it out?" Ned asked.

"Then at least we will be able to hide from the military without eating out of trash cans," I replied.

At about that time, I locked up again.

When I came to, Ned and Floyd were looking at me. They had gone into the garage, set up the power converter, and patiently waited for me to come to. When I did, we proceeded to set up the experiment. We all hoped that it would be a success. Everything would be more difficult if we could not find a way to make at least something happen. They moved me to the far side of the garage, as far away from the power source as possible and practical.

"We will not be able to maintain any reaction that happens for long. If we are able to power the device properly, then we could possibly gain some knowledge of how it works. Possibly even know if I will be able to gain some control. If we can't get it to do anything, then we will have to go back to the drawing board. Whatever the case, ARGO will most likely be on to us soon. Let's just hope that we can make progress quick enough to be able to relocate to a more secure location."

"I was talking to Mr. Schwartz, and he has property close to Houston. He was talking about moving there to get more business, and with the income we're providing him now it won't be long before he will be able to go. We could go there too. There must be someplace to hide there, and our only connection to Houston will be him. What do you think?" Ned spit out.

"I always wanted to see Texas," Floyd muttered thoughtfully.

I was simply mulling over the facts.

"How do you want to hook the leads to you?" Ned asked slowly, glancing between the large wires in his hands and me.

"Let's try hooking them to my fingers at first. We will only feed a small amount of current at first to see what happens."

The system was crude, but hopefully would achieve its intended purpose. There was a cord that plugged into a wall socket that led to a large square box. The box had a large lever that moved ninety degrees, with two smaller leads out the other side. The lever, when moved, increased the flow of electricity through it and into the smaller leads, then to whatever they were attached. On one ninety-degree setting, the flow was cut off, and was at full flow when in line with the leads. The smaller leads had been equipped with large spring loaded clips to secure them to their goal, which at this point were my fingers.

Once connected, the flow was initiated at its lowest level and held there to monitor the effects. At first there seemed to be none, then there was a loud pop and a bright flash. Streams of miniature lightning bolts flashed between the control and me, then they abruptly stopped.

"What happened?" Floyd asked excitedly.

"An overload." Ned returned slowly, attempting to look me over.

"I'm okay. Let's replace the fuse. I have an idea," I shot at Ned.

The fuse box was soon closed, the burned fuse replaced. The makeshift equipment checked out quickly as unharmed.

"Hook you back up?" Ned asked.

"No. We need to go to the store and see if we can buy a train set."

"Why a train set?" Floyd asked, beginning to enjoy the intrigue of the situation.

"It has a much smaller version of what I cobbled together. Lower voltage," Ned replied.

"Are you following me?" I asked Ned.

"*Yeah*! It's getting late, so we'll have to hurry. We'll be back soon. Come on, Floyd."

They were soon outside, and I heard the Ford spring to life. Floyd was starting to accept and live more like his new age, for the engine revved more and the tires cried from the strain put on them from his heavy foot. I sat in the chair, listening to the sound until it was gone. I was still feeling the effects of the last jolt of power. In my mind I could see everything they did.

Once they returned it didn't take very long to jury-rig the new device. The train control was stripped out and wired to some smaller output leads and clips. After some testing, Ned declared it ready to go. He reached out to clip the leads to my fingers, and I stopped him, opened my shirt, and started to explain.

"I want to feed a very small voltage directly into the unit," I said, exposing the square-shaped lump on my upper chest. "Hook one on each corner at the top."

Ned proceeded to clip one, then the other, with a look of torment on his face.

"That's gotta hurt," he said when finished.

"Now, feed as little voltage as you can. Hopefully it won't be able to draw enough through this thing to short anything out," I said, looking at the way my skin was distorted between the clamps and at the unit under my skin. I shuffled in my chair, and a small trickle of blood moved down my chest from the left lead.

The power was on. I felt it instantly. I could hear Ned and Floyd talking to me, but couldn't understand a word. There was a cloud that seemed to form in front of my face, and that was all I could see until the screen formed. The cloud actually covered me entirely, but I couldn't tell that. It was almost form fitting. I could not move, and did not try to for long, because I lost total control of my body.

There was a tiny television screen that formed in front of my eyes. On it was a line of the same symbols or letters I had seen before. They streamed across it slowly. It would start and stop. After a few times, it changed and a picture of me appeared on the screen. A series of letters popped up at the bottom. It became apparent that whatever this thing was, it was trying to communicate with me. Somehow, I knew that I needed to increase the power by only a fraction. It must have perceived the thought, for the cloud cleared around my face and I could see Ned looking at me, his face full of terror.

"Slowly increase the power. Slowly, until the opening closes," I struggled out.

Everything went black.

18

I WOKE UP IN THE back seat of a car moving at a rather high rate of speed down a dark, desolate road. The added sound of the loud exhaust Floyd had modified added to the assurance our traveling speed was high. The only light was the headlights bouncing off the telephone poles as they flashed by and the dash lights reflecting off the faces of the pair in the front seat. I was in a daze, and the poles passing seemed to help keep me there. As I gained more control over myself, I realized that I was sitting between the two girls. Floyd was driving, and Ned had the copilot's seat. Not a word passed for what seemed like hours. The miles passed, and I still could not move. I broke the silence with a slowly growing scream. Everyone in the car jumped, and the girls screamed with me. Floyd struggled to maintain control of the car.

"What was *that*?" he yelled at the back seat, looking in the rear view mirror.

My voice was booming. It sounded like it came from a loud speaker. It reverberated like it was in an empty recital hall.

"STOP... THE... CAR," came out of nowhere, but out of me.

I heard the tires squeal and felt the sudden controlled deceleration fueled by fear and understanding. We moved to the narrow shoulder, and I could hear the gravel rattling around under the tires.

I waved at Bea, who was sitting on the right, to move. She got out. I followed and walked, zombie-like, across the road to the closest telephone pole and started to climb. It was equipped with metal steps screwed in at the proper intervals. There was a roll of cable about halfway to the top, and I stopped at the bottom of the coil. I had heard the other doors open, and the murmuring and shuffling of the others as they looked and wondered. It was difficult for anyone to see what I was doing because the only light was from the car and the stars.

I fumbled with the cable, trying to free the end. When that was accomplished, I jabbed it into my chest at the device. I felt the power and energy flowed through my entire body. There was a thud in the air, like before at Bea's house, only smaller. My mind spun wildly, and the wires grew hot. The power failed, and I fell with a thud to the ground, my entire body smoking, my shirt ablaze, from the feed. I sat up unharmed, looked around, stood up, and started walking out into the wilderness, slowly turning gray as I went.

"Get the foxhole shovel out of the trunk and follow me," I said in a monotone voice, without stopping, my voice still booming loudly.

"Where's he going?" Floyd asked.

"Does it matter? I think we just need to listen and do what he says for a while. Besides, where else are we going to find this much excitement? In a factory or lab somewhere? Floyd, for now this guy has us in the most exciting place in the world. Let's go. Think about it! How did he know you put the foxhole shovel in the trunk before we left?" Ned said.

Floyd was always very well-prepared. In the trunk he always had a flashlight, a small tool kit, several small blocks, and added a small shovel for this trip. He had learned over his many years to be prepared, starting while driving a Model T. Roads were not very good back in those days, and you had to be smart or walk a lot.

I was walking slowly and precisely as if measuring my paces. There were distant noises behind me, the sound of things being shuffled in the trunk, then the trunk closed. Indeterminate voices bounced around, complaining about not being able to see and the occasional stumbling. The flashlight spot danced wildly around me, lighting up small bushes and the rocky ground, then back to where the rest were trying to catch up. I could see them in my mind as if I were with them.

"How can he see where he's going?" I heard Bea ask, her breath a bit heavy.

I stopped. They caught up. I took the shovel from Floyd and stuck it in the ground at my feet.

"Dig 3.5 feet," was all I said.

By this time, I was entirely gray, clothes and all. I stood there frozen as they decided what to do.

They looked at each other for a few seconds, smiled, and started to dig. I stood there, petrified. The ground was a mixture of sand and stones ranging from bits to rocks about two inches in diameter. It was not hard to dig, but it slid in on itself from the sides. That made it take longer than it should. No one asked what they were digging for. The only words traded were those when someone was relieved. When they struck something hard, I came to.

"Where are we?" I asked slowly.

"On the side of the road digging a hole!" Floyd said, breathing heavily and a bit irritated.

"No, where *are* we?" I asked.

"Texas," Ned answered. "Somewhere in West Texas."

"What are we digging up here?" Bea asked.

"One point two million dollars of gold bars. Estimated value in a few years," I answered.

It seemed that even the bugs went silent. The shoveling started, and it was quicker this time. The flashlight lit up a tattered, broken wooden chest. Ned, Floyd, and Edna pounced upon the hole, feverishly digging with shovel and hands until they had the entire top exposed. A few bumps with the shovel and the lid fell away. The dull rectangular shapes of metal bars stared at the light for the first time in many forgotten years.

"Get it loaded as quickly as you can. We will have company if we are not gone soon," I said, still without moving much.

"Do you think you can get the car out here without damaging it?" Ned asked Floyd.

"Let's take a look." Floyd beamed, no longer breathing heavily or irritated. The sight of the tarnished gold had repaired his mood. He and Ned took the flashlight and walked along, looking intently at the route that they would take. It checked out, and the car was soon backed up close to the hole. The bars were soon in the trunk, and we were all loading back into the car preparing to leave.

"Shut everything *off!*" I blurted out.

The engine died and the lights followed. A short time later, a car passed by on the road. Time passed, and Floyd turned and looked at me. We just sat there. About the time everyone started to fidget, I nodded and we started out. The car as large and powerful but still showed the load it was under. The trunk had been about full already, with the five of us and the added weight of the gold, it sagged badly in the rear. It complained but never wavered. We were soon on the road, and I asked to be filled in on what happened before I came to. The windows were rolled up, and the heater was blowing on high. I realized that it was cold. I was wearing only a light jacket and did not feel uncomfortable at all even with the entire front of my shirt burned off.

Ned turned to face me from the front seat and started to fill me in.

"Where did you stop remembering?" he asked.

"When I told you to increase the power."

"That cloud thing covered you for about an hour, then what was like a trap door opened and you told me to up the power. It closed, and you sat there for two days. We got real worried, but just like it's been since this thing started, we were scared to do anything. I mean, if we shut it off, there is no telling what would happen. The same with doing nothing, but you asked to do it, so we just watched, took shifts, and tried to make sure nothing else happened. Well, after two days you cleared up. That thing went away.

"You were all gray and cold. Even the inside of your mouth was gray. You didn't move. ARGO came snooping around again, but didn't come inside the house, so we ran. I went and talked to Mr. Schwartz and got directions to his warehouse near Houston. So we started out. We just put you in the car and got out of there as quick as we could. Then you woke up. Why did we dodge that car? Did we do something really wrong?" Ned finished.

"It was a highway patrolman. He would have searched the car," I told him.

"How can you be so sure?" Edna asked.

"At times, I can see into the future. The more I learn from this thing, the clearer things become. I'm not too sure about everything or anything that just happened, but the information about the car and the search just popped into my head. I knew that it was true, and that it would happen if we didn't hide. He would have taken us to jail, and our future would have been ruined," I answered.

"If you can see into the future, then how much longer is it to the next gas station? We're getting low on gas and I could use a soda," Floyd said with a chuckle. "And you could use a shirt."

"Breakfast wouldn't be bad either," Edna said.

"It doesn't work like that. It comes in flashes. It seems like it has something to do with the amount of power introduced to me and this thing. I guess it would be safe to start calling it us. This thing is intelligent. The time spent in the fog was an attempt for the two of us to communicate. I think that the basis for that was established. The problem is that neither of us can learn each other's language in an hour or even a month. Maybe never. You said that I was out for two days. To me it was almost instantaneous. I went in there and woke up here. Nothing was really clear until just before I said to shut off the car. It was like floating on a cloud. There was no up, no down. All I could see was a grayish haze all around me, then a screen just appeared in front of me and some sort of writing started to flow across it. It did that for a while, and then it started to show pictures and what looked like words. I think that it was trying to build an information base with my reactions to what I saw, because there was no true communication between us. I just seem to be able to sense things now, maybe more clearly now than I could before. It is still difficult to understand. When it happened last time, it was as though I was living the future right then. It was so real. It seems to read my mind in some way, because it keeps us safe. And I could use a shirt."

"I told you so," Floyd said

Ned looked at me thoughtfully, as if mulling over what I had just said. He was about to speak when Edna broke in. She was a little emotional.

"It's bad enough with all that's happened, without you walking around like some character in a bad science fiction movie. Talking all funny. Screaming after not moving for a couple of days. You were so stiff when we put you in the car that they dropped you, and you just bounced around. Didn't bend, move, or anything. I was worried that you were going to break. You stuck a power cable to your chest and fell fifteen or twenty feet and just got up and walked off like some kind of robot or something, still smoking, and how did you know about that gold? It must have been there for a hundred years. What is happening to us all? It just doesn't seem right or real," she finished and looked out the window, tears welling up in her eyes.

The only sound for the next few minutes was the V8 droning and the sound of road noise as we made our way along.

"We're coming up on a station. We'd better stop. I don't know if we will make the next one," Floyd broke the silence, still showing concern for Edna in his face.

The engine noise lessened as we reached slower speeds, and it became all but silent inside the car before we pulled into the station. We were out in the middle of nowhere, and this was a little mom and pop grocery store and gas station. There was a small row of houses on down the road, the probable reason the store had survived. It had two pumps in front with two large fluorescent lights high on either side, sweeping up toward the outside on metal stands. It was breaking day, but the lights still shone bright and lit around the pumps and the front of the store. There was an older Chevy Impala sitting in the outside lane, so Floyd wheeled into the inside, even though the filler cap was on the wrong side. He pulled up far enough to get the hose under the rear of the car and to the opposite side.

We slowly peeled out of the car, everyone stretching and groaning. It had been a long drive so far, I could tell, without knowing really where in Texas we were. The air was cool and smelled wet with the morning dew. Wet grass accented the air before the smell of the cooling fumes from the car took its place. Bea wasted little time retrieving a shirt for me from a bag in the trunk, and I quickly changed. The search was on for the restroom, and Ned headed for the door to find out where it was when we heard what sounded like a gunshot.

A young man burst from the door, running into Ned. They both stumbled and Ned fell to the ground. The other man only stumbled and fell into Bea, and both tumbled onto the sandy ground. There was a jumble of voices and activity. Bea was shouting and so was her assailant. Ned responded quickly to her rescue, grabbing the man by the arm and pulling him up and away from Bea. Floyd was there too, pushing as Ned pulled the boy upright. The stores door clanked again, and another dirty young man bolted out. He had a gun in one hand and a bag in the other. There was shock and anger in his eyes when he saw his friend in the hands of two others. He did not hesitate, but I was frozen. The entire world seemed to start to spin around me.

The second robber yelled, and Ned whirled to face him out of surprise, not bravado. The revolver responded to the mistake. Ned crumpled to the ground, and Floyd followed after the second shot. The first man grabbed Bea in an effort to take her with him.

The sight was now in slow motion in front of me. The closest thing I had ever had to friends were there, two were dead or dying and one, maybe two, were being kidnapped. I felt like a switch was tripped inside me. I screamed what must have been a blood-curdling scream. It froze everyone for a second. The gun suddenly was pointed at me. I raised my hands which made the gunman smile but not stop. This time he had the wrong man.

The lights above me exploded. Power flowed into my fingers then was pulled from the pumps and then straight from the power leads on the wall of the store. I felt powerful. I felt angry, and then I felt very calm. All motion ceased, the noise was gone. The blood staining the ground slowed and stopped flowing. All were frozen, their faces etched in the terror and pain of that one second. I was free to move. I did not feel pain, remorse, or anger anymore.

I walked past the group outside and into the store. Inside, there were signs of a struggle. Some of the smaller display stands had been knocked over. Suddenly I realized, of all things, at that moment that there was no smell. When you walk into an older store with wooden floors, there is always an assault on your senses. The smell of years of use and products give you a sense of walking into a familiar home or kitchen. A pleasant, warm feeling from a comfortable place, but it was not there. What was there was a scene of horror, much like the one outside. On the floor was an overweight, elderly balding man in a pool of blood. Kneeling over him was a woman, just as overweight and about the same age. Her face was a death mask of torture. Tears frozen on her face, blood staining her hands. Husband and wife, their long lives together ended by a senseless act. He would die, and her life would tumble into despair, poverty, a slow, lonely death. It was more than I could stand.

I realized that there was a line of electricity about three inches wide attached to me. It was not like a lightning bolt, but just a white line of power, bright in the center, fading at the edges. As I turned, it stayed in the same place. It had been touching me in the back, now it was in my stomach. I walked back outside, and without emotion I looked around at my friends and the evil men we had chanced into. I concentrated on what I wished happened, that we had not been a part of what happened here and that so many innocent lives had not been so irreversibly changed in such a short period of time.

The thread of power started to grow wider, ever so slowly. As it did, the scene before me started to back up. The assailants retreated into the store. Floyd, Ned, and Bea repeated their tragic moves in reverse. It was then that I realized that Edna had walked around the corner of the building, because she came back toward the car. They gathered at the side of the car, just as they had before deciding to go inside, but that is where it stopped.

The sky faded back to complete darkness, and the Chevy and its occupants backed out the drive and disappeared down the dark roadway. At this point the power stream faded away. Everything remained stopped after that. I roamed around, looking at whatever I could find to interest me. I could touch and move whatever I felt like, but no one or thing reacted to me. Outside, I found a jackrabbit. I picked it up and petted it. It seemed alive in my hands, but did not struggle, and when I put it down, it was still again.

I walked back to the front of the store. There was another thud in the air, and we were all seated back in the car and it was rolling silently back up to the gas pumps. Ned blinked and grabbed me.

"Wha-What... What just happened?" He gasped. "I got *shot*, then everything *backed up*!"

Then the others clamored in as well.

"I was looking for the restroom and heard *gunshots*!" Edna exclaimed.

"That boy had his hands all over me," Bea said in disgust, brushing her hands all over herself as if cleaning away his touch.

Floyd was feeling his chest and looking at me. "We would have died, and the girls would have died later too. Right?" he said calmly.

"Yes. It made me angry and I took action. I still don't know how, but I *did*. This is before the others arrived, and we seem to be functioning *outside* our normal timeline. The rest of the world seems to be frozen in time. You were too, until I got close enough to you."

Things started to move again. Floyd noticed that the bugs started to make noise and buzz again. It was strange, like a bubble popped. The world just jumped into gear.

"We have to prepare. They will be here soon," I said and started into the building. The others followed.

"Morning, folks," the woman that I had seen before said with a huge smile. Her gray hair and bright eyes showed her happiness with life. In her sixties, possibly older, and well past plump, she still moved with determination and purpose in the cleaning duties she was involved in.

"I've already turned the pumps on if you need gas," the friendly voice of her husband came from behind the counter.

I walked over to him, reached over the counter, and touched his arm. He instantly looked shocked, then returned to normal and went back to putting cigarettes on the shelf behind him. It was like nothing happened. We gathered up supplies, and they finally found relief in the room in the back. Floyd filled the tank with premium and checked under the hood. I just stood at the door, watching. The other three chatted and giggled as they browsed the limited contents of the store. Floyd finished filling the car and came inside.

Floyd paid. It was six dollars twenty-three cents.

"You got a pretty big tank on that thing," the man said as he took Floyd's money.

"Yeah. I ordered it that way. I'm real happy with it so far. This is really the first trip we've taken in it. Pulls the load real well," Floyd replied.

"I'll keep that in mind. Thinkin' about gettin' a new one myself," he said as his eyes went glassy. He picked up the phone. "I need you, Brock. There a couple of kids in an Impala that looked like trouble. Okay," he said flatly and hung up the phone, as the sound of a car with loud exhaust came from outside.

Floyd and I walked outside. I stopped, standing by the door, and Floyd moved to the car as if to fill the tank again.

One of the young men looked innocent, like a schoolboy fresh out of high school looking for his first job. Dressed in jeans and a denim jacket, he started to fill the tank quickly, looking at us as if frightened. The other had dead eyes. I had seen them as he had killed before. He was dirty, unclean. His clothes, hair, and skin plainly showed a lack of concern for his appearance, and his action showed that there was little for anything else. He started toward the door, steadily looking at me. His hand slipped into his jacket pocket. I knew his intent, for his eyes were fixed on mine.

There was some noise at the rear of the store that caused the crook to break his icy stare and look to his right. The revolver was already on its way out, and it had started again, this time with more intended victims.

A figure flashed at the right corner of the store that drew his attention as he got close to me. The gun was almost leveled at my chest, and that cold crooked smile started to show once more.

"Hold it right there, boy!" A voice came from my left.

It did not slow the killer down. He extended his left hand to grab me, .38 firmly in his other hand. I simply reached out and touched his approaching left hand with mine, and he crumpled in a heap to the ground.

His partner shouted at me, but was unsure whether to charge me or to run away because of the unseen voice of authority coming from the darkness to his right. After a split second of indecision, he took several quick steps toward me, and Floyd landed a right cross on his chin from behind the pump where he had been standing. The younger, lighter man fell with a thud. Dazed, but not out, he started to recover and was snatched up by a man in a uniform. He was a large, muscular man, strong and powerful-looking. His tightly fitting uniform accented his broad chest and showed taut muscles as he moved. There was no fight left in the boy. He limply complied with the force, was thrown on the trunk of the Chevy, and quickly cuffed. The officer then turned to the other unmoving target. He was still breathing heavily, looking at the pile of person at my feet. I had my hands raised at the elbows to show my intentions.

"What did you hit that one with?" the sheriff puffed. "He went down like a rock. He's still out." He lowered his hand from his holster, revolver still inside.

"Karate," I said, waving my arms around absurdly.

"Seen some of that before," he said, relaxing. "Back away from him and let me get him cuffed." I backed away slowly, and the officer, with a wary eye on me, collected the gun and cuffed the unconscious man. He looked at me, then at Floyd.

"Help me get him to their car," he ordered Floyd, after seeing his larger build.

Everyone poured outside, both owners and the other three who had remained inside chatting with the other two. They all looked around at the sights: two thugs cuffed and lying on the trunk of their car, and the rest just standing looking back and forth between them and each other.

"We would like to leave," I told the officer.

"You'll have to hang around, at least until I can get your names. I may need to keep you here till the highway patrol gets here. I think that I got a bulletin on these two. If these are the guys I'm thinking about, they've killed five people already. Not in that big of a hurry, are you?"

"We really want to leave," I said slowly. Everything slowed once again. "Let's go," I said.

We lost no time getting on our way. The small town quickly vanished to the rear, and those left standing around soon started to move again.

"Nice bunch of kids," the officer told the storeowner. "Good thing they got here after all this was over."

19

THE REST OF THE TRIP was uneventful. Actually boring. It seemed like an endless mix of gas stations and burger joints. I had no more "*events*," and we made it to where Mr. Schwartz had sent us in two more days. We had been in far west Texas and traveled into Houston, then made our way through downtown to the north side, close to a small town called Humble. The trip would have been a day shorter, but the added weight and fear of being stopped for speeding added a full day. We were not sure what had happened after we left the station, how hard the lab was still looking for me, or if they were looking for Ned. I said that we were safe after we left the station, but it was hard to be sure about anything. Anything at all.

It was made extremely clear upon our arrival that Humble was pronounced with a silent *h*. So it was actually "*Umble.*" We caught on quickly. Outside of the poor pronunciation, we were readily accepted and very welcome. It was a friendly little town. Mr. Schwartz had a warehouse on Old Humble Road just north of Upshaw Street. It was just walls and a concrete floor, but it would do for what we had in mind. Schwartz also had a house nearby for us to stay in.

He was making a large profit with our help and was an honest man, but loved his money. We had come to him for that reason. He was aware of that and fully intended to maintain our trust and our business. It was his chance to have the kind of retirement he had hoped for, and he would do what he could to preserve the chance. Ned assured him that if he helped us, things would only get better. That idea pushed him to new heights of cooperation.

Ralph Schwartz had joined the army at fourteen years old during World War II. He was too young and small for his age, but had used his brother's birth date to facilitate the lie. He had seen little combat, being in the transportation corps, and well behind allied lines. It was grueling duty but rarely dangerous. He served in the supply corps where he was trained in business in a worldwide theater, and from mid-1942 he served as such until the war was over. Afterward, he had moved from base to base and job to job until he was assigned as a supply sergeant at the ARGO Lab where he retired.

He met his wife, Carol, in town one day. Her father had the only local pawnshop, which fed off the base. When personnel transferred, they often pawned belongings of all kinds, expecting little but getting what was fair. It made for a decent living for the family, and once Schwartz began to take part, he added the coin and antiques. Profit skyrocketed. Carol was an only child, and the couple inherited the business after the death of her parents. They had turned over most of the control to Ralph and Carol years before and virtually retired anyway. Ralph Schwartz expanded the business as far as he could in such a small town, and looked to Houston as an alternative source for expansion, since he had connections in business there. He purchased several parcels of property in the area and had finally got the break he needed to make the move. It was a win-win situation for both parties, Schwartz with connections there and us with a seemingly endless supply of rare and very valuable coins to sell.

The building was a large, open area. The inside measured about one hundred fifty by fifty feet. There were no walls or ceiling inside, but the outer walls and roof were well-insulated. It was used as a truck repair shop by an oil field company for a short time and needed cleaning. It also needed some repairs and remodeling for it to work for us. Schwartz had several different companies already waiting to start.

We arrived at the old, wood frame house late at night. The air was cool and damp, very different than we were used to. It was a welcome change from home. The others were tired of traveling and just tired. We entered with the key provided and looked it over. It was clean and well-stocked. It had two bedrooms and a rather large kitchen and dining room. You entered in the left front into what was the living room. It had an overstuffed sofa, a couple of end tables, and a small television. That was the room I claimed. Floyd and Edna took the bedroom in the back, and Ned and Bea took smaller room behind the living room, also in the front. It had two twin beds, and while they were interested in each other, the relationship had a long way to go.

I said, and all agreed, that they should clean up a bit and retire. I had not slept since I woke up in west Texas and felt no need to do so. I volunteered to unload and unpack. It was not long before the sounds of soft snores came from both rooms. I took everything from the car and stacked it in the living room. I took the coins and gold and put them by the wall next to the television, then covered them with a blanket. The rest were suitcases and a few of personal items belonging to Floyd, Edna, and Bea. Ned took nothing for fear that he would send up an alarm, and said that he really had nothing worth bringing anyway. I had only a small bag of clothes that they had packed for me.

I felt normal in some ways. There were no flashes of any sort. No strange out-of-control sessions leading to anything, but I did not sleep or eat. I had no feelings about what happened, good or bad. There was a strange feeling that came over me from time to time, and we came to the conclusion that it was a warning of trouble to come. I felt it, and a police car stopped us, but luckily the officer had to leave on another call before he could ask more than a few questions. We watched ourselves after that. I let them know every time from then on.

The next morning, they all slept late. I sat up and watched the only all-night station on TV. It was a parade of old movies, none very good, but it broke the monotony of waiting for the others to wake. They had breakfast and then we made our way to the building down the street. After a short walk through, we returned to what was now our home.

Ned and I started to plan the renovations to what we started to call "the office." The cleaners stopped by the house for directions and instructions after confirming that we had arrived and being properly advised they were soon working. It would be a big job. There were used engine oil stains on most of the floor and in spots on the wall, with grease accenting the stains. We also requested they contact Schwartz and someone to mow the grass and clean the overgrowth from all the property. Our intention was to fence at the property line to add security. The property needed to be clean for visibility, and we wanted to give a good impression to whoever came by. Floyd took control of the project, supervising the work. He was good at it. He organized the situation well and helped speed things along.

The project would be large. We had to make an office at one end and floor the rest of the building. We had to insulate the entire building in an aggressive fashion. We learned much of what we had to do already, but were wary of what was to come next. It could only get more bizarre as we went along.

Floyd would make it all happen. He was a master at taking the idea and making it a reality. Edna often commented that he had not seen him that happy, even when he was young before. It was her belief that he liked the new technology that he was now working with. It was a far cry from the old mule and sled that he had hauled water to wash with to his family's house as a boy. He had worked hard in his former life and never been able to move out of that type of labor-intensive jobs. He had always wanted and tried to move up the ladder, but had not been fortunate enough to succeed. He now had a unique opportunity and was making the best of it. He intended to prove that he had been capable before but just passed over.

The work went slow and tedious. There were revisions at every step of the way. Our need to keep the final purpose secret made things even worse for those working on each particular part of the project. It was explained that we were not sure of what we wanted as a finished product. That was little consolation to any of the different foremen. The only thing that helped when we had to rip something out and start over was the generous salary and promise of added bonuses for an accelerated pace. It still seemed there was more time spent going backward than forward. Time dragged along as slow as progress did.

There were long periods where there was little for us to do but observe. We got bored. Floyd did the most, and he even started to pace the floor. He would stay at the site a few hours in the morning after opening and come home for a long lunch. In the afternoon, he would go back and forth until time to lockup. As always, he and whatever crew foreman was there would review progress and plan the next day's work. Floyd would bring the information home for us to look over as a formality. We had grown to trust his judgment, and that added to his drive and confidence. Looking back, it would have been almost impossible to do all this without his help and guidance. He had a grasp of things because of his age and common sense, which eluded the rest of us on most occasions. He could explain anything, so it was easy for all of us to understand.

We had to do something to occupy ourselves. We could not really socialize outside our group for fear of being discovered. Ned and I had to be extremely careful, because we were certain that law enforcement would be, if not already, informed to be on the lookout for us. It stood to reason with the loss of several men that I was somewhat of a priority for at least the department that was over the ARGO Lab. We could not be certain how large or aggressive the search would be. It would be very hard to justify any charges with no evidence, and the explanation of stolen alien technology would probably be a hard sell, but murder of a government agent would be good enough.

One of the foremen at the site told Floyd how to get to the Houston Public Library. It was in downtown Houston, and with our three friends having new identities, getting a library card and a stack of books would not be difficult. It sounded like the diversion we needed.

I refused to go. It was too risky for me to expose everyone to some unknown and unexpected event. Ned and I had tried to make something happen to gain some control. It was useless. Nothing we could do, including low power at home, would work anymore. Things had started to appear normal for a while, and Ned and I both had hoped that it was all over.

They brought all the books the library would let them have. It was a wide variety of subjects. Ned was a good judge of what to bring for me. We had talked at length about what we wanted to research, and I had given him my other interests as well. The books on physics and alien visitors were limited in information and numbers. They were both outdated and lacking in any real information, but they reinforced what we knew already in physics and were entertaining about the aliens.

I read through the books at an incredible rate, most of the time. My usual reading speed was fairly fast before all this started, but it had at least tripled now. There were times, though, that I had a hard time reading at all. It was almost like the words did not make any sense. After a few hours of reading at a third grade level, my reading and comprehension level would get better. After a month, I could just look at a page and know what it said and have complete recall of all information acquired. Ned and I decided that the device was trying to tap into my brain, and that was why the increase in ability and erratic pace at times. The only reasonable explanation for the periods of inability was it trying to interface with my brain. It made sense at the time.

With my ability to read dozens of books in a day, everyone else restricted themselves to one book per trip. Ned and Bea had started to make visits to the library almost every day and started to order other books through the system. It took at least a week, sometimes more, to get anything in. Some of the books gave us a bit more insight. There were some obscure books they found on alien technology and theories on who they were and where they came from. Most were nothing more than creative writing, but there was a fact or two in a few that made sense and gave us a path to pursue.

To fill the gaps in time while waiting for more important books, I started reading about the American Civil War. It turned into an obsession. Within a two-week period, I had read every book available through system. It seemed to run through my mind all the time. Different scenes played like a movie. An entire day would play in the back of my mind while I went through my day. It was like having the TV playing in the background, and from time to time it would get my attention. Names and faces that I had no way to know came to me and stayed with me in almost a haunting manner. It seemed as if they were calling to me from the grave. I could almost hear their cries as they died on the battlefield. Finally, it slowly tapered off until it was just a voice in the back of my mind, nagging at me, like it was something important that I had forgotten.

Things crashed around us. We had to back up and almost start over on the construction. The ventilation system was not sufficient to handle our cooling needs and filter out our estimates of radiation. We were devastated with the delay. It meant that we would have to endure more months of the tedium, waiting to try to make me free of this thing or make something out of it. Either was better than hiding in a strange town and having nothing to do, always afraid of being found by the lab.

Floyd decided to work extra to get us back on track, but didn't want to work all night as not to attract too much attention. As night fell in the area, activity slowed to almost desolation. It became so quiet by ten in the evening that it was like being back in the desert. Our project running twenty-four hours a day would be like a beacon, drawing local attention. Certainly the police would at least stop by to check us out. It also did not seem too prudent to have plants or even animals dying suspiciously around our new facility because we had not filtered out the radiation properly. That kind of scrutiny we could not afford. Things would just have to go slow, and we would just have to wait and be bored.

At the other end of Upshaw Street, Bea and Edna had made new friends against our urgings. They were two brothers and their families, the Benders. Both women were housewives with large families and welcomed the company of the two new ladies in the area. After making an acceptable excuse to keep them away from me, their relationship blossomed. They had dinner on a regular basis, played cards, and drank a few beers. Everyone fit right in except for Ned, who did his best. It was the actual age of the other three that made it all possible.

Jack Bender and his brother Jim were union truck drivers and were away at times. The time alone gave their wives and our girls more time to fuss over some project, and made all of their lives a bit more tolerable. Ned spent more time with Floyd at the office, which was profitable and productive for us too. Ned was taken with Bea, and she with him. The time apart may not have been good for them, but it got Ned back on track and our project moving much faster.

It was me that had the problem. With the others starting to acclimate to their surroundings, it left me alone more and more. That gave me time to think about things, all kinds of things. My mind wandered from one end of everything to the other—the beginning of time, to what the movie stars in Hollywood had for lunch, who won the first armed conflict, to the end of the world. I kept getting a vision in my head of a man in a mechanic's uniform, preaching in some kind of a shop that the end of the world was tomorrow, for days on end. For him, at least, it never came when he said. I saw people on the moon and further out in space. It was a bit disturbing, seeing all these strange things, not knowing where they came from and, in some cases, what they were. Some images were from the world wars. Some were from other wars around the planet, but I was unsure about the date or exact event. Then there were visions of someone's everyday life.

I started to play solitaire. It did not take long before I could anticipate the cards ahead of time. Still I played. Soon the cards would play the game by themselves. I just sat there, and the cards played and danced in the air as the game progressed. It was a bit unsettling for the others, so I restricted my playing time to late at night or when they were gone.

Then one night, as everyone was going to bed, it started. I was sitting on the couch, trying to be part of the furniture, and starting to feel sleepy for the first time since all this started, when a small thread of light crept, like a snake being charmed from a basket, out of a wall socket. It slowly, deliberately moved in my direction, touching everything in its path as it went, as if sampling its surroundings. When it reached me, it touched my entire front, slowly surveying all it could see, starting at the top of my head and slowly sweeping down to my feet, covering everything as if to see what it was that surrounded what it was searching for. After the tour, it settled center of my chest and stayed. I was no longer sleepy. My mind started to move at an accelerated rate again. It was not out of control, but it was moving at least triple my normal capacity almost instantly.

Ned saw the light and came to investigate. He was shocked and quickly moved to see if I was all right. He mistakenly moved between the ribbon and me. He stiffened as if in pain and stood up straight. The power ribbon danced around his back then moved over his shoulder, back to the center of my chest. It stayed there no matter. Everyone got up and no one went to bed for a while. I moved around the house at Ned's request, and it followed me. As I left one room to the next, it would change sockets to one in the next room. The next step was to go outside and see what happened. It was not good.

I stepped outside into the cool, humid air, and the ribbon attached to my back. I walked in as straight a line as I could away from the socket I was connected to. The screen door closed with a flash. The ribbon cut through the door, wood, screen, and all. It became more intense trying to sustain contact. The door started to burn, and sparks started to erupt from the electric breaker box on the back wall.

Floyd and Ned each grabbed an arm and rushed me back into the house. Everything calmed down, and the ribbon resumed its smaller, calmed state. Floyd quickly removed the remnants of the door.

The power did not leave me for the next several days, and that added to the need to get the office up and running to protect and hide me even more.

At first, I tried to move around the house as normal. It didn't work because it was too disturbing to the others. The ribbon didn't hurt anyone, but it tingled as it passed over them to get back to me. They didn't like it. The long, virtual imprisonment was starting to take its toll. I resigned myself to the couch and just sat there. How long I sat there lost in my dreams was uncertain, at least to me.

20

THE FIRST THING THAT SHOOK me was Ned, trying to monitor the power stream. He sat different materials in the way first, and none made any difference. He tried larger panels. It just felt around and bypassed those like the others. Failing to interrupt the process in any fashion, he next tried to monitor and measure to gain more insight. There was nothing to find. No matter the method, nothing worked. He could not find a meter or procedure that would show the ribbon existed. It tingled when it touched your skin with the voltage of a flashlight battery, but the only other sensation related to contact was a slight feeling of pressure. He finally gave up.

They started to bring me books, any kind of books. I read them all. Ned and Bea would just grab whatever they could find and bring it. They would empty an entire shelf. They started on one side and worked their way around the room. By the next morning, I had gone through them all. It began to wear on them, all the trips downtown with little else to do, but it also gave Ned and Bea a chance to be alone. That had become a regular occurrence as well. They were now a couple, no matter how much they tried to deny it. They were both excited about it, but did not want to admit it.

On Wednesday nights, there was a regular card game with the Benders down the street. All four couples engaged in penny poker and a rather large amount of drink. I, of course, was not invited. It did not bother me to stay home as it were. I read a lot and watched what TV there was. I seemed to be quite content doing basically nothing for the most part.

This Wednesday night I had a large number of American Civil War books to read. It had become a passion. I felt a connection to it that was hard to explain. I was sitting on the couch with the TV churning away on some pointless program while reading through a particularly interesting book when I noticed that the power thread was growing brighter. In the low light that I preferred, it was painfully obvious that it was ever increasing. As the light increased in the room, there was another thread that joined the first, then another.

The room started to turn and twist much like a slight to extreme case of vertigo. I felt ill for a moment, and then it went away. The TV went off, as well as all the lights. The power drain on the circuits seemed to limit itself to a point below the level of causing a problem. It was as if I was drawing all the power I could get without shutting down the source. Now the threads were coming to me from every different outlet in the house.

I somehow knew that I had to go outside to the breaker box. I walked slowly to the back door, with the threads following the entire way. I walked down the steps toward the box and lost the connection from inside. It was pitch black outside, but I had no problem seeing somehow. When I reached the box, I opened the outer door and removed the inner plate, exposing the cables. I raised my right hand, palm out, and placed it in front of the opening, very close to exposed cables. A soft glow appeared between my hand and the box. It increased ever so slightly, but never became intense. I really don't know how long I stood there, but I felt exponentially better.

In the glow from the drain, I could see that my skin was turning a dull gray. It did not seem odd to me, but then nothing seemed to bother me. It was as if I had lost the ability to feel or care about anything. I stared at my left hand and watched it go from pasty white to light gray to almost black. It seemed quite normal.

It became hard to move. It felt like I was trying to walk around neck deep in mud. I could think with untold clarity and knew that this was nothing abnormal. *Abnormal!* My mind suddenly realized what was going on, and for a split second it rebelled. I should have been burned to a cinder! It was like screaming at the top of your lungs and not getting any sound to your ears. It was gone. All the panic and fear was just there, and then *gone*. I was focused again. *It* was in control now.

I turned to the west and looked up at the stars. I seemed to get my bearings and took a step forward. I was standing at the doorway at ARGO when my foot hit the ground. I felt a shock wave pass over me, then seemed disoriented, but was not deterred. I entered the door with a determined attitude. I seemed to know where I was going and what I needed to do. The problem was it was not clear to me at all. It was like not being in control, but being there. I started to think of *me* as *us*.

We were looking for something and came to get whatever it was. The people that we encountered were frozen like before, no one moved at all. They were a bit blurry at times. *We* made our way through the halls and in various labs collecting small devices. *We* started filling our pockets.

Suddenly *our* vision went white. There was a sudden flashing of the characters *we* had been seeing. *We* had a sudden vision of an army MP and a man in a lab coat. Both had an astonished look on their face and seemed to be staring at *us*. It seemed to have put *us* on alert. All the streaming letters turned red. We picked up a last few pieces and *we* were back outside in an instant. *We* paused, looked up, and took a step to the east. *We* were back home in Texas.

The alert script seemed to go away when *we* got back. There was a short, frantic flashing of red, then it returned to the normal black and white. From there it settled to a simple line in the bottom and right side. They would move around, some would flash, and then they would stream for a moment and stop. It would start over again, and that is what it did when it was there.

I simply walked stiffly back into the house and resumed my regular position on the couch. The program on the TV was at the exact spot I left it. I had looked up from the book I was reading when I started to feel the effects of the change. The actors were still in the same place, moving toward each other to embrace. I simply accepted the fact that it had all happened in less than a second.

I sat there for, well, I'm not really sure how long, but for a while, and the stuff that was in my pockets started to hurt. My pockets were full and now digging into my legs. I started pulling them out one by one and lining them up on the coffee table like trophies.

21

NED CAME IN THE DOOR first. He drank less. The others followed, grumbling about how late it was and how bad they would feel in the morning. They stumbled around, getting comfortable at home before Ned stopped to check on me. There was normally little need. I just sat there. He was surprised when he saw my color. It was still a bright gray.

"What happened this time?" he asked, as if questioning a child about a scraped knee. The others came to see.

"I'm not sure what all happened, but *we* went to ARGO and got a few things," I said and waved my hand at the table.

Ned quickly took inventory of the items.

"All marked as from H 333. Must be connected to your unit," Ned said and continued slowly. "You said *we* went to the lab. You mean tonight? Who is *we*? And there is no way to get there in the time we were gone, let alone there and back. What are you talking about?"

"*We* drew power from the house supply and *We* were instantly at the entrance to the ARGO Lab. Somehow *we knew* what to get, and did so. When *we* were done, *we* got back here the same way. *We're* not too sure what all happened, but *we* recovered this stuff and was back here in less than a second. The show *we* were watching, *we* never missed a bit of it. It was like *we* never left. I know *we* went, *we* have those things to prove it, but *we* really don't understand."

"You're gray," Bea broke in.

"That was part of it. The more power *we* drew, the darker gray I became. It seems to be getting lighter now," I replied.

"Is there anything we can do?" Floyd asked, standing with Edna behind the couch. "I've got to be at the office early. I knew this was a bad idea."

"*We're* fine. At least I think *we* are, but there isn't much you will be able to do," I said

I'll stay with him and do what I can. The office is too important to put off. Go ahead," Ned answered.

"*We* should try to connect these items to the main unit. It will help *us* process the situation," I said.

"How do you know that?" Ned asked.

"*We* just do."

"It's in you," Bea said with a twinge of disgust in her voice. "How do we connect anything to it?"

"She's right. It's under your skin, or at least out of sight. How do we do it?" Ned asked.

"They are lined up left to right. They are to be attached at *our* breastbone in order. We will do the rest," I replied.

"If you say so. Get your shirt open," Ned said reluctantly.

Each piece was placed on my breastbone, beside the device, one at a time. The same gross phenomena repeated itself each time. My skin would cover the item, and when it spat out the new device, it was empty. My chest would boil and bubble and contort itself, then settle down to wait for the next. When all were in, the original cases that had adhered themselves to my breastbone were spat out, and I lapsed into what seemed like a deep sleep. Ned and Bea sat on either side of me for the rest of the night to keep watch, trying to take turns staying awake.

22

IT TOOK TWO DAYS FOR me to stir. Ned and Bea had given up their watch on the couch about noon the first day, but did not leave the house. One of them was in the room at all times. Floyd had gotten up reluctantly and gone to supervise the construction crew. Edna fed everybody. I simply sat on the couch with my head down, chin to chest.

It would be impossible to describe the feelings related to having friends who cared enough to watch after me the way they all did. We were in an impossible situation. Ned was simply my friend, and in the world we had made for ourselves, it was rare to be able to call someone friend. I was never sure, like Ned, until all this started, just how good of friends we had become.

The others were a different story. They had lived a life already and had started to prepare themselves for the inevitable. Through me, all that had changed into an unexplainable miracle. They handled it with incredible poise, but the generation they were from had that quality. Most seemed to have the ability to accept and adapt to the cruelest of circumstances, and if it turned out to be euphoric instead, all the better. For both reasons, they had taken me into their fold, and that would be almost impossible to change. I had been fortunate to fall in with such exceptional people. If I hadn't, I would probably be locked in a lab somewhere, or on a medical examiner's table by now.

Despite all their constant and continuing concerns, all anyone could do without getting all of us locked up was watch and wait. The second day was better, but still a repeat of the first. Floyd was in a much better mood and condition, but still left on time. Edna kissed him at the door and said that lunch would be ready when he got back. The watch continued and all conversation resembled ones in an ICU ward or a funeral home. All were hushed and had an air of sorrow. It was genuine concern, laced with a touch of what would happen to them if I were gone.

About two in the afternoon on the second day, I woke up. You would have thought that a parade had come to town with all the excitement. I just raised my head and started talking like nothing had happened. I didn't get out three words before Ned yelled at the others and they came running. The overwhelming question was, "Are you all right?" but since I didn't know I had been out, the question was difficult to answer.

"How long was I out this time?" I queried.

"A little under two days," Ned answered with reservation.

"You turned gray and were as cold as *ice*! We thought you were dead! *Again*!" Bea exclaimed, her eyes welling up.

Edna said nothing, but her face reflected the same amount of bother.

"I'm hungry," I said flatly.

They all looked stunned.

"Anything to eat?" I asked with a smile, looking at their frozen faces.

"The gray is gone," Edna said slowly.

"It just drained out of you like you sprung a leak," Ned said, not moving anything but his mouth. None even blinked, until suddenly they all looked around the floor, as if looking for the gray they had said ran out of me.

I slapped the tops of my knees with my hands and smiled broadly.

"Should we go out? I'm really hungry!" I asked, almost beaming.

"We better stay here. Can you fix him something kinda quick?" Ned asked, quietly looking at the women.

"Sure," Edna said, and they both left the room in a rush.

"Hungry, huh?" Ned said with a smile.

"Famished!" I said with gusto.

"Are you aware of what has been going on lately? You haven't been yourself," Ned said with caution.

I pulled open the front of my shirt and tapped breastbone.

"You talking about my little friend here? Yeah, I remember, but it doesn't change the way I feel right now. I think it is turned off, and do not ask me how I know, I just do. Now, how about a cookie or something? Water sounds good."

"You haven't eaten or drank anything in weeks. Are you sure you're up to all this?"

"Oh, yeah. Let's go!" I said, standing.

We made our way into the kitchen at the back of the house. The smell of bacon frying filled the air and delighted my senses. We moved to the small table to the left of the elongated room and sat down. The kitchen proper was at the other end, where both women were feverishly at work.

"I hope bacon and eggs are okay," Edna shot our way, not missing a beat.

"I'll have some biscuits ready shortly. I know you like them," Bea said, smiling at us. I was not sure which of us she was talking to, but I had hopes that it was Ned. She was beautiful at twenty-one, but my mind still saw her as the other elderly Bea. It was strange. I had no emotional attachment to any of them anymore, to anyone at all really. It was and still is hard to explain. It was just gone.

I ate. I ate more. I continued to eat until there were no more eggs, bacon, or biscuits. I ate it all and wanted more. There was left over meatloaf, and the two girls started to make me sandwiches. The sandwiches were quicker, but not considered first, because it would not have been a hot meal. Ned was still watching cautiously. When the meatloaf was gone, I seemed to have had enough, so we just all sat at the table and talked and laughed. Everything seemed to be fine, normal, if you will.

There was none of the strange writing in my vision. No flashing signals either. I looked at my skin from time to time, and it looked as pale as ever. I never thought that pale would sound good, but it did this time. It seemed like the nightmare may have been over, or at least taking a better turn. Ned broke up the festive mood.

"You feeling okay?"

"I feel great!" I shot back with a smile.

"Do you think that it may have turned itself off after we added the other components?"

"To be honest, I'm not too sure. It all seems to have truly turned off," I said thoughtfully.

"You ate an enormous amount of food. Almost two dozen eggs, a couple of pounds of bacon, a whole pan of biscuits, and six sandwiches. You should have gotten sick long before you finished. I'm just concerned," he finished.

I lifted my shirt and patted my flat stomach.

"See, still just as skinny as ever, but I bet if I keep eating like this, I'll be looking healthier sooner than later," I said with a laugh.

We all laughed, but Ned's face was still full of concern.

The conversation started up again, and we talked for a while longer. I regaled them with stories I had read recently, and the girls told of things from "the days of old." Ned was sort of left out. Like me, he had spent most of his life in a classroom, but he still got in a few stories about the lab.

"I'm thirsty," I said suddenly. Edna started out of her chair.

"That's okay. I've worked you enough already," I said, stopping her with a two-handed gesture. She sat down slowly and then turned back to the yarn Bea was spinning. It was something about a mule.

I walked toward the refrigerator and heard them laugh. It sounded like it was coming from inside a drum. I could feel it starting again, then it was gone. I stood still for a few seconds, waiting for it to overtake me, but it didn't.

False alarm, I thought, and opened the door to get a drink. When I stopped, there was no liquid left except beer. For some reason, I just didn't want any. Milk, juice, water, or soda, I drank it all. No one noticed. They were relaxed for a change and having a good time. I finished, returned to the table, and joined the revelry.

I started on a story about the battle of Shiloh, which Bea's uncle had been a part of, when I got a shocked look from all.

"What?" I asked slowly. My voice sounded a bit odd.

"You're not going to start doing something strange again, are you? I don't think I can take any more of it," Edna said with a small sob and left the room.

127

Everything just stopped. Bea and Ned were frozen, except for their ever-increasing look of horror.

"*What...* WHAT!" I stammered out, and then I noticed why I sounded funny. The left side of my upper lip was coming to view. It was slowly moving out from my face, like it was swelling rapidly. It just kept swelling, but did not hurt. There was pressure, but no pain.

Bea and Ned both jumped from their seats and backed away as if I was going to explode on them or something. It must have looked horrid from their viewpoint. From mine, it looked like something was trying to push off that side of my face. The protrusion was so large now that my nose had flattened out and just become two ever-expanding holes. It looked like a baseball under my skin, and then it started to move. It crawled slowly to the other side of my face, then to the top of my head. Once there, it moved around slowly, then down to the side close to my right ear, and then moved slowly around the back of my head to the other ear. It sat there for a short while, and then started to grow again. It got bigger, and ever so slowly it moved back to the top of my head. It didn't take long before it looked like I had two heads, one on top of the other, but only in size. The other was a misshapen ball of hair and skin, pulsating with activity. All the openings on my face, along with my skin, were stretched to their limit.

My skin would crack, then pop, and blood would start to flow, then it was gathered up by black ooze and both were absorbed back inside. I felt no pain. I should have been writhing on the floor, but I was only vaguely aware of what was happening. The pulsating stopped, and my face was a grotesque mask of upward flowing lines. The hair on my head was spread so thin that it was no longer a cover, but horrid patches that sprigged on the bulbous growth.

Bea had buried her head in Ned's chest and was holding on for dear life, trying to escape the overwhelming urge to run away. She wanted so dearly to comfort us both and make it go away, but could not quell the fear and revulsion she felt.

Through a small slit over one eye, the scene registered. I made an effort to ask what was wrong, not really knowing. With the skin down to my shoulders stretched to the breaking point, my jaw would hardly move, and there was no place for the sound to go. All that came out was a low muffled, "*Whaaa.*"

That was it for Bea. She shot me a split second glance and left the room sobbing. Ned was trembling, forcing himself to stay in control. He came closer and kneeled down to level his face to mine. Through the slit, I could see the strain in his face and tears welling in his eyes. Rapid footsteps on the hard wood floor sent a chill up Ned's spine and caused him to lose his balance as he looked for the source. His tense state caused him to release a slight yell as he lost control and his balance at the same time. He fell at Floyd's feet.

"What's wrong with *every*"—Floyd started as he took the short step in the room—"*Holy!*" he almost yelled as he staggered back at the sight of me. "That has got to be killing him… in more ways than one!" he finished, with excitement still filling his voice.

Ned was a heap on the floor in front of Floyd still, and neither could take their eyes off the apparition that was now me. For a few seconds, we were all frozen in the moment.

Floyd, of course, was the first to recover. He grabbed Ned by the arm without looking and dragged him to his feet, his stare still on me. Ned found his feet, but stood crouched as if unable to stand straight. At the sight of them, I slowly reached a hand up to try and feel out the problem. *It has to be horrid* ran through my head, just as my hand made contact with the bulb. Little did I know that this was nothing of what I would endure for the next hour.

As my hand made contact with the swelled part of my head, there was an audible electrical crack. It was like the sound produced by a static electrical discharge from a spark plug or something similar. Instantly, it was as if the air was let out of a balloon. Whatever it was on top of my head started to flow down my neck and into my body. It left quickly, leaving a mass of loosened skin hanging in a layered pile just off my shoulders. Ned tried to take a step back, but made contact with Floyd. Their faces were contorted and ashen.

There were small electrical pulses that would appear and move systematically across the pile of loose skin. It started to tighten. It took very little time for it to look normal again. It seemed to just move back into place, with sparks passing over the surface as it grew back.

The mass of unknown, what seemed like fluid, was now pulsating under my shirt. It would make a long lump up the side of my neck then recede. Lumps would show under my shirt and move side to side, then shrink. The pattern changed. They would form and move in a pattern all the way around my chest. It seemed to be systematic after a fashion. After covering the inside of my upper body, the bulge targeted the rest of me. It took in every inch of me eventually from under my skin.

"What's it *doing*?" Ned asked, finally starting to recover.

"I... think... it's... cleaning... my... insides," I said spasmodically.

"How do you *know*? Are you in contact with *it*?" Ned asked excitedly.

"No."

My left foot started to swell. It grew so large that my shoe burst. My toes grew ten times their size and then started to return to normal, and a protruding ring formed at their base. The ring traveled up my foot to my leg and proceeded up the left and down the right, growing to a full two inches over the muscles on all sides. It repeated the procedure for the right shoe and foot, and then it just receded back to nothing under my skin. My skin was sagging and badly bruised but recovered slowly.

My right foot started to shake. It grew ever more violent. It quickly spread to both legs, and I fell to the floor—arms, legs, and neck flapping and my torso twisting every way possible. It seemed like it would never stop, but it was only for a minute or so. As violent as it was, I still felt no pain. Then it was over. I just lay there, not really knowing what to do. There was too long a pause for Ned and Floyd, and they each grabbed me under an arm and put me back in the chair I had fallen out of. I just sat there with a blank expression on my face, blinking my eyes and breathing heavily.

"Is it over?" Ned asked to both Floyd and I while looking back and forth at us.

"I think so. I feel okay... really different. Strange," I stumbled out.

"I have no doubt, after that. I know I'm wasting my time asking, but are you all right?" Floyd asked cautiously.

I nodded my head slowly, signaling that I was. Everything was still. There was no sound. I was looking at my feet. My shoes were gone, socks torn, but my toes seemed to be fine. They wiggled like they were supposed to. I looked up from my feet to my two friends standing in front of me. They jumped back when I stood up with incredible speed. My arms began to flap and whirl in odd rhythms. I stood and began to walk. Somehow I made it out the back door, arms still flailing. I fell down the steps and began to convulse on the ground like I had before in the house, but this time it grew ever more violent. My joints began to move in unnatural directions. Soon I was a sickening sight. My arms and legs were flapping back and forth and side to side until it was physically impossible for them to go further, bending almost a full 180 degrees in both directions, as well as side to side.

My left arm shot up and locked itself stiffly at the sky. Each finger started to dance. Each would move round and round in turn, reminding me of a ballet troop, each taking their turn. It was as if they needed to get a bearing for what came next. This was followed by each joint in each finger moving the same grotesque pattern as the others before. They moved slowly at first, in all directions, one at a time, then started to move in unison. If it hadn't been for the awful cracking and popping sounds, it would have been almost entertaining. My right hand joined in, catching up quickly.

My fingers curled slowly around in separate directions, giving the appearance of wilting flowers. After reaching my hand, everything went wild. All the connections in my hands and fingers broke down. Everything jumped, undulated, and twisted from a ball to a mass of flexing digits. The frenzy intensified to a blur, moved back down my arms, and then stopped. My entire body swelled, showing bruises, and then within a few minutes everything looked normal.

Ned watched, finally succumbing to the horror, ran to the corner of the house and wretched. Floyd had a pained look on his face, but outwardly seemed to be unaffected. He was the strongest of us all and kept watch on Ned and I until it stopped.

They let me lay on the ground for about fifteen minutes. I did not move. I just lay there looking up at the sky. The clouds were doing their usual dance in the summer Texas sky. It was a real sight to see. It seemed fantastic, even though I had watched the less intense version at home many times before.

When they thought they had waited long enough and Ned had sufficiently recovered, they once again helped me to my feet. I was shaky and weak.

"He feels all rubbery!" Ned exclaimed.

"Not surprised after all that. It would be nice to be able to take you to some kind of a doctor," Floyd shot at me.

I let out a shadow of a chuckle and slowly said, "What would we tell them? This guy has some kind of alien paste in him, and it makes him do strange things, makes his joints move in ways that would make a normal person crippled for the rest of their life and seem to have very little effect on him shortly after it does all this. You would be sent the insane asylum with me, and if ARGO ever got wind of us, we would never be heard from again. I would probably be dissected, and everyone else would either be locked up forever or suffer the same fate as me. Regardless, I seem to be no worse for wear. Think of it this way, if they find me, they find you. If this stuff kills me, take me out of state and just leave what's left of me somewhere, hopefully never to be found. Reap the benefits of what we have done already and be happy that you all have a new life. It should be a good one with what money we have gathered already. My life is a small price to pay to save the rest of you. I'm sure the army would love to try to find out how you lost thirty years or so."

There was an awkward silence, and then the two of them half carried, half dragged me back inside to the kitchen table, where this had all started. I flopped limply into the chair, barely able to maintain my seat. I had little control over myself. My entire body was as numb as my mouth the last time I had gotten a filling. My mind worked, but nothing responded very well to any request or command. I just sat there in a lump.

"I'm gonna get a beer," Floyd said, looking at Ned. They had both been in a trance, staring at me, I suppose waiting for the next show. Floyd made a gesture at Ned, asking if he wanted a beer too.

"No, I don't think I should. I'm still a little sick," Ned said, touching his palm to his stomach.

Floyd went to the refrigerator and collected a beer, opened it, and took a couple of large gulps before closing the door and rejoining Ned. He realized that he had the bottle opener still in his hand and pitched it back onto the countertop by the sink. The silent stares began again.

"I feel sick," I said slowly. It took the frozen pair time to thaw, and before they could, I opened my mouth and retched slightly. A large lump filled my throat and then my mouth. A black wad around the size of a tennis ball forced its way out of my mouth. It slowly contorted its way out past my teeth and fell to the floor. Ned and Floyd were moving to grab me and take me back outside, and it fell between their feet, shattering into thousands of BB-sized pellets. Both men jumped back. The sound of the pellets rolling on the floor was the only sound.

I sat back in the chair, feeling really sick now. I was turning pale again, and the room was starting to spin again.

"How much more of this can he take?" Floyd insisted.

"I have to believe that he is past his limit. I can't see how he has survived this long. There's nothing that we can really do but watch. We are witnessing history at his expense and still have no idea what is going on," Ned said slowly. He paused, as if pondering the situation, and seemed to regain some of his composure.

"We are not even sure that this won't somehow start to affect us. Do you have that movie camera out where we can get it? It may be wise to record some of this for later if it does get around to us," he finished.

"I want to get the girls out of here if this stuff is catching. The last—" Ned cut Floyd off in mid-sentence.

"Not catching that way, I don't think anyway. It would be more like standing in a ray of light that stays with you. Like radiation, but different. We all have been exposed to it, just at different levels. Nothing we can do now, except wait and see if it gets to us. How about that camera?" Ned said coolly.

"No film or batteries. It's still packed away too," Floyd said thoughtfully.

I flinched and sat up. Both men backed up in anticipation and fear. My head wobbled on my neck like I was trying to stretch out a kink. For a second, I screamed, then long pointed spikes shot out from all over my head. Some were over a foot long and an inch at the base. The others were smaller and shorter. My eyes were not even immune, a black bump formed in the center and expanded to cover the entire surface of both eyes. They grew to a length of about six inches and formed a perfect point. My head looked like a porcupine or a heavily spiked mace, and continued to wobble slowly. I was moaning lowly the entire time.

The spikes instantly crumbled into the same small pellets as the ball had before and scattered on the floor with the others. The exit wounds oozed a black-looking paste, and it too transformed and fell. My neck was next. It shot out only a few, and they were gone quickly.

With a gurgling yelp my torso was next. The number of protrusions was so great that it literally ripped my shirt to shreds and pushed me almost out of the chair because of the mass from my back. One in the center of my breastbone kept growing slowly, and once it reached about two feet they all fell to the floor. I had stopped watching my two friends. Their reaction had started to trouble me in some odd way. The only sound in the room was the sloshing sound of Floyd's beer as he took a large gulp. The lower part of my body fell victim next. I was now naked, sitting on a group of spikes from my waist to my toes.

The instant they fell away, I felt fantastic. I felt new, well, energized. Color returned to my entire body quickly and to my face faster than the rest. There were random red blotches all over me that slowly faded. I sat back in the chair and leaned forward modestly, trying to cover myself.

"Think I might need some clothes?" I asked firmly.

Still stunned, Floyd reacted first and much quicker than Ned. As he walked out of the room, his footsteps caused vibrations in the wooden floor, and the pellets moved around, looking for a new resting place. It made an odd sound.

"I'm getting tired of asking this, and I'm sure you are tired of hearing it, but are you all right?" Ned asked sheepishly.

"Outside of having my butt stuck to this vinyl chair and sitting in the kitchen naked, I'm just fine, believe it or not. I honestly feel… *wonderful*. Really alive." I started to stand, then thought better of it, given my lack of clothing.

Floyd came back with a pair of his pajama bottoms and tossed them to me.

"That's the best I could do in a hurry. Your stuff is still packed up."

"Thanks. This will do just fine for now," I said, standing quickly and stuffing each leg in the pajamas in rapid succession. They were too big in the waist and too short, but at least they covered me up. The black nodules stuck to the bottom of my feet and rolled around all over the floor as I moved, but as I stepped out of the mass, everything stuck to me fell off. All three of us stood looking at the patch of black giving a dark tint to that portion of the floor.

"Do you think it's dangerous?" Floyd asked.

"No," I said. "I think it is just waste. It's all that stuff I ate and the rest of the stuff that *it* deemed unnecessary."

"You mean that's crap?" Floyd said excitedly.

"Not the kind you mean, but in a way, yeah," I answered. "I want to get my clothes and shower. I'll clean up the mess when I get back."

"Let's get this picked up. I really don't like that stuff on the floor," Floyd said, as he moved toward the cupboard where we kept the broom. He returned with the broom, dustpan, and a grocery sack.

"I would like to keep this for analysis. That is, if I ever get to a lab again," Ned said, taking the dustpan and opening the thick paper sack.

They spent about ten minutes gathering up all the little pieces they could find. As they finished the last pan full, Floyd noticed the bag looked wet. He threw a quick look at the dustpan, and the pellets had turned to putty.

"Let's get this stuff outside!" Floyd said excitedly.

They dropped the bag several feet past the walkway and dropped the dustpan in the bag. After watching for a short while, Floyd waved a hand at it in disgust, returned inside, and got another bottle of beer.

"Not planning to go back to work today?" Ned asked.

"No need. We had to tear out the last two weeks work to redo the ventilation system. It wasn't self-contained the way you drew it up. We need to consider putting glass in double layers. I have the plans for you and Newton to look at," Floyd returned between swallows.

"I'm going to sit down in the living room until we get ready. Unlike our friend in there, I could stand to calm down for a little while," Ned said wearily and wobbled off. Floyd took a couple of swallows of his beer and went to the cupboard and got a jar and spoon. He went to the bag outside and took a few spoonful out and placed them in the jar. The black tar was almost liquid now, and despite the contorted look on his face, there was no odor. He screwed the lid on the half-full jar and went back inside. He placed the jar on a shelf in the dining room, thinking it was out of the way for now, and then he joined Ned on the couch.

23

I HAD GONE INTO THE living room, opened up a cardboard box of clothes, got what I needed, and gone into the bathroom before Ned headed that way. The bathroom was a horrid pink color. Even the tile around the tub was bright pink. Being the well-coordinated ladies they were, the rest of the room matched. It almost hurt my head, that is, if it would hurt now. It smelled hospital clean and looked that way too. Everything was in its place as usual.

I let the water run to get the hot water to the tub and put my finger in the flow to check the progress. To my dismay, I could not tell if it was hot or not. I heard the gas water heater ignite. It was in closet with the towels inside the bathroom. That meant that the water should be as hot as it would get with the heater so close. There was a wisp of steam lifting from the tub now, so it was obvious that the water was hot. I quickly ran my finger through the stream and watched as a large blister formed, then retreated back into my finger.

I turned off the hot, turned on the cold full stream, and checked it for some odd reason. Habit, I think. It didn't feel any different than the hot. I turned on the shower, stepped inside, and closed the curtain. The water ran over my body and washed off what little of the black paste that was left. It ran black streams across the tub floor and down the drain. It turned from black to crimson. That sight startled me. I looked for the wound. It was not hard to find. The water was entering the wounds on my upper body formed by the spikes, flowing down under my skin, through my body and out the lower wounds. They had been only red patches when I entered the shower, but now had opened up, taking in the flow. My skin was stretching again as the water made its way inside me. I stuck my head under the flow. The water filled my skin but did not collect anywhere but my feet. It chugged its way all inside of me, and my feet swelled until I stepped back out of the spray. They stayed oversized for a few seconds, then expelled the fluid in one burst. It was a combination of blood and the black compound, accented by lighter streaks.

Relief swept over me, and I stepped back into the water, my eyes closed as I did. I stood there trying to access the strange feelings I had. I cocked my head, my eyes still closed, still attempting to grasp the situation. I was not sure if I couldn't feel the pounding water or it was not there. All the sounds were right, but I felt nothing.

Finally, I opened my eyes to get this next shock out of the way. I half believed that some part of me had fallen off, and I just had not heard the clunk when it landed. After a glance to make sure all parts were still attached, I started to try to find the problem. The shower was working and water was flowing in the way it was supposed to, straight at me. It just wasn't getting to me. Some unseen force deflected the water before it touched me. I extended my hand, and the water still ran off the bubble around me. I crouched and let the shower spray fall directly on the top of my head and gauged the effect. It appeared that I was inside a clear cone, and the water even ran around a perimeter on the tub floor. I stood back up and called to Ned. Before they could arrive, a thread of light wormed its way over the curtain and danced across my chest.

Ned and Floyd cautiously entered the room.

"Are you okay in there?" Ned asked.

I yanked back the curtain and just stood there, throwing my hands out palms up in a sign saying, "*Look at this.*" All modesty was gone. Ned slowly reached out and touched my left arm. His hand and arm were instantly soaked, but as his fingers entered the bubble, they dried too. He had no problem touching me, and as he withdrew he became wet again.

"Is this ever gonna *stop*?" Floyd asked.

"Yes," I said, stepping from the tub.

Ned handed a towel my way, but I refused. There was no need. I was already dry. The thread followed me as well.

"We must get the design flaws worked out at the office. It will end your part of this misery. We need a heavy-duty extension cord. That will help end the threads. We may have to get someone down here to wire in one at two hundred twenty volts. We will just have to wait and see, *but*," I said while tugging on my clothes, "I think that the show is over for a while. You can tell the girls," I finished, leaving the room. Ned and Floyd just looked at each other, shrugged, and then followed.

I went to the couch, found a legal pad, and started to draw. I continued long after all four of my cohorts had joined me. When I looked up, all eyes were on me. I should have felt awkward, but noted the stares and started to explain.

"These are the changes we need to make to the lab," I stated. Threads had formed and started to multiply. Floyd reached down and lifted the heavy-duty extension cord I requested. I went to him, threads in tow, took it to a receptacle, plugged it in, and returned to my seat, extending it as I went. After getting settled, I looped the end of the cord through my belt so that the plug would be near my skin. I felt the power touch my skin and the threads that helped light the room faded away.

"Now, as I was saying, these are changes we need to make." I paused as everyone gathered around the coffee table and me.

"The second layer on the floor has to come out. All power to the lab needs to be run through the first layer, and a second layer of plywood needs to be added. We will need six of these," I paused to write down a number. Edna turned on the rest of the lights in the room.

"An AC529 connector will allow us to run power through the different layers without compromising the seal. It is unclear what form of radiation will occur during the tests, especially if we actually have a sustained run. We need to be sure that the office is well-protected from all forms. Protection is not guaranteed, so be aware of that before we start. We will have to install as large a layer of glass as possible and completely enclose the entire lab with at least six inches. It would be advisable to have a double layer, both six inches thick. There will need to be a twelve- to fourteen-inch air space between the layers. I know this will be difficult, but it would be best if we could use glass." I paused and looked at Floyd.

"Getting a six-inch layer of glass that large is not going to be easy. I will check with Reggie when you get done," Floyd replied.

"I will work on alternative materials. The cooling system needs to be completely enclosed, sealed inside, no outside outlet. We need to devise a fresh air system that can be sealed while tests are being conducted. We need to wire inside and outside with equipment to monitor radiation, temperature, light, intensity, humidity, and air density. Any other measurements can be added as you think necessary. All equipment will be wired with the same type connectors as the AC529 but sized as needed, to ensure the seal as stated before. They are essentially an all-thread bolt and washer setup that go through their respectively sized holes and seal layer to layer," I explained, showing all a crude drawing. I paused to look at everyone, then continued, "The doors will be the most difficult to seal. It will require two doors, each opening opposite of each other. The same principal as a bank vault door should apply. A steel reinforced, glass door will be acceptable. It is imperative to use as much glass as possible. Some sort of layered seal on the doors would be best. The original 880 volts will not suffice. We will need to get 1320 if possible. Now, I'm open for suggestions.

"Most of this just came to me as I left the shower. All this information just pops in my mind like turning on a light. It's just there. I just know it," I said, and started to draw again. When I had finished, I passed it to Ned.

"This is what I see now," I said.

The artwork was crude but made my point. It showed a square like a TV screen, and in the center was an attempt at people, but all around the edges were odd-looking figures. Everyone looked with amazement and blank expressions.

"Glass it is," Floyd said, breaking the awkward silence, and started asking questions as he worked his way to my side.

"What about a layer of lead?" Ned inserted.

"A one-inch layer on all sides except for the side facing the office would be sufficient. We will need to add some form of protection to the office. Even if it is some sort of door that closes, but the front of the lab area needs to be left where you can observe what is going on inside. There can be no compromise there," I finished.

For the next several hours, there was an open discussion on how to make this a reality.

"I need to get back and get some of this started. We were tearin' stuff back out when I left, so no harm done. It just has to go a lot further than we had planned. Don't want to cause any unneeded delays," Floyd said, gathering himself to go.

"It is a becoming more critical every second that we finish the lab and confine me there. The risk of detection and the possibility of contamination and capture grows every day. Speed is of the essence, but quality and security are most important. Try not to raise any red flags," I said, then turned to look at the TV and stared at the blank screen. The others dispersed. Ned and Floyd started out. Edna kissed Floyd and told him to hurry back, supper would be ready soon. Ned and Bea exchanged looks and hugged. The men left and the ladies retired to the kitchen. All took a last look at me mindlessly staring at the blank TV screen. I didn't move for the next two days.

24

ON THE AFTERNOON OF THE second day, Schwartz arrived and knocked on the door. This seemed to break the trance I was in. It was all a blank. I just lost the time like it was only seconds that had passed. When he knocked, my eyes fluttered and I was awake.

Bea answered the knock. We thought it necessary to at least hook the screen door to provide some warning of someone's approach, in case of something else happening with me. There was an exchange of hellos, and Schwartz entered.

"Just wanted to come by and check on you kids," he boomed, smiling from ear to ear.

"We have some coffee in the kitchen if you would like a cup," Bea invited.

"No, no. I just wanted to see how you were doing and see if there was anything I could do. Although I would like a word with Ned, come to think of it. It could be nothing, but I would like to see what he thinks," he said, his smile fading.

"There's not a problem with any of our business with you, is there?" Bea asked uncomfortably.

"Not a problem at all with any of that. Don't worry your pretty little head over those things. I was in good with the auction house, but now I'm almost a celebrity in their eyes. I can't foresee trouble at any time dealing with them. There—" He stopped as he heard footsteps on the small front porch out front.

"That should be the boys. They called a few minutes ago and said they were through for the day," Bea said with joy evident in her voice.

Floyd entered, saying something, but stopped and greeted Schwartz. Greetings were passed all around again, but Schwartz cut things short.

"I don't mean to be rude, but I'm a little short on time. Business and all, you know." He looked around sheepishly and settled on Ned. Floyd took the hint and ushered Bea toward the coffee.

"Mr. Hooper has sent me a letter," he said slowly, looking at the back of my head.

"Whatever it is, Mr. Schwartz, you have my word that it's safe to say in front of Terry." Ned said with authority, nodding at me.

Schwartz continued slowly. "There is a young couple that has shown up several times in town looking for Bea Baker and asking for a young man. They say he was renting a room from her some time back and wished to visit with her. He thought it odd that the only name they were willing to give was Scooter. They said their name was Sutton and kept coming back. With Bea away and all, he started to call the police, but was a little afraid to with all the MPs that had been around there before. Anything to worry about, you think?"

Ned rubbed his chin and looked at me. I turned on the couch and looked over the back at both men.

"They are looking for me, and we need to have Mr. Hooper tell them to start asking about antiques around town. Fein interest in something that you can advise us on, Mr. Schwartz, so that it will not look suspicious for them to contact you here. Please advise Mr. Hooper to have them stop looking for Scooter and Mrs. Baker. Please call as soon as you can from your office here and inform him of this plan. We need to get them to come here without alerting anyone," I said flatly.

"I have a couple of estate sales coming up in a week or so. There are some lovely pieces in them. Sounds like a good excuse to make a trip, to me that is, for a true collector," Schwartz said with pride, not really wanting to ask too many questions.

I stood, walked over to the trunk in the corner, and removed a small pouch. Returning to the front of the couch where I had been sitting, I handed the pouch to Schwartz. He looked inside and gingerly poured its contents into his hand. He took a finger and gently spread the coins around his open palm, assessing their value as he went.

"My word!" he exclaimed, breaking into another wide smile.

"Please sell them individually, a week or so apart, longer if you think necessary. Take an extra bonus for your cooperation. Whatever you feel covers it," I said.

"No need to delay. I have a collector who will take them all today, no questions asked," he said quietly, still astonished at what he was looking at.

"Please be as discreet as possible with Mr. Hooper," I said.

"We go way back. It won't be a problem. We've... had a few shady dealings before. Nothing illegal, mind you, I won't be a part of any of that. He is my friend, and we will take care of it I promise." He returned the coins to the leather pouch, gave us both a nod, and went for the door

"Mr. Schwartz, we are in competition with the ARGO Lab. We are trying to develop sensitive electronic instruments for a government contractor. That is why we must be so secretive. I hope we can count on you to give your cooperation," I said flatly.

"I understand and I won't give you any trouble. You should know that by now. Never really liked those people at ARGO much anyway. Seemed to be... the wrong kind of people. I'll give Hooper a call. We go way back. We saw Europe courtesy of Uncle Sam. There won't be any problems on our end." He went out the door.

"I didn't think you could lie like that," Ned said, when he heard Schwartz's car engine start. "If the lab finds us, we won't ever see the light of day. Especially you."

"The people looking for me are my parents, and you heard what Mr. Schwartz said. If we tell him we stole things from the ARGO Lab, he would probably turn us in. At the very least, he would probably stop dealing with us. For now, we need him, but not for much longer. This is a strange turn of events. I do not understand," I said.

"I don't either. I've seen your parents. They are as old as mine. Midfifties, I would guess. It can't be them unless you *zapped* them too," he said, his voice tapering off at the end.

"It is obvious that somehow I did *zap* them. I will have to give it some thought, but somehow I did, it seems," I said slowly, settling back on the couch.

"Hey!" Ned almost shouted. "Can you fix my parents too?" He bolted around the end of the couch and looked me in the eyes.

"Sorry, Ned. At this point I don't know how I fixed mine."

Schwartz called a few hours later and said that he had talked to Hooper and covertly conveyed our wishes. There had been a message at the office when he arrived there, so he thought the return call would not raise suspicions. Hooper said he would relay news of the estate sales and their location.

25

THE NEXT FEW WEEKS PASSED without incident. Work at the lab moved along at a rapid pace. Reggie, the foreman, by chance knew a designer who had been stiffed on a huge job and had almost all the glass we needed. While curious, we did not ask why someone else needed that much glass. It worked out well because the subsequent orders would go unnoticed, and his knowledge of how to fasten and seal the panels was invaluable. His addition to the staff made up for a large portion of the delays we expected. Things seemed to be proceeding well, even though no one really knew what we were doing all of this for. I felt that I would know what to do at the proper time.

With assurance from Reggie, we added another twelve-hour shift. He knew the local police and assured them that it was nothing but a deadline that was causing the extra work. He explained that he had another big job that would start soon and could not afford to lose time on either. The explanation seemed to suffice, because there was no interference from them, just occasional checks for security purposes, and Reggie kept them at bay by buying them dinner occasionally for their troubles.

It was now more routine than anything else. Floyd and Ned left as if they had a regular job. The last infusion of cash provided by Schwartz gave us the funds needed to finish the job and much more. The coins were rarer than we thought, and even with the extra amount paid to Schwartz, we were well set for the time being.

Their lives began, to them, to seem normal. However, I still did not eat or sleep, unless you counted the periods that I seemed frozen. Every so often I just locked up, sometimes for days. That started to seem normal as well. I stayed on the couch, and they just lived around me.

One night, Ned, Bea, and I were up late watching TV. I was now on the end instead of the center, Ned and Bea now sat together. Floyd and Edna had gone out to eat, something they had started to do more and often.

Bea and Ned joked that they were frequenting the local motel to get away from me, because I never left the house. True or not, they went out often.

The large budget, epic late-night presentation was playing. A romantic movie with the American Civil War as a backdrop, it was good but far from graphic, like some movies of the time.

I really became engrossed in the show. It seemed to reach out and touch my mind, as simple as the plot was. The mass of troops it depicted somehow affected me. I couldn't take my eyes off the screen, even as Bea brought in refreshments for the two of them. The hoof beats seemed to echo in my head, and I started to think that I could smell the horses and the mud they were in.

I started to lean closer and closer to the small screen, which attracted the attention of my friends. It was like my legs were pinned to the couch, so I leaned forward at the waist, craning my neck as I went. I went as far as I could, which laid my chest on the top of my legs, my face still forward facing the TV.

At first they paid little attention to me. This was too little an oddity to cause much concern with my past record, so the show progressed. The lead character's screen presence engulfed me, and when the next commercial came on, my eyes started to glow an eerie blue glow. It started to show on the floor in front of me in the low light of the room. Ned jumped up and moved almost in front of me, looking at the effect. A small amount of smoke began to escape from my nose, and the show returned to the screen.

"We skipped the commercial," Bea blurted out, and Ned jerked his attention back to the show. I sat back up, eyes still shining the penetrating blue light. The smoke started to encompass the rest of my body, and small flashes like distant lightning started to fill the cloud. I was completely engulfed now in a cocoon of gray smoke with a blue hue at the top.

Ned took Bea by hand and led her toward the front door, ready to have her exit for her safety. Neither took their eyes off me, until there was a thud on the floor behind the couch. Bea let out a blood-curdling scream.

A Confederate and a Union soldier were in a death struggle in the living room. Rifle shots rang out, and the sheetrock exploded over the top of the TV. The odor of blood, smoke, and gunpowder started to fill the room. Ned made a move for the door, but a shout and a gunshot made him grab Bea and dive to the floor in front of me. They did not seem to notice us or the fact that they were fighting inside our living room. It seemed likely that to them they were still in the proper place and just were overlaid onto our reality.

The sound of the struggle behind the couch died away with the gurgling sound caused by a knife wound to the chest. There was a slight pause and the Confederate soldier stood, knife in hand, still looking down at the lifeless body at his feet. Before he could move, another gunshot rang out, his body lurched, and he fell across the couch, coughing blood. His body retched as blood turned the cushion crimson. A volley of shots ripped the wall by the front door, and the sounds of running soldiers filled the room.

In desperation, Ned reached out to shake me grabbing my ankle, thinking that he could stop the madness. It was his turn to scream this time. He withdrew his hand from the cloud, smoking as if it had been on fire. He tried to stand, but Bea pulled him back down. He rolled over on his back, holding his hand up, yelling at the top of his lungs. It looked burned to the bone and still smoked. Bea joined him in screaming when angry soldiers from both sides appeared through opposing walls and clashed over the top of us.

Shouts and curses drowned out the screams of my friends, and the rank smell of body odor and blood became stronger by the second. Ned and Bea stopped yelling as they covered themselves, trying to keep from being trampled as more troops appeared through the wall and joined the fight. Bodies fell and joined the pair on the floor, but were unseen as they had their heads covered, dodging the boots of the combatants.

There was a flash, and what light there was in the room was gone. The fury of battle never faded, but slowly the participants did. Their ghostly figures faded away as if they were lit by a faraway torch that had no fuel left. The glow from my eyes faded, and the only light that remained was the glow from the overheated extension cord. The smell of the battle and bodies, mixed with the modern smell of burning insulation, and the faint glow of a thread from another room cut through the darkness.

When the thread touched me, I leaned forward and my palms started to glow the same blue light as my eyes had before. I reached out and placed each hand on either side of Ned's injury. His torture eased as light engulfed the damage and his hand slowly returned to normal.

"It absorbs the energy back into itself," I said

Floyd burst into the door, ready to fight. He crouched low and looked around the room for the threat he expected to be there. Bea raised herself from the floor, looking over Ned first, then the couch to finally seeing Floyd. She jumped up and ran to embrace him. The glow had caught his attention, and he grabbed and held her as she wept, without taking his eyes off the pulsating light.

"What happened? I heard what sounded like a fight and gun-fire. I thought you guys were in real trouble. What happened to the lights? What's burning? It stinks in here," Floyd raved.

Edna entered. Floyd handed Bea off to her and went to the bedroom and retrieved a flashlight. When he returned it was dark again. The glow was gone. He swept the spot of light around the room, finding the melted cord on the floor along with splatters of blood. Muddy boot prints littered the hardwood floor, along with handprints that smeared the rest. Ned was in a heap at my feet, and the coffee table was thrown against the wall. Bullet holes were scattered over all the walls. Ned stood and Floyd hit him in the face with the spot. His face was streaked with mud and blood.

"I think that we have blown a fuse or something. We need to get power back on in here and see what the damage is," he said slowly.

"You're kidding!" Floyd shot back. "What happened here?" he demanded.

Ned moved forward, heading to the back of the house. "You would have a hard time believing me, but we need to get the power back on and make sure we are not going to have a fire. We'll talk about it then." He turned and looked at Bea. "Sorry, dear, but are you injured? Are you okay?"

She took her head from Edna's shoulder and sobbed. "They kicked me and stepped on me. One of them fell on top of me, but I don't think anything is broken." Her face was stained with mud and a small amount of blood too, and when Edna saw that in the light she led her toward the bathroom.

Floyd snapped to and pulled his handkerchief from his back pants pocket, then gently placed it on the cord and pulled it from the wall. It took part of the faceplate with it, but the receptacle looked intact. The pair then went out back toward the meter box to check the fuses. Part of the power was still on, so they had hopes that there was no serious damage. Fortunately, the power was still on in the bathroom so Edna could care for Bea. I called the pair back into the living room after a few moments. Edna gingerly escorted Bea back beside me. My eyes started to glow a pale then brighter blue followed by my palms. I reached over and passed my hands slowly close to the injuries Bea had received. All wounds began to fade.

"I could not let you suffer," was all I said.

Bea looked at Edna and they embraced in disbelief.

It was only a fuse, and the guys discussed the incomprehensible events of the last hour. Things seemed to be getting worse as time went on, or maybe it was just the storm in the center of the calm. Power was soon restored, and they went back inside to inspect the damage.

A total of twenty-three bullet holes littered the wall in the living room, but only two had penetrated both walls. The blood on the couch and floor had remained somehow, but the living and the dead had vanished as strangely as they had appeared. On the floor at my feet was a pistol and part of the blade of a sword. We surmised that these pieces had slid on the floor and into the cloud that surrounded me and were captured here from wherever they came from or went to. Why, we were not sure, but it was all we could come up with at the time. Why the blood, mud, and smaller artifacts remained was unclear.

Edna helped calm and clean up Bea. She was badly bruised on her back and arms from being kicked by both sets of soldiers. Ned got the worst of it because he had successfully shielded her from some of the fury, which left him open to more punishment. The injury to his hand had also lessened his concentration, causing him to be even more vulnerable. Both would have been sore for a few days and bruised for weeks, if I had not repaired them both. All evidence was gone within a few hours, and the pain was gone instantly.

The house would be much easier to fix. The couch was beyond help and would have to be replaced. The sheetrock could be fixed with a little plaster and some paint. The outside wall would have to be repaired so that all traces would be covered, and so that if we did have visitors, no questions would be asked. Reggie would be called and have to be trusted if the need arose. Repairs to the electrical receptacle were a simple replacement of parts. There was no visible damage to the wires. A good wash and wax took most of the marks on the floor and was called good enough. Ned also added a device to limit power to my cord to rid us of the threads of electricity.

Floyd and Edna went the next day, purchased a new sofa, and had some of the workers from the jobsite bring it to the house. They left it on the front porch and went back to work.

As soon as they had left, Ned and Floyd removed me from the old sofa. They took it out back and quickly set it on fire to hide the bloodstains. I was still standing where they had left me when they came in with the new one. They moved it into place, removed the protective covers, and I sat down. Both stood looking at me in a mix between wonder and caution. After the last episode, they had started to be a little afraid of where all this would lead. Fear for their mates was creeping into their minds, and the thought of moving them or me had been discussed. It would never be necessary because our lab would be ready before any other incident occurred.

Reggie showed up that afternoon to finish the repairs that were beyond our capabilities. He was rather tall at six feet and had a huge mop of black hair. He always seemed to be unshaven but never with a beard, just a heavy five o'clock shadow. He always wore bib overalls, a t-shirt, and a painter's cap. He spoke with a rather heavy New York accent.

He was working on the plaster in the living room after placing an order for the siding to repair the outside walls. He would work awhile and stare at me every chance he got. I started to concentrate on him and his life. Ned entered the room.

"Good afternoon," Ned said, admiring Reggie's work.

"Hello," he returned, stopping to look at me, then continued. "What's up with this guy? He just sits here all day or what? Kinda gives me the creeps, if you know what I mean," he said without taking his eyes off me.

"Perhaps we should tell Reggie the truth about me," I said slowly and mechanically.

"Do you think that's wise?" Ned asked honestly.

"Look," Reggie started, "I ain't never been in much trouble. What little I did find made me move down here to get away from it. I get paid too good to cause you guys any problems, okay. Sorry I said anything." When he finished, he started back to work, but the TV program changed. The images and sounds made him stop. On the screen, scenes of his childhood started to play. His day in court that prompted his move and his tearful departure from home was shown.

"Hey, how you doin' that? I ain't made no home movies," he asked, craning his neck toward the screen.

I mechanically twisted my head in a jerky fashion and turned to face him and Ned. I let the blue light fill my face and die with a twinkle from my eyes.

"I am a robot. That is what our facility is for. We are trying to develop more like me and repair my flaws. I have the power to look into your past. I know what is in your heart. I know you are a good man, deep down, and you will not betray us. It will be extremely profitable for you if you comply. Please keep our secret. Only Mr. Schwartz can know," I said loudly, trying to sound like the television robots I had observed. I jerked my head back facing forward and lowered my chin to my chest acting asleep.

Reggie dropped the tools he was holding along with his jaw. He stood there for a second and said, "He don't look nothin' like that broad on TV."

"We did our best," Ned replied, with no clue that Reggie was referring a TV show about an attractive female robot that aired each week on a local channel.

The work was soon finished, and Reggie was safely added to the group. I was complemented by all on my improvisation when Ned told the story.

There was enough progress that we needed to put the finishing touches on our project. Everything was fine-tuned and the overnight shift was no longer needed. Production slowed, but the end was near. Our last main hurdle was the chair. We decided that this was the best way to deliver power to me, since I wanted to sit all the time anyway. Floyd was in the lead, but all revisions were run past Ned and I just for good measure. We had a marathon session on how to modify some sort of chair to meet our needs.

A barber's chair was what we decided on. It could be modified to accept the multiple electrical contacts we needed and had the basic design to facilitate power and padding. It looked like this would be the last holdup and it would a rather large one. It was the only piece of the puzzle that had not somehow fallen into place. We were fortunate that Reggie knew a company that could make it for us. It would just take some time, and they couldn't give us a firm estimate of how long it would take. We were now at their mercy. We were negligent for not having it built already.

A concern arose over the fact that there was no real way to attach anything to the glass floor without compromising the seal, and the glass was very slippery. For safety reasons, something had to be done. It was decided that a ceramic tile could be glued to the glass well enough to solve the problem. It would fit tightly together and be cemented firmly in place. It was basically glass and would provide the traction needed to move around inside safely.

26

My parents arrived much too late for the estate sales, but the plan had worked anyway. It seemed that there was no attention paid to them by the ARGO Lab. They had been discreet enough to avoid suspicion. They made their way to Schwartz's Texas office, and my dad carefully made contact. He was told to go to a local motel and someone would be in touch. He did as he was told without question. Schwartz then called the house and informed us of their arrival. Ned decided to meet with them since they sort of knew him.

He said that there were lots of questions, and he gave them only as many answers as he had to. With the basic information that they had and a limited explanation, they still accepted their fate. It was helpful that Ned lied just a little and said that I was fine.

My father was an engineer and my mother was a schoolteacher. Both retired after long years on the job and settled into a comfortable retirement. I was born late in their life, left them early to go to college, and then to work at the ARGO Lab, so our adult time was next to none. They had come to see me at school and ARGO a few times, but only a few days at a time. It was almost awkward, but enjoyable. Now everything had changed, and in ways no one would ever believe.

Conrad Samuel Tupnic had been drafted into the Army Air Corps during World War II as an engineer. He entered as a lieutenant because of his education. He was in charge of construction crews that were building air bases in England. His job was to build a base and move to the next. While witnessing the comings and goings of the aircraft assigned to some bases, his only exposure to combat was the air raids in the area. When construction stopped, he repaired some bases after damage by air raids and then was reassigned to the United States to train others.

After the war, he returned to his private business.

After several trips back and forth to make sure there were no misunderstandings, a face-to-face meeting was set up. It seemed strange to be so cautions with my own parents, but things were different now. Ned was having a good time telling them about all that had happened in the last few months. My father seemed to be thrilled to hear them, and my mother became more reserved as the stories progressed.

I remembered my father at the time as an older man, who was just under six feet tall and rather thin. The picture that came into my mind was him sitting in the den, smoking his pipe and reading a book. He was always reading, and only smoked that huge pipe when he was. He had a favorite hand-knitted sweater that he wore in the winter months and always sat in an oversized lounge chair. His hair had almost gone all gray, and there were many wrinkles on his face.

Cynthia Ann Sutton Tupnic was my mother and a tall woman. Dad always said that was the first thing that attracted him to her. She had retained her girlish figure and had only gone up two dress sizes since high school. She, like him, was going gray, but she had not wrinkled as badly. They lived for each other for almost all their lives. Both would always say that there was no one else in the world. She taught school long enough to get a healthy retirement, but never really thought about it until she did. A few days a month she would volunteer at the same school, just to break the monotony. Her persistence was part of the reason I did so well in school.

I felt a shock when they finally walked in the door. It was the first thing I could remember feeling in quite some time, but it was gone in an instant. I didn't stand; I just sat there and greeted them as if I had seen them yesterday. Dad, as usual, shook my hand and sat down beside me on the side farthest from the door, while Mom grabbed me in a bear hug then sat on the other side, tears welling in her eyes. Dad looked like me, and Mom looked young and lovely. There was an uncomfortable silence.

"I understand that you may have had something to do with our... uh... condition." He choked out. Mom was still trying to squeeze the life out of me from her seat at my side.

"There is some connection. I cannot be certain what it is. I feel that the first time it was activated, in my mind I thought that I was going to die. I remember clearly a snapshot vision of you in the den in your chair and Mom serving you coffee. The sight of it is as clear as this room. That is the connection that I see. I can only surmise that energy from that activation was transferred to you then. I cannot explain it any more than that," I said in a monotone voice.

"What was it like on your end again?" Ned jumped in.

"That was about it. I was reading. Cindy brought our coffee into the room, and there was a growing blue light. We both felt a little funny and then passed out. We woke up in the morning like this. Your mother first thought that I was you then started to club me with a lamp. The thought crossed my mind to do the same to her. It was clear that a doctor couldn't do anything, and we felt fine. It took a few hours, but we finally got a handle on things and tried to get in touch with you. We wanted you to come home, to be able to contain the situation there and try to sort all this out. We got the run around when we called ARGO, and after a while we decided to see if we could find you ourselves. We got no answer at the phone number that we had for you, and no one was at the house, so we asked around. I thought that anyone that knew you well would know that we called you Scooter. It looks like I was right. So what happens now?" he asked, a bit anxious. Mom tensed too.

"I think that the two of you are the missing pieces of the puzzle. Your knowledge of engineering will be most helpful in our future endeavors. I would be most grateful if you would work with Floyd and Ned and review our projects down the road. Any refinements you suggest will go through those two. Mom, your knowledge of history will be invaluable. There will be many surprises to come," I said.

"A bit cold, aren't you, son?" Dad returned.

"Five people that I know have somehow became many years younger in an instant. I have killed many men, and I don't know how I did it. I have changed ten thousand times more than any of you, and more than any of us can imagine. As much as it should pain me to see my own indifference, it is just how it is and what I have become. Get to know your new friends. They are all good people and are the only friends that I have. All our lives are connected now and will be forever," I declared and slowly went into a frozen state.

27

IT WAS FINALLY TIME FOR me to go to our lab. The trio that had come together by chance was an awesome team. Dad had gone over the systems and made some improvements. Ned added his expert knowledge gained at ARGO, and Floyd saw that it was done. Everything would have worked as it was, but the systems were much better now. Tests had been run on all systems, under any and all conceivable conditions they could test for. It was not on the level of what Ned and I had worked in before, but it was still top of the line. We had had the money to buy the best, and it showed.

Mom, Bea, and Edna had forged a great friendship as well. They busied themselves taking care the men, the house, me, and what little research projects I could come up with. It seemed like there was nothing they could not do. Mom had gone to the library and somehow gotten fifty or so new books on the civil war, something they told us before they could not do. The three of them had searched and found a few used bookstores in the area and had luck finding a few more in Houston. There were things, though, that they just chose not to do and made the guys do when they got home. I am still amazed at what all six could and did accomplish in such a short period of time, especially under the circumstances they had faced in the past few months. Today it seemed not to bother them one bit.

I had become frail. The limit to the power I absorbed seemed to be the key. We were all afraid to increase the limits because of the last incident. The thing inside me seemed to have a knack of drawing what it needed when it chose to, so someone was always with me to try to make sure that did not happen. Everyone had been drilled on how to shut down the power, but if it decided to draw from the main power lines, there was nothing any of them could do but try to get away and wait for it to stop. I seemed to have a very limited amount of control over it. I just had to stay passive and not become overly interested or enthused about any one thing. It seemed to work, but I was listless. I would read and go blank. Everyone started to call it sleep, but I just stopped. I preferred frozen, maybe in time.

I had to be helped out of the house and into the car. All of me was weak, but especially my legs. Maybe because I hadn't walked anywhere to speak of in months. The car died when I got in because I drew all the power from it as soon as I made contact. The trip was finally made possible when they brought a pickup truck and a portable generator with it. I was hooked to the generator and the truck was spared. Floyd's car had to have a battery, alternator, and voltage regulator before it would run again.

I was genuinely impressed when I stepped through the doors of our new workplace. It looked futuristic and utilitarian at the same time. To the left of the entryway was a staircase leading to the office. It sat atop the storage and bathrooms, which included showers and a first aid station. Floyd had basic medical training during his time in the service. Both were about thirty feet by thirty feet. The top floor had a small kitchen and lounge. All the comforts of home, someone had said: food, sleep, and the bathroom. What else could you ask for? In reality, it was there so if things went awry, there was the ability to have shifts and meals. The two sofas would suffice as beds, and quick but limited meals could be fixed. The pantry was stocked with canned goods, just in case a lockdown was required.

The structure was walled with plywood and painted white. It was a large square box with large plate windows at the far end facing the inside, overlooking the rest of the internal structures. Two four by eight sheets of one-inch glass allowed sweeping views and added protection, if needed. Thin layers of lead lined the entire structure behind the plywood walls, and plates could be released to cover the glass if needed.

The room with the windows was a state of the art monitoring station. Three of the four walls were covered with meters to verify levels of all forms of radiation known, as well as temperature and barometric pressure inside and outside the lab. There was a closed circuit television system to watch and record what happened in both places as well. Three large clocks were installed: one at the bottom of the lab wall closest to the office, one in the monitor station, and the last in the lounge. All were synchronized to the second, and were the best we could find. It was an attempt to check for any time discrepancies inside the work area. We had no idea what was going to happen, but were well-aware of what had already occurred.

To the right was a large, cavernous glass-enclosed room. It had a short set of stairs going up about four feet. There was a small entryway deck at the top to facilitate the large doors' swinging radius. It was like a bank vault door in glass. Thin strips of steel lined its edges to add strength. It even had the large locking wheel in the center, and the locking mechanism could be plainly seen through the layers of glass. Past that was the same type of door, but opening in the opposite direction, although the latching equipment also faced the outside.

Once inside the great glass room, all outside sound was subdued even more. With all the insulation outside the room, it was very quiet outside, but the silence was almost overpowering with the doors still open. The sounds of our footsteps on the ceramic tile sounded like drumbeats resounding through a canyon.

The modified chair was to the rear, but centered about ten yards from the rear wall. The lights mounted between the walls, a large TV camera in the front left hand corner, and the chair were the only things in the massive, open room. The glass front was the highest polished finish available, but still gave a limited view inside because of the thickness required to secure the radiation's signal.

The chair had a different type of tile around it, one that was smoother, which formed a ten-foot square of different colored and textured floor. It was the only interruption in the floor, which was made even more apparent by the flood of lights that lit up every square inch of its contents. The two panes of six-inch glass gave the dreary outside walls ghostly hue, and with lights focused inside, shadows obscured all details of what was really outside.

The clearest panes and most highly polished were reserved for the side near the office. While intricate details were washed out, there was still remarkable clarity. Any lost information was expected to be collected from the camera system, and all would record everything that happened, good or bad, for review later.

The chair bore little resemblance to the barber's chair it was designed from. The basic design was what we needed, but that was where it ended. The wide base and strength made it a great place to start, for wires were easy to run through the center of lower structure and integrate into the upper part. Pads were removed and others were added. The new cushions incorporated multiple conductors and extra padding for my expected extended use of the chair. We had hoped that a multiple contact system would relieve the stress of transference and even out the process. All was conjecture, and now was the time to start turning it into fact.

As I had requested, there was no hesitation putting me in the chair. Dad and Ned had helped me from the truck and steadied my slow walk inside. It was only interrupted by my occasional stop to peek at the wonders around me. Floyd had gone to the control room to start everything up so someone would be isolated in case the unexpected happened, again. It went smoothly.

We removed my shirt and pants, and I donned a special pair of short sleeve coveralls. The cushions groaned and exhaled as I slipped into position, and my skin tingled as the copper made contact. I shuffled around to get more comfortable, and then Dad reclined the chair to a point where I was just above lying flat. He and Ned exchanged looks, went to the doors, and began to seal them. This started a week of tests that went better than expected.

28

I FELT ALIVE AGAIN WHEN they started to feed in power. They did it slowly and in intervals, slowly increasing the duration and intensity. There seemed to be no ill effects to me and no strange things happened. After each test, a detailed report was made and film was reviewed, labeled, and filed. This process was repeated time and again, and the results seemed to be the same. A low voltage current was finally left in place to quell my low energy pangs.

It sharpened my mind and I started to give more input into the tests. I felt so much better that at one point I wanted to walk and left the chair, walking toward the front wall and the office. The threads that followed were not small this time. If the others were threads, these were ropes. It was almost a solid, man-shaped silhouette of blue light following me, but it started to fade and thin out the further I moved from the chair. The reduction in transfer made me go back and sit down.

We were in the middle of a review when the ladies showed up with a meal. It was in the afternoon and the men had missed their usual lunch appointment, so the meal came to them. As the data was reviewed, conversation was interrupted by the muffled sounds of chewing, and alternating voices came over the intercom. I could almost smell the aroma of the food I knew was there. The mood changed, and so did the process. There was less of the clinical review, and a lighter mood prevailed. Laughter rang through my enclosure many times before the session was declared over. It pleased me to see that they all were happy.

The sound of thunder rumbled through the com system, and this caused a small panic in the control room. When the girls had entered the safety door, it had not been closed. In the heat of the afternoon, and with an approaching front, the weather in southeast Texas turned ugly very quickly. The storms could be intense, with strong winds and even hail. The wind was gusting intermittently, and when Floyd checked his car to make sure the windows were rolled up, he reported that it looked very dark to the northwest. He came back inside and closed and latched both doors. The joyous mood returned as the meal was finished while the storm brewed outside. I was included in the conversation and even told some jokes. Although I had no sense of humor at all, I still knew that they were funny. We all seemed to be adjusting to the circumstances well.

A break was declared and everyone pulled chairs into the control room. The conversation ranged from what was next to getting some other form of housing. Our financial situation was still sound, and my father was discussing the possibility of purchasing land and building houses for everyone when the first lightning bolt struck.

The first was only a small explosion that shook the entire building and rattled everything in it. The second changed everything! Even though there had been forethought enough to add a lightning rod and ground the building itself, it had little effect. A bolt hit the rod at the rear and jumped to the building. It burned through the outside metal skin and hit the outside of the glass wall. The alien technology took over again at that point.

The lightning took the form of a massive thread. It looked like a glowing white snake two feet wide with spires extending everywhere, giving the appearance of hairs. It gathered in one place and made a large ball on one end, as if trying to penetrate the glass wall then crawled along as if looking for a crack to enter through. It stopped at each joint and tested its entire length until moving on to the next. Other bolts joined in the dazzling display, until the entire visible sections were laced with the shining, undulating snakelike bands of raw power.

The ladies were quickly herded into the lounge, the safety doors were closed for their protection, and the furor in the control room started. There was a brilliant white light that lit the entire inside of the building, and portions of the instruments were dancing out of control. The feed from the cameras was fuzzy but still there, and audio volume had to be drastically reduced because of the roar of static. Every effect steadily increased as bolt after bolt hit and joined in the unimaginable images laid in front of us. Everyone was concerned for our safety as all of the glass in both sections of the building began to become crystal clear, polished at the molecular level.

It was an infusion of comfort for me, outside of the worry for my friends that still lingered inside me.

The trio inside the control room soon fell silent and motionless. There was simply nothing else to do but watch. Everything was out of their control, and none of the instruments readings were recordable. They were reduced to an unwilling audience. They stood at the TV screens, watching the light show.

The bands had flattened out to where they almost covered the entire surface of the glassed-in lab. The brilliance was almost impossible to look at and the temperature inside was climbing rapidly. The energy began to pulsate, as if tugging at the glass, and then started to gather at the lower part of the wall. It breached the floor joint insulation, finding the power couplings feeding me at the chair.

It came in waves and seemed to burn into my very soul. It made me scream as jolt after jolt coursed through my body. I started to lose control of my body and thought that it was finally over and I was going to die. I slowly felt as if I was losing consciousness. It was only interrupted by the regular agonizing scream that accompanied the next surge of power.

An instant puff of fog filled the room, making it impossible to see what was happening inside the lab. Everyone strained to see, and then as quickly as it appeared, it was gone. I had finally gained enough control to stand by the chair and was now clearly visible to all. I leaned against the chair, touching it with the tops of my thighs and my butt. I was bent at the waist, my hands almost touching my ankles. Blue tendrils of light started to dance over my entire body, fed by the intensifying power of the lightning bolts. I screamed once more, and it echoed throughout the building, magnified by the intercom system. As I released the bloodcurdling yell, I began to straighten out my body. I raised my hands, arms outstretched, palms outward. The dancing blue strings of power followed, and the scream turned into a long, loud unstopping assault on everyone's ears. I had assumed a stance with feet shoulder width apart, arms over my head, slightly spread away from my shoulders. The blue bolts had followed my movement and formed bat-like wings between my legs and arms. When the last bolt fed into the system, I started to turn into a brilliant blue silhouette of light. Starting at my feet and slowly moving upward, all detail of myself was replaced with only an outline filled with the blinding blue light. When it reached my forehead, the lab was instantly filled with the cloud that was so common with increased power intake. Unseen by anyone outside, I returned to the chair and simply sat down.

Dad was frantic, trying to figure out what to do and how to get inside to help me. It was an absurd thought, given the circumstances, but no one could avoid concern. Floyd, as usual, took action bounding out of the control room and down the stairs to the space between the two rooms, still having the composure to re-latch both doors on his way out. He watched as the flow of pure power drained down the glass sides like water out of a broken glass. To his surprise, the doorway was clear, even though the white lace still danced over most of the other walls. With forced deliberation, he jumped up the few remaining steps to the entryway and tapped the great wheel that locked the outside door to check for what effect it may have on him. There seemed to be none until he grasped two of the outstretched rods and tried to make them turn. He was awestruck by what he saw inside as he positioned to apply more force when the wheel refused to move, and was oblivious to the pain in his palms as his mind focused on the spectacle before him.

Small tornados seemed to be forming in several places around the floor. They did not seem to be rotating with any great speed, but almost looked like escaping gas. A wave of black passed in front of the door like someone had passed a cape across his vision, and that made him release his grip and step back. The tornados turned into a slight mist over the floor, and grass started to grow from the tiles. The fog worsened as Dad and Ned, at last, joined Floyd at the door.

All three acknowledged each other and strained their eyes to try and see me through the varying visibility.

All three jumped back at the sight that sprang out at them from the mist. A man dressed in a World War II GI uniform sprang from the fog, crashed into the inside wall, and fell back onto his back. He lay there for a moment, seeming to be in shock, his haggard young face reflecting the obvious strain of his situation. He threw a look over his shoulder and jumped to his feet. The uniform too showed that it had seen hard service. The olive drab clothes were soiled head to toe; his boots and helmet were streaked with mud. He rubbed his unshaven chin, adjusted the ammo belt around his waist, raised his right foot, and tested the wall with its muddy bottom. He threw another frantic look over his shoulder and raised his M1 Garand and fired two shots from the waist. The bullets hit the glass and left crack marks on impact. He turned to face the unseen terror that seemed to be pursuing him, and a string of blemishes peppered the glass over his head as enemy fire was directed his way. He turned, his face twisted with effort, and plunged at the barrier that he could not fathom. As he charged, he seemed to see the frightened trio just outside, and his expression changed to one of shock, but his progress never slowed. When he made contact with the wall this time, he simply passed into non-existence. The entire building started to rumble and shake. No one could believe what they saw next. A World War II German Panzer rolled at the glass wall, and it too faded into nothingness, as it should have crashed into it.

Dad and Ned pulled Floyd back inside to the safety of the office, and he was now very aware of the radiation burns on his hands. Dad was the most composed of the three, mostly because he had lived through a worse combat episode before. He took Floyd to the lounge for care, and Ned latched down the doors.

Their attention turned toward Floyd for a few moments, and they lost track of what was happening in the chamber. I seemed to be able to somehow store the power flowing into me. When it reached what seemed to be the proper level, the equipment inside of me activated. My eyes glowed blue, with ever increasing brilliance, and to the point that even in my semi-conscious state I could see the glow above the other lights. I opened my mouth to scream, but the sound never came. I felt my body grow stiff as if it was the morning after a marathon, and then I felt nothing. My vision, the lights from my eyes, everything, was suddenly blanked out by a swirling gray cloud.

After their attention turned from the quick bandage job to Floyd's hands, everyone turned back to the maelstrom outside. To their surprise, they saw me standing at the front wall, waving at them. One by one, they froze where they stood when they saw me. Behind me was a boiling cauldron of multi-colored smoke, clouds, or fog. It was all and none. It crackled with energy and boiled, turning from a gray color to pitch black.

Mom slowly raised her hand to wave back, but Ned caused her to stop and look his way.

"That's not Terry!" he shouted.

"Of course it is!" Mom shouted back, in fear that he was right.

"No, he's right," Dad said, just loud enough to be heard.

"He has on his lab coat and safety shoes. There's no way he could have gotten them in there. He was in coveralls and barefoot. It must be that stuff he has in him again. More power means more strange things happen, and there is no telling how much has hit him now," Ned said, following Floyd toward the control room.

I locked eyes with my dad first, then my mom, stepped back one step, and was swallowed up by the cloud. My voice crackled over the com but was unperceivable, so it started to repeat.

"Feed me power. Feed me power." Finally understandable, it just kept repeating.

The massive breakers on the back wall under the bank of gauges were all thrown to the on position, and one lever after another was pushed forward until all the voltage wired in was fed into the system. A second after the last connection was made, a wave of blue energy blasted through the glass but did not break it. It came through like a four-foot-high section of a ring. Penetrating both walls, it crashed into the office and the outer wall, and dispersed like water, splashing onto the sidewalk. It swirled round and round until it finally hung in the air like a fog.

They all felt it when it hit. It was like a static charge in the air. Their hair became charged and began to stand on end like the age-old science fair showpiece. A blue wall of light passed over them and filled the room. It made them feel like they were underwater, but that was the only ill effect. They recovered slowly and started to check the instruments, but all were off the scales and useless.

Inside my real body had become rigid and turned bluish-gray, clothes and all. My face and hands were twisted in a frozen mask of pain. It felt strange to stand and look at myself, let alone in that condition. When the last bit of power flowed into the device from our stable power source, there was a flash of blue light and the fog began to clear around the chair. I was just standing there looking at myself. I should have been horrified at the sight, but I simply, slowly walked over to myself and looked intently. After satisfying whatever made me look in the first place, I turned my attention to the space that was clearing in front of me. The cloud was receding to the edges of the walls. It formed an enclosure on all sides, including a light mist on the floor.

I felt better than I ever had in my life, maybe because it was not really me. What was really me was an ugly colored lump of clay, cast into a freakish mold of terror and pain. In the far recesses of my mind, what happened to me bothered me, but it was only a small voice in the distance. What was foremost in my mind now was what had laid itself out before me, not just what I could see inside the room, but the connection that had been made with what was inside of me. It seemed to be alive at some level. How I knew that was not clear at the time, but it explained much of what had happened so far. The warnings had seemed to be a voice from inside, but it seemed to be my voice. Maybe it wasn't mine after all.

The fog on the floor moved as if wind had disturbed it, and a pale blue glow penetrated what was left. Large cuneiform symbols, the same ones that were in my vision, shone through and started to blink, and then they would change and repeat. I stood watching, unable to understand. I'm not sure how long I watched. It just seemed to draw me to it.

My trance was broken by a crackling voice over the com. When it caught my attention, it cleared up, and Dad's voice broke the silence.

"Scooter, can you hear me? Are you all right?"

"Yes," I returned.

"What's going on in there? We've been trying to contact you for hours," came the reply.

"I seem to be better now. What is happening inside here is, at best, difficult to explain. I'm inside some sort of vortex that seems to be contained by the walls. How much power are you feeding to me?" I asked.

"We are at maximum feed," Floyd's voice answered.

"I cannot say that I am all right, but I am as well as I am going to get."

"We are covered in some sort of a blue power field it seems to restrict our movements. Can you tell us if we are in any danger or how to shut it down?" Ned broke in.

There was nothing but silence.

"Terry! Are you there?" he called.

The blue tint began to fade around them.

"Look!" Bea said with excitement, pointing out the window.

There was a blue line of energy fog that was flowing slowly through the wall and back inside the lab. It continued until everything was clear on the outside, but the swirling turbulence inside grew more violent.

"I have contained the field. I believe you should not feel its effects, at least for now. It felt it was protecting you. You will not be able to leave the building yet, but I will make every effort to make it possible. Will you be all right for a while? I need to… make some calculations," I told them.

"We seem to be fine now. Floyd has some kind of burns on his hands. We have food and drink, so we will be okay for a while, provided there are no ill effects from the blue stuff," Ned returned.

"Hey," Floyd said, holding up his exposed hands. "No more burns."

Ned and Bea replied together slowly as if in a temporary trance, "It absorbs its energy back into itself."

"That's what he told us when he fixed my hand before," Ned finished.

They could not get a response from me after that, and as hard as they tried they could not open the door to the outside.

29

INSIDE, THE LIGHT DISPLAY OF alien writing continued. It called to me, but I could not seem to breach the gap to understand what it said. It repeated itself an untold number of times, then seemed to become more insistent, as if angry or eager, then stopped.

The floor cleared quickly and completely, all the way to the walls. Grids appeared, defined by blue lines, then they flashed. One to the left and outside stopped, enlarged to push the others away and filled the entire floor. In this view port, for lack of a better term, I started to see images. A breathtaking view of earth from space came into focus. My thought was that I was the first person, or human, on earth to see the Earth from space, but that was overshadowed by the sheer magnitude of what I was looking at. It was *extraordinary*.

The view turned away into space, then to the moon. I took in the entire surface at a close proximity, and then it moved on to what I believed was Mars. A detailed survey was made of the surface from a high orbit, then it moved on to the other planets, ending up with the oblong rock we called Pluto.

It did not stop there, but when we were outside our solar system, there would be flurries of the writing appear and flow all around the window as it had in my vision before. When it stopped, there was another planet under my feet. There was a similar amount of time spent at each stop, as if whatever was happening was timed, or the job, whatever it was, took about that length of time.

I saw many civilizations of human-like creatures, and as many others with strange and frightening creatures that defy description. It happened so quickly that it was hard to retain any real knowledge of what I was seeing, but the images were so striking that I could not help but remember most of them.

I reached a planet and this time stayed there. I surmised that this was home. Partly from the duration of the stay and partly from a feeling that came over me while in orbit. There started to be flashes of human-like creatures going about their daily lives, but only bits. Covering their thin muscular bodies was a shiny, metallic cloth-like material that made me think of the science fiction movies I had always liked. They had upside-down, teardrop-shaped heads with huge diamond shaped eyes that never seemed to blink, and their skin was a pale gray. Plants decorated their homes, and there were sidewalks filled with these "people." Great buildings of unbelievable height littered the landscape. Like everything else, they were all silver or a gray in color, looking part metal and part glass.

There seemed to be no plants or even grass outside, just buildings. It was like the entire surface of the planet was covered by the city. No animals or vegetation were obvious anyplace except on the inside, and these were only in homes, not in public. I found no photos, no adornments of any kind, personal or otherwise, in any of the scenes that I viewed. Their lives seemed to be drab and functional only.

After an extended stay on the tour, the writing returned, and then suddenly I was looking at Earth from space again. The view still astonished me, but then it moved closer and closer to the southern part of the United States. Texas passed under my feet and New Mexico drew closer. As Texas disappeared from view, everything changed. It appeared that the camera that was taking the pictures began to tumble out of control as if dropped. There was Earth and space in turn in ever increasing speed. The letters turned red and became quicker and more numerous. There was a flash of what looked like a flying saucer floating in space above the camera, then one of the human-like creature sitting at a console, and then the screen went blank.

The grids returned. One in the same left outside location engulfed the floor, and I started to view all the strange things that had transpired since my incorporation into this alien realm. It was more bizarre watching things happen from behind my own eyes than walking over the top of alien planets. At the times of power input, a certain "letter" would appear and flash blue. As the limited supply of electricity faded, the letter turned red again, fell to the bottom of the row, and then disappeared. This, I thought, was worth remembering. It proved interesting when the lightning found its way to me. The same letter appeared, flashed red, then green, and broke into three different sub-columns. The first flashed both colors and turned a brilliant pale blue. The second repeated that same process, but the third started flashing yellow, then stopped and stayed that color. At that point, the cloud formed and the pocket inside followed.

In New Mexico at the ARGO Lab, there had been a watch setup at the H333 console on the intact ship after it was activated before. When it came on this time, everything was ready, but what happened was unexpected. H333 lit up, and so did three other stations scattered around the circular room. That caused a flurry of activity from men, trying to get to them to observe. Everything stopped when the wall above the H333 station flickered and presented a roving presentation of what was happening to me. Everyone stood aghast as I sat in the chair screaming, presented on a screen ten feet in height and thirty feet wide. The scene would change from looking at me to looking from my point of view. Someone came to their senses and moved the TV camera back away from console to get a wider shot, including the projected images. This served to bring the rest to life.

A collective groan went up when a GI ran past in combat gear followed by a clacking sound, and he fell back into view. When he stood back up, he was gone from sight again, but when shots were heard, they all shuffled, knowing that there was nothing that they could do. The soldier had encountered some sort of force field protecting the doorway and tried to shoot his way outside. It did no good, but the field dissipated quickly and he was on his way with little delay. The next thing that they saw was what I had seen: the ceiling of our lab, swaying back and forth. It was the result of me shaking my head.

Before any of the military commanders or lab supervisors could arrive, there was nothing to see on the huge screen but a gray cloud with strange lines of odd figures on three sides that continued to move and change. The other two consoles flickered and closed down. H333 stayed active, but progressively reduced activity until only basic functions remained on. No one there knew what made it activate or remain on, at least for now.

A colonel walked into the ship, slowly followed by an entourage of burly men in uniform. No one had to ask who he was, they all knew. He bulled his way up to the console and took a long drag off his cigarette. His henchmen roughly moved the startled scientists out of the way and took up their stations behind their leader. When there were only a few minor sections lit up, the colonel reached over and touched what looked like a button, but was only an illuminated spot on the console. With obvious frustration, he turned and took a brief report from the officer in charge, then walked around the circular row of control panels. Satisfied, he nodded to the others as he reached the door and they all followed. At the end of the ramp, they all gathered and he told the group to conduct interviews, gather all information, especially the film, and meet him later. He made his way toward the exit and the others returned inside. Back in Texas, I had just finished my first look at the Earth from outer space.

30

THERE WAS NOTHING AFTER THE show. It was like stepping into, where I was, a large, quiet room. It was as quiet as I had ever heard, and the desert in New Mexico is very quiet at times. I'm not sure how long I stood looking at the blank floor. My mind did not wander. It was focused on one point in the floor like it was important. I blinked my eyes, and a table with a glass of iced tea was just there. I started to drink from the glass and moved around the table, looking at it. The tea tasted good and was very cold. I placed my hand on the table and it was solid. I looked over at my real self and surmised that this was either all in my mind or generated by the machinery inside me. Either way, to me, this was real.

I started to review the information I had looked at from outer space. There was a planet that, for some reason, had intrigued me. It was the plants that seemed so fascinating. Only at certain times was anything other than an orbital view shown, but this particular planet displayed a wealth of data on the life forms.

I zeroed in on a yellow plant or tree, which was the closest related shape. It was about five feet tall and two feet in diameter. It had two short branches, one on either side of the trunk, which looked dead. It had no foliage of any sort and a jagged top. I was fascinated. I could not take my eyes off it. The two-dimensional image jumped from the floor and was suddenly standing in front of me. I sprang back in surprise, but slowly moved closer to investigate.

I cautiously touched it. It was cool to the touch. It felt like refrigerated putty. While stunned by the beauty of the plant, I was equally amazed by the way it felt so real. My mind jumped back and forth between reality and what was before me, then settled back to the investigation. I stared at it intently and then it split into two pieces, it just opened up. It was as if it was split in half, top to bottom, by an unseen knife and its halves opened like a book.

Inside, it resembled a pumpkin. The color was lighter, but still yellow, and had a row of what looked seeds down the center. I reached in and touched the inside, and a small piece sliced off, floated up, and stopped at eye level. It floated there, then dissolved into smaller pieces, and finally into little sections of powder. The letters followed each division and now floated in the air beside each display. After several sections were dissected in this manner, the letters flashed several times and then everything vanished. I felt my curiosity was satisfied, even though I still knew nothing factual about what I had just seen.

Again I stood there, feeling lost. The intercom crackled and my dad asked if I was all right. It broke the trance.

"Yes, Dad, I'm fine," I responded.

"We've been calling for half an hour, and all we were getting was some strange beeps. We're all worried. This is uncharted territory we're in, and you're the one in the most danger," his voice crackled back.

"You should see the things I have just seen. Somehow I have seen parts of the universe that should be impossible. It was so real that I feel like I was really there. I wish I could describe it properly, or that you could come in here and see it for yourself," I said, with only a hint of excitement in my voice.

When his voice came through the intercom this time, he was standing there beside me. He jumped at the sight of me.

"Hello, Dad," I said as if I expected him.

"Glad to see you're okay, but what's going on?" he stumbled out. His voice echoed in the chamber, sounding like it was coming out of the intercom and from him too.

"Not sure, but I'm happy to know that you can come in here without getting hurt. Ned got burned when he touched the cloud before. It must be different now," I replied.

"But I didn't come in. At least not by the door," he said, slowly trying to figure things out. "I was standing in the control room and then I was here. What did you want me to see?" he asked, still deep in thought.

"Watch this," I said, and started the show with a view of the Earth from outer space.

In the control room, Dad had been standing close to the microphone to the intercom when he stiffened and let out a low grunt, as if he had been struck with something. At first, no one caught on to what had happened, but when his voice started to reverberate through the room, everyone moved to see what had happened.

He was standing there, rigid as steel. His eyes were glowing a pale blue color with growing intensity. The glow was increasing and soon took in his entire face, but he continued to talk as if he was having a conversation with me. They could not hear what I was saying, only his booming voice and static from the intercom speaker.

Floyd tried to move Dad, but could not budge him. The blue light continued to expand and started to emanate from his fingernails. Floyd started to feel the tingle of the glow on his skin. With that, he started calling roughly to me trying to get my attention. After a few calls, he got no response and tried another plan. He punched Dad on the arm. No results. He slapped him on the face lightly and repeated it with growing force.

"Wait," Dad interrupted the tour. "I think Floyd wants to say something."

Floyd could hear what he said, so he went back to the intercom.

"Terry, you have to let go! Stop whatever it is you are doing to your dad! I think you're killing him," he shouted, trying to get through.

I stopped the show and leaned my head back, looking up at what should be the level of the control room. In my mind, I could see the frenzy there and what was happening to my dad. There was a whirlwind of activity in my mind, part of which I did not understand, but the connection with the outside was severed, and my dad fell to the floor. He was scooped up immediately by the others and taken to one of the sofas in the lounge. He was comatose.

The calculations in my head completed themselves, and I started to give instructions over the intercom.

"Move away from him," my haunting voice crackled into the room. They slowly complied.

"I can repair the damage," I said, sounding like a ghost from a bad horror movie.

They stood and watched as a six-inch tube of cloud snaked its way through the glass wall and into the lounge, looking alive. The leading flat end seemed to take in all their awestruck faces, one by one, then found Dad on the sofa.

It struck him like the snake it resembled. It hit him in the face first, then passed slowly over his entire body. As it left a section, there were no more effects from the connection to be seen. When it was done, it quickly passed over Floyd and then retreated back inside the glass chamber.

"We are in danger of being discovered. We must power down. Slowly reduce output to ten percent. Hurry," I ordered flatly.

Floyd and Ned complied a quickly as possible. Dad sat up and seemed unaffected, but was excited about what he had seen inside. The women insisted he remain on the sofa.

"It has become clear to me that when any part of the field leaves the chamber, there is a signal sent to the other ship that the lab has. When I sent a thread out to repair Dad, communication was made. Our location will be compromised if the connection is not severed."

The power level fell and the field in the chamber grew less violent.

In the other ship, the console fully lit again and so did the screen. The inside of our building filled the wall and another console began to come alive. To the dismay of everyone there, only shadows of the people inside were visible before everything powered back to its previous lower level. There was not even enough time for much activity by those on vigil. They slowly checked to make sure that they had recorded everything and returned to their seats.

We decided that it would be better to power down as far as possible, to try to reduce the risk of any further detection, and to basically take a rest. They were all tired and wanted to go home to eat and sleep. I was the opposite. I wanted to go on and continue to explore what I could now do, but gave in to the better idea of waiting to see if we were still safe.

31

ALL THE CLOCKS IN THE building were wrong or not working at all, so no one really knew how long we had been inside. We all agreed that it had been several hours of extreme stress and a break would be advisable. Thinking that it was early evening, Ned and Bea volunteered to stay with me while the others went to eat. It was too late to start cooking a meal, so everyone agreed that a trip to the diner was the best idea and a takeout plate for Ned and Bea would solve the rest of the problem.

The door to the outside swung open, and a rush of frigid air jolted the quartet preparing to leave. They were all dressed in light clothing as it was a warm autumn day when they entered and in this part of Texas that felt like summer heat in most places.

"That must have been a cold front that came through instead of just a thunderstorm. It's really cold out here," Mom said, her arms clasped close to her chest, and like the others she started to shiver.

The air was crisp and the sky was crystal clear. The stars shone as if they had been revitalized by the influx of clean, cold air. Smoke rose from the breath of everyone as scurried toward the waiting car parked on the south side of the building.

Floyd pulled his keys from his pocket and they jingled clearly in the still night air, but he stopped before he unlocked the door.

"Hurry up, I'm cold," Edna shot Floyd's way.

"The doors aren't locked," he shot over his shoulder, looking at the side of the building.

"Yes they are! Now get them open we're all freezing!" Edna half screamed, showing her irritation.

"Reggie cut the grass and trimmed around the building yesterday. Look at it now," Floyd said, still transfixed on the wall. He spun around quickly and thumbed the door release button, but it didn't work. It was locked. It seemed wrong, but he unlocked it anyway and fell into the seat to start the motor. He felt like something was wrong. Everything was just not right.

He unlocked his door and let the rest in. When he touched the starter, the engine strained to turn over, but did start reluctantly.

"That's not right," he said, staring at the dash as if looking for answers.

"You're right. The grass is high and weeds are all over the walls. What's going on?" Dad asked.

"Not sure, but we'll think better on a full stomach. Let's hope it's not too late to eat," Floyd said, backing out of the parking place.

"Can't be much past seven," Mom said, snuggling closer to Dad.

Floyd moved the car toward the street, but stopped quickly when he got a clear view of it in the headlights. After a short pause, he eased up to the gate.

"There wasn't a gate here when we came in this afternoon," Dad said, sliding forward in the rear seat to get a better look.

"No, but it was on Reggie's list. Let's see if he did this," Floyd said, leaving the car.

He walked to the lock side of the gate, which was only an elongated pipe triangle. The lock was hanging on the outside, connecting a short length of chain wrapped around a pipe post, and the end of the gate connecting the two. Floyd looked things over, squatted down, and retrieved a key from under a large rock a few feet away. The key worked and he let the lock hang on the chain, once released, and swung the gate open before returning to the idling car.

"It must have been Reggie that put it up. The key was where we decided to put it," Floyd said as he sat back down behind the wheel.

"Maybe they just got in a hurry and finished it ahead of time," Dad replied.

"Not unless it rusted up overnight," Floyd said sarcastically.

"Something more happened today than we know. Terry and that contraption of his has messed with everything again. We'll just have to get through tonight and see if he can fill us in the morning. I'm too tired and hungry to start anything else now."

He pulled through the gate and was sitting in the space allowed for a vehicle to sit while opening and closing it, keeping the street clear. While traffic was almost non-existent most of the time, it was thought that the space was a wise idea. With the gate closed and locked, and the key returned to its hiding place, they pulled out.

Old Humble road was a narrow, two-lane blacktop street that had been used for many years. It had been a muddy dirt road years before and was well-used after being paved. It had been State Highway 35, and while at one time it was an important route, the creation of US 59 had rendered it a back road, after dark traffic on both roads slowly dwindled to nearly nothing, as it was now.

Floyd turned left, which was south, out of the gate, and headed toward Homestead Road. It was the quickest route to the local restaurant that they all had fallen in love with. Along the way, they noticed that nothing was open, and the cold just seemed to creep closer and closer to their bones, despite the car heater's best efforts. At Homestead they turned right, and after half a block, turned right again onto the US 59 feeder street. There was no need to slow down for the turn into the parking lot because it was obvious that the diner was closed, so they proceeded down the service road a few miles and turned right onto Upshaw, which would take them back home.

The oddities continued once they reached the house and found a steel gate installed and locked across the driveway. Floyd repeated the procedure of retrieving a key from under a large rock nearby and then opened the gate. The headlights gave him the ability to see what he was doing and also revealed the fact that the grass needed to be mowed badly. The gate was left open, and they all hurried into the house to escape the cold.

It was wasted effort, for it seemed colder inside than out. All three gas space heaters were soon lit and pouring out heat as rapidly as possible. The bathroom was soon the warmest room in the house, but the two pairs were gathered around separate heaters, wondering what had befallen them now.

After warming for a short while, their attention turned back to their hunger. Clocks in the house were working, unlike the ones at the office and their watches, and knowing that it was two in the morning made it seem worse. Nothing in the refrigerator seemed fresh, and all the bread in the house was nothing but piles of mold. The anxiety mounted.

After a short discussion of whether to return to the office for fresh food or have canned Spam, fatigue settled the debate. A couple of cans were opened, and by the time it was fried, the biscuits were ready.

"I said I would never eat this again after the war," Floyd said, looking at a slab of the meat held at eye level on his fork.

"I know it's not much, but it was quick and it will fill you up. The only reason we have it is because Ned likes it," Edna said, taking her seat beside him.

"He never had to eat it cold out of a can for a month. I had to chip it up and thaw it out in my mouth just to have something to eat. At least it's warm," Floyd said, taking a bite while making a painful expression.

"It's good," Dad said simply, and Mom nodded while taking a bite.

The hurriedly prepared meal was just as quickly devoured, and little time was spent around the table afterward. Mom and Dad elected to take Ned and Bea's beds for the rest of night. Floyd tried to call and check on things back at the office, but couldn't get through. He had the operator check the line, but it was a problem with the phone, not the line. She then explained that they had been plagued with problems over the last few months, and it all started when a sub-station somehow burned up. There had been problems in the area ever since. Floyd thanked her and hung up the phone, accepting the fact that the phone would have to be repaired and there was nothing he would be able to do tonight. He was tired and wanted to get some sleep.

He went into the bathroom to wash his face before bed, more to clear his mind than to get clean. Things were spinning again, and he had to keep a handle on them, if for no other reason but for Edna.

He rubbed his face with the warm water and looked up into the mirror above the sink. He still could not believe what he saw. It was him, but him from years ago. He thought about people who had told him of looking in the mirror and suddenly seeing an old man, but never the other way around. Then he noticed his fingernails. They were blue. He held his hands down, spread his fingers, and looked at all his nails. They were growing brighter blue, quick enough to see the increase. He let out a long breath and aroused the others.

It was common to them all. After a short discussion and the lack of ill feelings, it was decided to just retire, since there was really nothing that could be done anyway. The consensus was that it was an aftereffect of exposure to radiation, or whatever it was, at the office. If there were any other negative effects, no one was aware of them, so they just tried to rest.

I was, in a fashion, resting myself. The cloud that surrounded me was almost a fog now. I seemed to be at peace with all that had happened, and I was well on my way to accepting my fate. I was almost pleased with the outcome. My life was forever changed. That was a powerful understatement, but words could never do justice to what my future seemed to be.

I felt a calling suddenly, and using only the power of my mind, I reached out and increased the level of power flowing into my body. I felt the energy as it flowed in, and the cloud around began to grow in size and intensity. I could see in my mind's eye the levers controlling the electricity flow moving to feed more into the system, into me.

The area cleared once again. The image of me was standing, looking at my real self once again. The floor took on its TV screen appearance and a blurry picture of Ned and Bea appeared under my feet. As the power increased, the images became clearer, and finally were a three-dimensional image before me. Ned was on one knee, and Bea was sitting on one of the sofas in the lounge with tears in her eyes. I heard him ask her to marry him, and then she launched herself at him, knocking him to the floor. Clinging to him as if dangling over a cliff, she showered him with kisses and a steady stream of yeses. I interrupted their joy, and both let out a short yelp as a hazy image of me appeared at their feet.

"I need help. Go to the control room," my ghostly voice moaned.

Ned sprang to his feet and bounded into the next room.

The intercom crackled. "Increase to full power," came my voice.

Ned wasted no time. He gently shoved all three power controls to their uppermost stops. The meters showing output fell to the maximum reading, and then bumped the high side peg. The smell of burning insulation soon filled the room.

"You're pulling too much power!" Ned shouted, watching a wisp of smoke appear near the panel.

Seconds passed like hours as Bea joined Ned and stood behind and to one side, looking at the panel too.

"Shut it down now," came my reply finally.

Ned forced the levers to their low output positions as quickly as he could.

"I must leave now. Open the doors," my voice now boomed through the speaker. It was deep and reverberated with power.

The couple looked at each other with large smiles and broke into a dead run toward the door. They shuffled down the stairs together, and at the bottom stopped to look at the lab. It was starting to clear and show the devastation inside. The large TV camera was just gone. Where it had been was only a spot on the floor where the wires and mounts were run through. Nothing not connected to the chair was missing, as if erased. Fortunately, the air conditioning unit had been installed between the floors and survived. Nothing else did. Strange small piles of mud marked the floor in two distinct lines. There were cleat marks in the mud as well as muddy boot tracks that led to the front wall. Ned stopped and whispered in awe, "That tank was really in there!"

They noticed me standing by the inside door, beckoning them to come my way. Ned moved ahead and started to turn the large wheel to unlock the outside door. Once finished, he repeated the process for the inside door, and with great effort, swung it open too. He started to move toward me, but I stopped him with a simple gesture. Somehow with that gesture, he knew not to come closer and stopped in his tracks. I stood still and lowered my hand, standing straight up with my head lowered, arms now at my side. Ned backed out of the lab and watched from the floor outside as a gray specter of me appeared from the remaining fog and, as if in slow motion, moved forward and absorbed what had appeared to be me.

"Do not be afraid. I must leave. I must retrieve it," I said, my gray face a frozen mask, hardly moving.

"What?" Ned slowly forced out, not able to absorb what he was seeing.

Without a response, I stiffly moved out on the entryway and down the steps to the floor.

"Open the door," I said with a slight slow nod to the door that led to the outside.

Ned quickly complied.

I started to take a step forward and seemed to freeze. Small wisps of smoke began to rise from my body, and then I was gone. Ned and Bea looked at each other in astonishment.

To me, I was instantly back at the ARGO in New Mexico, standing at the main entryway. When I touched the door, I was instantly inside the complete ship twenty-five floors below. I slowly walked around the interior of the ship on all levels, mentally recording what I saw. The figures in my vision had returned and formed different configurations with each floor and object I observed. On the top level, which I assumed to be the bridge, there was a small contingent of men in lab coats, some uniformed soldiers, and some large, unsavory-looking characters in black suits. They were all frozen in their respective poses. I simply made my way past them as if they were part of the ship.

As I approached the console with the largest number of men nearby, it lit up. The letter streams in my vision flashed and increased in speed. The entire bridge came alive in just a few seconds, and a three-dimensional image of Earth and another planet floated over the open area in the center of the room. After a long look, I started out the door, and then I was in a large warehouse.

There was what seemed like endless rows of shelves that reached at least twenty feet high. I started at one end and with each step moved hundreds of feet. Somewhere close to the center of the structure, I turned and went down an aisle. When I stopped, I was standing in front of what looked like a glass bell. There was a black, one-inch-thick base at the bottom, about two feet in diameter, and the thick glass cover was connected to it. The glasslike material was thick, but the distorted shape of what appeared to be a bell could be made out inside. There were three metal rods that stood equal distances apart with connecting metal fins that formed an open shade effect around the outer glass shell. It lit up in a brilliant blue light as I stood looking it over.

I could not believe it, but I reached over and lifted it as if it were made of paper. I tucked it under my right arm, took a step, and was back in Texas outside the door to our lab. I stepped inside and felt the weight of my burden. I sat it down and looked as Ned and Bea, in slow motion, started toward each other.

As they sped up, back to normal speed, they gasped as they realized I was sitting there. The sight of me momentarily froze them as I sat there, appearing to be smoldering. There was an excessive amount of steam escaping from all over me, and parts of me were slowly returning to my normal color, but only in patches.

"What happened?" Bea shot my way.

"I thought you had to go somewhere! What's that?" Ned asked, almost talking over the top of Bea.

Both started toward me, but I waved them off.

"If you touch me you *will die*! I must get back to the chair and feed. My power level is growing dangerously low," I said as I stumbled forward toward the open door.

"Feed low levels of power in. Maybe I can pull a thread from the door," I said, still struggling to get inside.

Ned ran up the stairs and inside the office. As I reached the threshold, a thread of power found me. I stood and moved to the steps just outside the first door. Another thread appeared, then another, and soon I felt refreshed. I stood there, gathering my thoughts. The steam was gone, and my color returned completely to normal. The threads danced around on my back like on the static machines you would see at the science fair.

"Enough?" Ned's voice boomed over the intercom.

I waved at him that it was okay and to come back down. When he got there, he put his arm around Bea's shoulders and pulled her close. She leaned her head onto his chest, and they both stood there, not knowing what to do or say. They did not even flinch when my eyes started to glow blue. It was beginning to seem normal, the abnormal. When they returned to normal, I walked over to the device I had returned with.

"I must get this inside. Seal me back in. They will be able to locate us if we do not hurry," I said, walking slowly toward the object.

"I'll get it. You go on inside," Ned said, grasping two of the rods around the outside. When he lifted, it was as if he was trying to lift the whole building. The strain was obvious on his face, and he gave up the futile attempt quickly. I lifted it with ease with only one hand, turned, and entered the lab, the wooden steps creaking from the strain. My footsteps echoed loudly through the cavernous room until there was a soft thud when I placed my trophy next to the chair. I sat down.

"Seal me in. They will locate us if you do not hurry," I said again, settling in.

The sound of the door closing, then sealing, rang through the empty room, then a softer report from the outer door followed.

"We are safe now. Raise the level to forty percent and let it settle there. Congratulations to the two of you. I saw the proposal. The two will have a long and happy life together. I will not disturb you before morning," I said and switched off the intercom, not waiting for a response.

32

THE NEXT MORNING, A POUNDING on the door awakened Floyd. No one else stirred, so he quietly padded to the sound of the noise. When he opened the door, he found Schwartz standing there with shock then relief on his face.

"Thank God you're all right," he gasped. "Where have all of you been?"

"We were at the lab until late last night. We got back here about two and just went to bed. Is there something wrong?" Floyd asked, still tired, and invited Schwartz to have a seat on the sofa.

"Forget last night! You have been gone for the last *three months*!" Schwartz shot back, taking his seat.

"*What?* We were just in there for one long afternoon! *Three months!* Whatever you been drinking? Next time, save some for me," Floyd returned, smiling with the last comment.

"You might have told us you put an electric door on that building too. Reggie almost died when he tried to get in there. We got worried after a few weeks and wanted to check on you. He grabbed the doorknob and went straight out. The doctor at the hospital said it was the strangest kind of shock he had ever seen. His fingernails turned *blue* for a week. Heckins, he was laid up for a few weeks. Said he was just tired, had no energy at all. That thing is dangerous!" Schwartz rattled out excitedly.

Floyd thought about the situation for a second or two and started apologizing.

"It's about time I filled you in I guess. We are doing some real secret research. It could be worth some real money. Nothing illegal, I assure you, but if word gets out about what we're doing we could lose everything. I didn't realize that Reggie was hurt, and we'll cover any of the money he was out, including the work he missed. This must be kept quiet at all costs, and I will see if the others want to let you in on all of this. Frankly, we could use some more help, but I'll have to see what they want to do first, okay?" Floyd said, feeling like he was lying, but in a way he wasn't.

"There is the matter of the bills I took care of while you were… uh… gone," Schwartz said, standing up when Floyd did. "And I have another large check for you that needs to be cashed, or we will have to have it re-issued." He really didn't want to offend, but business was business.

"We will be by your office later today. We were up late and need to rest this morning," Floyd said, starting toward the door, trying to hide his hands so not to expose his blue fingernails.

"Of course, of course. The last thing I wanted to do was intrude. We were all just worried that some of that weird stuff that you do had hurt you or worse. Just concerned you know," Schwartz said, shuffling his way nervously toward the door. He stopped at the doorway and leaned close to Floyd, asking in a hushed voice, "Is this some of that robot stuff?"

Not really connecting the story told earlier, but seeing his opportunity, he just said, "Yes."

Schwartz seemed to be elated. "Reggie told me about him. Will I be able to see him too?" he asked, patting his hands together as if clapping.

"I'll talk to the others and see what they say," Floyd said, one hand behind the door and the other behind his back.

Schwartz was on the porch in a state bordering euphoria. "I can't wait… for you to come by the office that is… with the news about the robot… you know."

"Just keep quiet about all this or we will have to pack up and leave again. We can't afford to lose what we have done so far," Floyd said sternly.

"Oh, not a word, not a word, I swear. See you later today," Schwartz said, hurrying back to his car.

Floyd just shook his head and went back to bed.

For the next few days, things were uneventful, at least on my part. I felt tired after my little trip and just seemed to rest. It was probably for the best, because the three diesel-powered generators arrived and had to be wired in. Power could be switched from circuit to circuit to maintain a flow into me, and a floor to ceiling curtain was installed to hide the lab from the workers. After the work was completed, we were called to a meeting of sorts.

33

It was determined that everyone had been exposed to too much energy or radiation from the wave that had penetrated the lab walls. There seemed to be no long-lasting effects, but real tests were impossible to obtain because no one knew what test to run or what to look for. The discoloration of the fingernails was the only real symptom, but while all were concerned that it could be serious none knew what to do about it. Limited exposure for each individual was the only option since I had to remain connected to some kind of power source for the time being. A reduced or more controlled power flow was another option that was explored, but was not a real possibility, since power was drawn without our ability to stop it.

The last option and the best long-term solution was to find some way to determine what type of energy we were dealing with and find a way to protect people from it. The first problem with that project was to find a way to detect and monitor whatever it was. I decided that I would go to work on that part of the problem and feed any information out to whoever was monitoring at that time. Dad was an engineer, so he took the lead on the project outside. He quickly delegated assignments and started gathering the equipment that he thought he would need. Little did we know that his efforts would soon be found antique and useless. The technology we were dealing with was so advanced that there was no equipment available to test even the smallest part of what we were looking for.

I adjusted the power input to a level that I could function at and started to research what kind of radiation we were dealing with. I found that I could create equipment and actually do comprehensive research just by thinking about it. I started by doing experiments that had easily verifiable results to make sure I was not dreaming the outcome. As I did more, I needed more power, and when we reached another increase, the unit that I had recovered on my last trip activated. At first I was afraid that the others would be injured because of the effect that I saw inside. The clarity and solidity of everything that I had been doing was increased by hundreds times. It seemed that even my IQ level was going up. The level of light in my make-believe lab went so high that it hurt my eyes. I had to figure out a way to lower them and finally did.

Once I could see clearly again, I went to the intercom and called out to see if everything outside was still okay.

"Yeah," Ned replied. "We're okay, why?"

"The last unit that I acquired just lit up. Things in here really became more intense. I was worried that the field had gotten out again," I replied.

"It's not out here, the best I can tell anyway, but… the cloud looks more intense. Thicker and more turbulent, but nothing like before when it came through the glass," Ned stammered out.

"Lower the power some. It's starting to give me a headache. Not much, I want this thing to stay on. Leave it there for now," I said, paused, and continued. "If you have a radiation suit, it would be advisable to keep it on for the next few days, and if there is anyone with you, send them home. We need not risk more than one of you at a time. I wish that I could do this alone so that all of you could be safe."

"We will be fine," Ned reassured me. "None of us would dream of leaving you like this. Now go back to work. We need to find out what we are dealing with."

I did go back to work, and the things that I could see and do were unimaginable. It did not take long to devise a way to detect the type of power we were using. At least, it seemed simple to me. When I explained it over the intercom, the reaction was like I was speaking a foreign language. No one understood a thing I was trying to say. There was no way to write it down or send it to them, so I had another problem to solve. Finally, I got Floyd prepared and had him watch the wall of the lab in front of him.

Letters and figures began to appear on the wall, and he copied them down best he could. It took Dad a month to decipher and build a detection device. He had trouble believing what it was, let alone that it would work, but it did and that started a flurry of new devices that we needed. That took a lot of the worry out of being in the office and gave Dad a whole new world to explore. He was soon planning a company to market some of the ideas.

Once the safety issues were out of the way, I returned to the information that I viewed about space. This time, the information was considerably more detailed.

When I got to the tree-like plant, I was overwhelmed with curiosity again. It was so fascinating that I was completely captivated. The process that dissected it before did not start this time; it was just there, so I started to examine it myself. I could feel it like it was really there, and after due consideration, I decided that it was. I was some kind of projection, and to me I seemed real, so given that premise, this plant had to be real too.

It felt soft and rubbery. Its yellow surface felt more like skin than bark, sort of like cold modeling clay. After a thorough external examination, it was time to continue inside as the display had done before. I wanted to split it open and look inside like before so that I could actually examine firsthand what I had seen.

I concentrated intently on the equipment that I would need to open up and make a comprehensive analysis of the specimen. The interior of the room modified itself into a lab stocked with all the equipment that I needed. Somehow it was not a real surprise. Everything was laid out and in place, just as I had wanted.

I reached down and grabbed the plant at the center on each side and lifted it toward the table. I felt a warm sensation grip my palms, and the dough-like yellow bark seemed to reach out and make an attempt to surround my hands. I sat it on the table and tried to release my grip, but found it difficult to separate myself. I seemed to be glued to it. As I twisted my right hand, trying to free it, the smell of honey overwhelmed my senses. It was so strong it was sickening. My hand slowly became free, trailing thin strands of clear mucus, and the odor became more powerful. I freed my left hand, which proved to be much easier.

I started to review the information I had looked at earlier. It was extremely detailed this time. The additional equipment enhanced the available data, was my guess. It was still difficult to make out the information being displayed. I had to read by pictures and improvise the best I could.

The first section I watched was an examination of the outside and really told me little. The next was a partial look inside. It showed the plant split in half, as if cut almost in two, top to bottom, and folded open like a book, showing a cross section of both sides. This was what I was going to try to duplicate. I selected a large knife that seemed suitable to the task given for what I surmised to be the consistency of the plant, but as I turned to the table to start, the plant was on the wrong side of the table. It took a second to recover. After all, I was in what seemed like my own fantasy world, or so I thought.

It occurred to me that this might be an accurate representation of reality, and if so, then I was dealing with whatever this plant really was. I quickly watched the entire report, scrutinizing every aspect of the external sections. Afterward I took a scalpel, moved around the table, and cut a small sample from the top edge of my subject. The smell of honey flooded the room, overwhelming me again. I was anxious and excited at the same time. It seemed out of character for me to be this overwhelmed. I raced back around the table to a waiting microscope to see if I could prove my theory. I placed the sample on a slide, gently placed it on the scope, and focused in with the lowest power. After a quick look, I moved up to the next, then to the highest magnification, and studied for a long time. It was clear now why the smells and the mucus and why it was on the wrong side of the table. It was alive! It was an animal, not a plant. With this revelation, I reviewed the information again, paying even closer attention to the internal parts. It still did not tell me that this was an animal, but now knowing that it was, I could see signs of a circulatory system. It would have been all too obvious if only I could read the large amount of script that scrolled around the displays.

I moved back to the treelike animal and gently rubbed its side, as if petting a small dog. My fingers would stick and slide at first, then they stopped sticking and its skin smoothed out. It seemed to know, somehow, that I intended it no harm. The smell of honey faded and was replaced with the scent of sour apple candy. It was one of my favorite kinds of candy, and it seemed to indicate that the odd little animal was happier.

I was a bit irritated that I could not seem to get any information out of what was apparently there. I played the entire recording over and over again, which just added to my frustration. It was odd I did not feel anger, but fighting disgust, I slammed my hand into the display. It did not hit the screen as I had thought it would, my hand simply passed into it. The image distorted, and what I thought was the surface of the screen was only a thin layer of air with images in it. There was a sparkling static circle around my wrist and it webbed out like small lightning bolts over the display. It was a magnificent sight, until there was a jolt through my arm. It was so intense that I heard my real self groan out in pain. My mind was suddenly shocked with the information that I had been trying to access and millions of times more.

It hit me like a ton of bricks, and my mind was instantly on fire. More and more information filled my mind. It was like having millions of books read aloud at one time and being able to understand each one as if they were the only one, but it was images and feelings and impressions along with the facts. I finally passed out and fell to the floor of the lab.

How long I was out I could not say, but I was still suffering the effects of the transfusion when I revived. It took several minutes for me to gather my wits. My consciousness seemed to expand. I started to get a small amount of control over the swirling influx of data I had been fed. It was a capsule of pure information instantly unloaded into my mind, and like a wave running ashore, it was spreading out, finding a resting place as its energy dissipated. It was like looking through a keyhole all your life, then stepping out onto the edge of the Grand Canyon. I could see all things with a tremendous clarity I never thought possible.

34

I HAD APPARENTLY TAPPED INTO some kind of memory cell when I touched the projected display. It felt like warm water was being poured through every atom in a progressive line down my body. I turned to look at my real self and could see a blue line of sparkling energy slowly moving down that was directly linked to the wave I felt. Its effects, I found, would never wear off.

The information I wanted so badly about the tree-animal now played out in my mind in staggering clarity. It was almost as if I could actually see into any and every fiber of its makeup. None of my questions were to be unanswered. I traveled through the primitive circulatory system and major organs, each cross-sectioned from every conceivable direction and angle. The layers of skin and the odd scent glands were there, dissected well enough to eliminate any doubt of what they were. Even the color was explained with a short video clip of it growing and hiding in like-colored plants and brush. It obviously moved too slowly to outrun any predator, so concealment and scent were its only defenses. It drew water from the soil like a tree, but attracted, captured, and consumed large numbers of a fly-like creature that were abundant in its marsh habitat.

I was popped out of the information system by a buzzing insect. One circled my head making a tremendous amount of noise. It was about the size of a bumblebee, but the best I could tell, it looked like a huge housefly. It flew round and round me at higher and higher speeds, then shot straight at the little yellow tree. It landed and started to crawl around on it, and after a few seconds became trapped in the mucus that was secreted after the bug had landed. It struggled, buzzing louder and louder as the skin nearby parted and overlapped the insect, pulling it inside the outer layer for consumption. The powerful smell of sour apple candy filled the room.

"Well, George, looks like dinner is served," I said, as more and more of the pests began to appear.

As "George" consumed the fly-insects, my mind started to wander from what I had just learned. Curiosity was again beginning to overwhelm me, but all other emotions seemed to leave. I could feel them flowing away like water down a drain. I do not know how I knew this; I just did, like so many other things before. I began to ask what caused this to happen to me and why I was now like I was. There were no answers, but one word came to the forefront of my mind. "Dane." I started to concentrate on that word alone.

Information flowed into my mind again, but this time it was soft and controllable. I was surrounded by vivid images of a world and its satellite. It appeared that I was standing in space, looking at the pair from a vast distance but moving ever closer. At first, I thought that it was a view of Earth from the ship I knew came here and that this apparatus was a part of, but as I got closer I realized the difference.

Both the planet and moon were larger but still close to earth-size, but the planet was barren and pockmarked like our moon. In fact, it looked like it was our moon, just much larger. It too appeared to have little or no atmosphere and did not spin. The real surprise was the moon. It was lush and green, a smaller version of the image that gives Earth the name Big Blue Ball. It was cast in the shadow of the larger sphere in a permanent orbit. The sun struck only a small portion of the surface, but lit one hemisphere, although partially shaded.

I moved ever closer until I was at ground level, floating around all I could see. Animals were strange, smaller versions of what could be found on Earth. Small cows grazed, with little difference besides their size and their eyes. They had very large eyes. As I looked at odd forms of pigs, bison, and other such animals, I noticed that they all had larger eyes. The thought came to me that it was a bit dark. Most of the time it was like dusk on earth, with the bright sunny part lasting only a few hours early in their morning. The people and animals stayed indoors or undercover for that part of the day.

To me, it explained the larger eyes. It was to give the visual acuity it took to survive in a hostile predator-filled environment. With that thought I moved on from plants and animals to the people who lived there. They were, like the animals, a smaller version of us and had larger eyes. They farmed and raised livestock, formed communities and then towns. Their civilization moved along similar lines as ours, but much faster and with major differences.

After their first steps toward civilized society, there had been no wars on the planet. They had avoided our violent past and had a true benevolent progressive society. They were all one race and color, so they avoided that divisive factor too. The landmasses were all connected in one way or another, so progress passed around the globe; sometimes slowly, but it did. Without war to put a strain on population, they voluntarily controlled their own numbers and learned the hard way that they had to marry outside their own village to help vary the genetic pool. Advances in science and medicine soon had them facing overpopulation on their small planet, despite set controls, so they turned technology toward the larger celestial body nearby. They reached out to their version of our moon, out of necessity more than curiosity. At that time, they looked much like us. Except for their eyes being twice the size of ours, very few other physical differences existed.

With the entire scientific community devoted to the venture, answers came quickly. Domes could be added to the dark side of the terminator, which was a permanent day-night line. Robotic probes had reported that the soil was suitable for growing crops and preparations followed quickly. Some large deposits of ice existed around the planet that would provide a suitable supply of water, although a limited one. The terminators provided enough suitable light for the crops but did not blind the settlers. The plan was put into place and soon the dead planet was alive with activity. An armada of rockets dropped supplies on the proposed site, and soon the intrepid settlers started arriving. First came the workers. They set up the temporary housing and marshaled the supplies, reporting every step of the way so changes could be made and plans could adapt. It worked well, and the revised changes were implemented at every level, which only accelerated the progress. Within a few years there were crops growing and a permanent presence living in the ever-expanding domes.

The technology for the domes improved exponentially. At first, tint was added so that the existing domes could be expanded into the brighter, sunnier sides of planet. Then filters were invented so the expansion could continue into blazing light of full sun. Domes sprang up past the terminator, and then moved farther into the sun side as better filters could be created. Lights and better temperature control technology followed that allowed for settlement of the dark side of the planet. Heat sources were invented, and progress flowed into the darkness as well.

With the progress to the filters came the need for better, quicker machines. At first, their machines were physical extensions of the people who ran them, similar to hydraulic robotics, but they were too slow. Computers were added to enhance response. Quicker meant more progress. Soon, instead of reacting to the physical commands of the user, the machine could receive commands and proceed on verbal orders. With that step came the next—an actual mental interface with the machine. At first it would kill and maim the operator when a malfunction to the system occurred, and then another breakthrough changed the entire race forever.

A radio wave connection to the machine was created. One powerful idea from a lab changed everything, and once put into practical use, progress at every level leapt ahead to staggering levels. It was as if the machines and the Dane were one. The machines started to streak around at all hours, for all physical requirements had been eliminated. More time could be spent producing and not resting. Unskilled labor could be added, because there was no experience required. The user just had to think of what needed to be done, and the equipment would do the work. This led to having excessive time and excessive food.

With little else to conquer on their two worlds, some of the improvements to the shuttle system between them were turned toward space, in hopes of finding another suitable planet to colonize. With their plasma drive propulsion, it was not difficult to advance to interplanetary travel. At first it took months to travel to the nearest planets, and true to their past, their prior progress times were cut to days, then moments. The two closest planets were suitable for limited habitation even with domes, and this feat soon fell to the juggernaut that was now *The Dane*. The ever-increasing technology and the drive to succeed race-wide made them all but unstoppable. With their own solar system conquered, they turned their considerable talents toward the stars. Levels of technology increased still, as schools turned out more brilliant students trained from childhood in the latest concepts. Food was abundant and prosperity was race-wide. All enjoyed the benefits of each invention.

When the first long-range ships returned, there seemed to be a downside to the latest interface with the computers. It directly linked the user to the onboard computer with a highly developed radio system. It seemed to make the crewmembers more machine-like. At first it was blamed on the rigors of the journey, but changes were soon made to try to alleviate the symptoms. With each upgrade to the system, the problem just grew worse. With no real options, volunteers were asked to continue usage for the progress of society. There were plenty of those who wished to do so. The allure of deep space was worth the risk, most believed. The side effects were small and temporary, or so it was thought.

With new refinements to the equipment, there were fewer side effects during deep space travel, so the system was soon installed in every instrument that was manufactured. The system revolutionized the effect of every instrument it was connected to. It was so efficient and productive that it became an aid in every school on every planet, but soon the hidden toll began to show.

Life spans began to increase, reproduction went down, and intellect was spiraling upward at an alarming rate. None seemed interested in relationships. There was no hostile intent. All emotion seemed to just slowly fade out of the culture. The changes were so gradual that it took almost a generation to realize what was really happening, and because it happened to all, no alarm was sounded. All the citizens of the Dane empire were stripped of the things that made them human, and with their focus on progress and expansion, no one was aware until it was too late to repair the damage.

At one point, the applications for reversal of the process were tested, but found impractical because it would require a total reconfiguration of their technology. To return to the agricultural life of their ancestors was unthinkable. Some genetic experiments were tried with ghastly results and soon abandoned. So, in a sense, they gave in to the belief that expansion took priority. Their idea of spreading out into all of space was important enough for their race to sacrifice this small part of themselves to succeed. It was only logical. It had been their goal for generations to move out from their home world and expand for the good of their entire race, and these few sacrifices were insignificant compared to the benefits and the alternative.

The link between man and machine was given priority after the decision to waive the side effects in the name of expansion. It was given more power, permitted to tap deeper and deeper into the mind of each user. Every aspect that the instruments controlled was enhanced to the point that it was possible for some to actually feel what they were learning or studying. It was almost hypnotic at times. So their focus was placed even more on enhancement.

The old side effect of graying skin was returning, but all thoughts of abandoning the enhancements were long past. It now was a part of progress. No thought was given to side effects unless they interfered with lifespan or were a direct threat to one's life. All without question sanctioned the slow, subtle changes to the Dane race. Their bodies soon lost all of their hair and became frailer with the lack of physical labor, but were still more human than the representation of the aliens known by the general populous on our planet. Regardless, they were what we were introduced to as "The Grays."

35

Long ago on their journeys they found Earth. It was of particular interest to them because of the similarity to their own home planet. They were interested in watching it develop, to chart the related differences in the two cultures. For eons they had observed the progress of humans on our planet, carefully documenting progress, being cautious never to interfere so as not to change the natural process that was taking place.

Then, one of three Dane ships on a scheduled observation tour had a mechanical malfunction and crashed in New Mexico. The other two came to their assistance, but found that residual radiation from the atomic test performed nearby had a tremendously negative effect on their technology. They were trapped without resources soon after they landed.

Communication was possible for limited time, so a dispatch was sent and received. All occupants soon succumbed to the bright light and the heat of the desert. It took only hours for most to die. The instruments on one ship recorded its transfer to a government facility before it shut down to protect the ship from the intruders that made their way inside.

The latest advancement to the ships had been the addition of a new bioorganic memory system. It was new enough that all the bugs had not been worked out yet, and they did not realize that it retained not only, but also absorbed partial memories of each user it came in contact with (which explained my fascination with George, the tree plant). He must have fascinated the operator of the station making the survey, so the imprinted curiosity bled over onto me. I often have flashes of his life, at home and on the ship.

There are large gray stone buildings with large numbers of people scurrying around living their lives, then the disaster on the ship. There is the soft blue light of the interior of the ship, giving way to the bright sun of the earth, and a desperate plea for help from all on board, as well as the ship itself. The ships were almost alive in a sense. The living tissue centers used to store information were a form of synthetic brain tissue, patterned after samples taken from the inventor himself.

As everything returned to a relative norm, I found myself back in my lab. I stood there taking in my surroundings. It seemed as if nothing had happened except for the chaos and a burning in my head that told me otherwise. I looked at my real self, frozen in torment. I thought of the people of Pompeii and their casts left behind. I wondered if I was locked in perpetual agony and did not know it or if it was just a reaction to whatever had happened to the real, physical me. I did not know, and likely never would, for I still did not fully understand what had happened or was happening to me. Hundreds of people had handled the equipment I possessed, but why did I have this reaction to it, and why did it seem to single me out? I resolved myself to find out one day, so I could return to normal and have a life of some sort. While completely unbelievable and more like a bad dream, even a dull laboratory lifetime seemed preferable to being a frozen fugitive in some hellish nightmare.

I noticed that I moved slightly. My real self I mean. As the artificial me, I felt like I was going to pass out. Then both the "mes" started to move together. It was like the device was taking stock of me again. Every joint in both my bodies moved one by one, then all together, and finally it was a repeat of the first time at our home on Upshaw: a grotesque flapping, twisting symphony that continued for several minutes. When both stopped, I sat up and watched as a swelling started at my real feet and slowly moved up my body until it reached the top of my head. My entire body was badly misshapen like a bloated rotting corpse. Slowly the swelling receded, feet first, then slowly upward, leaving only the portion of my head directly around my brain still swollen.

I felt my mind start to burn as if being seared by molten lava. Both of us were wracked with an unspeakable pain. I started to see flashes of my childhood and then it began.

It seemed that it had shared some information and now it was looking for some in return. I watched what seemed to be a very pathetic life flash around me. *Mine!* After the wonders I had just witnessed, even my own birth seemed mundane. My life passed quickly, and I saw everything not on a screen but as if I was an unseen spectator, knowing but unable to communicate. It was almost funny watching myself get into trouble, sleeping and learning. There was little else in my short existence until that day in the colonel's office. I was stricken with keen interest when the alien devices took control of me. I hoped that I could learn something from the outside that I could not while living it. Nothing. It was just a frighteningly bizarre freak show with me at the center, and then my life became *now*. I stood looking at a mirror image of myself looking back at me. We reached out to touch and there was a bright blue flash and I was alone again. There was only the two of us in my new lab as before.

36

I SAT DOWN ON ONE of the close-by chairs, and my mood sagged to depression. I started to regret my early graduations and my slight build. I had long blamed my high IQ for most of my social difficulties. I had really had only one friend as a child; her name was Jodi. We attended the same private school for our first years and seemed to get along as if we had grown up together. Our grades and mannerisms were all but identical, and then one day she was just gone. I asked each day about her, until I was told that her mother had become ill and Jodi would no longer attend school with us. I later learned that she had started to attend public school.

As all these things ran through my mind, they started to be played out in the lab. It started on a small screen in front of me, and it stayed in front of my face no matter where I looked or how I turned. As I became more distraught over the possibility of never having any kind of a life, the images grew until they were life-size, then became real again with me as a phantom observer. I watched as Jodi and I played outside and worked in class, then observed my strange fascination with a woman on some kind of an ad for a cleaning product on the television. I felt the pains of my friend missing from my life and wondered why both had been important to me.

There was a sudden jolt, and I was now part of the scenes around me instead of only watching. I was still reliving pieces of my life, but I was looking at them through my own eyes. I could hear myself talk, but had no control over anything. The three years that Jodi and I spent together in school we were ten, eleven, and twelve, working at high school level and above. The distinctive music of the commercial and my rush to catch a glimpse of the actress selling floor cleaner. It played over and over, until I began to think of how difficult it must have been for Jodi to adapt to a public school. There was no possibility of her being put in a curriculum advanced enough for her level of education at her age. It must have been torture to have to slow her education to such a snail's pace. Did she move on to some valued career or fall victim to her circumstances? What was her life like now?

There was another flash and Jodi and I were in a classroom, but a different one than we had attended. I was not the thinly built child I really was, but more muscular. The work I was doing was simple enough that if this had been reality, I could have done it in first grade. Jodi looked back at me from the desk directly in front of me and smiled. There was another slight blue flash and she and I were in a 1958 Ford car entering a school parking lot. We were teenagers, about the age I was at that moment. The Ford throbbed underneath us, making me think of the Mustang I had borrowed at the lab in New Mexico. The powder blue dash and hood shone, giving the indication of hours of work and layers of wax. We waved and yelled at students as we passed them by and they returned each one.

As I parked, there was another flash and we were on stage at graduation. Jodi was giving a speech. We shared top honors of the graduating class, and things started to speed up as she finished speaking. The flashes came faster and faster. It was our wedding next. It was a grand affair, flowers and people everywhere, and next I was coming home from work to our house. We had two children, and I was a salesman for a local chemical company. Suddenly, I was middle-aged and executive at the company, still arriving home to my loving wife and teenage children. There were four now, all soon to be adults. There was some sort of gathering with all the kids and grandchildren, and then the house was empty. Just she and I in our golden years, spending each day together. Then I drove into the driveway, looking at the '58, still polished, facing the street, and ready to go. I stood by the car I was driving, looking at it for long moment, and retrieved my cane and a package from the seat and made my way slowly toward the door. The face that greeted me was framed with gray hair and covered with wrinkles, but it was still the same girl from school underneath. She took my arm, led me to my favorite chair, and helped me into it. There was a short conversation about a doctor visit, and she took the bag from me and returned with a few pills and a glass of water, which I downed quickly. I looked around the room at all the photos on the wall. It was a mural of this life. There were photos of us as children, then our children, and then a recent portrait of us again in our old age. I could hear her talking to me from the kitchen, as always. I blinked my eyes a few times and I was back in the lab. My mind reeled as I felt as if I had lived that entire life. I knew that I had just died in that life.

What was this thing doing to me? I missed my children, my grandchildren, and a girl I hadn't seen since I was thirteen. It was madness. I just sat there for what seemed like an eternity, not knowing whether to be angry or to cry. That problem was solved as I watched my real body stand, dissolve into a puddle of blue liquid, and move toward the door.

The lab disappeared and I was standing in the empty, glass-encased room we had built to hide me. Only the chair and the large bell-looking structure were there along with my real-life puddle and me. It moved with deliberation toward the door, and all I could do was watch. It arrived at the six-inch-thick glass interior door and moved up from the floor to cover its entire surface. It seemed to pulse and sat there for a few seconds. It then moved through unseen openings in the seal and passed to the outer door and repeated the process. Once outside the room, I felt my artificial self fade, and then I seemed to be above the fast-moving, glowing, sparkling misshapen pancake that was my real self.

37

AT THE GOVERNMENT FACILITY IN New Mexico the alert went out. All the systems in the other spacecraft came to life as had never been seen before. Everyone that was assigned to the project was quickly brought to duty and was crowded around every station. Our location was clearly and consistently marked on an earth-like map, surrounded by the cryptic alphabet in red. It would start with a view from space, then move down to street level, and actually show the outside of the building. Armed forces of all kinds were scrambled to the location indicated, starting with the local police. Both Houston and Harris County dispatched units to the general area, quickly located the exact building the lab was in, and reported by radio that they were in position. Orders came back to secure the location and to observe and report suspicious activity, no interference. Soon there were several cars there, with their flashing red light slicing through the night as they intently observed the building and formed small groups, wondering what they had stumbled into.

A few houses down from our rented home on Upshaw Street, there was a family that also rented from Schwartz. There was a seventeen-year-old girl who lived there with her parents, two brothers and two sisters. She was the oldest and was preparing for a night-out at the local drive-in diner. While not a prostitute, she was very sexually active and looking forward to the night's activities. The only detail left was what dress to put on. She was standing at the closet door trying to make up her mind, dressed in her undergarments, when a strange blue light enveloped her and the room around her.

I had no control and was again just an observer of my own fate. On the way I could smell every smell and feel every stone on the road, as well as the texture of the blacktopped street. After quickly circling the house, I entered her room by a partially open window. As if a predator closing in on its prey, I sprang on her as she turned to find the source of the light that filled her room.

The blue mass of energy rose as a wall of light and fell over her before she could scream. She staggered and fell to the floor in fear, not from impact. She did not struggle; she could not, as this glowing cover of energy filled every pore of her body. I could actually see inside her cells.

I sat on a beach, legs crossed, looking at her sitting in the same position looking at me. The sound of the gentle surf in the background, she asked me, "Who are you? What are you doing to me?"

"I'm not sure who or what I am anymore, but my name is Terrance. I mean you no harm, but I'm not so sure about my... friend. He has control of us now."

"I understand," she said without panic or even stress in her voice. "I will have your child now. Somehow I know that it is yours only."

She was on the floor again, and I was looking at her from floor level again, moving away. She stood, looked around, shook her head slightly, and returned to the task of deciding which dress to choose. It seemed as if nothing had happened, and she was oblivious to the blue glow that was still in the room.

As my flat essence flowed through the small opening in the window, the glow faded, and I turned to see her holding a pale blue dress in front of her with a satisfied look on her face. Her night seemed to be set now. I stared for a long while as she finished dressing and left the room, calling to her parents as she headed for the front door and the street. I realized that most of me was on the ground, and just a string was at the window affording me my view.

With the room now empty and what seemed like mission accomplished, I (or we) started back to the lab. About halfway back, we stopped and pulsed a few times and then exploded outward. With a burst of reserve energy, we began to cover the entire neighborhood.

At the functioning ship, there was a group gasp and one of the men let slip an "oh my god."

From their view on the console, all they could see was an ever-increasing blue field spreading across the Texas landscape. Everyone's immediate thought was that it was a detonation of some sort. With the military's hostile intent toward the wayward employee, their first impression was retaliation. There was some slight relief when the display enveloped their location and they were still alive. More relief came when reports from outside, then elsewhere, seemed to show no ill effects at all. I knew better as the unseen energy field closed back on my position, totally engulfing the entire globe. Then it was gone, and I (we) started back to the lab. I somehow knew that every child on the planet conceived that day would be mine. The device had satisfied its curiosity.

As I crossed Old Humble Road to get back to the lab, there was one military and five police cars blocking the street. The sight of the blue blob floating across the ground made all the seasoned officers of both services jump. One drew his revolver and snapped off a shot before he could think. The bullet had no effect, but we (I) stopped anyway, pulsed for a time or two, and then continued into the street and into the building. The army captain tried to fire a shot as I (we) slid under the doorway, but his pistol failed to fire. None would work. The gunpowder had been rendered inert.

I sat in the lab watching the number of men and vehicles grow outside. My real self was back in the chair and I was free to roam the interior once more. I had opened up a screen on that side, as if the wall had been removed, and the situation began to look bleaker as each hour passed. As my concern for my parents and my friends became greater, another screen opened on the opposite wall. Unfortunately, they had all gathered here for dinner against my advice. After studying it, I discovered it was all of us, a few hours from now. I was actually looking at the future. There was no way to be sure how far in the future it was exactly, but I could tell that it was not days, only hours. I did nothing but try to think of options, until the future screen showed the soldiers attempt to enter the building. It was a repeated number of short attempts.

They first tried to storm the door with an assault team. It would not open, so they used explosives to blow it open. As they rapidly entered through the missing door, Floyd threw open the door to the control room to see what had happened and was greeted with a rifle shot to the knee. He fell down the stairs, writhing in pain. As the shot rang out, all the soldiers turned to dust like the ones at Bea's house months before. There was a rally outside when they discovered there was no more activity inside besides Floyd's cries of pain, and they started to send in additional troops. Everyone outside with a weapon turned to dust as the next team started in the door.

The army evacuated all civilians out of the area, and police had been reduced to traffic control. They set up television cameras hooked to trucks with recording stations in them to document such things just in case they happened. The few officers and advisors that were left fled to the trucks to watch what happened on tape and hoped to have some protection, not realizing that they were alive only because they didn't have weapons. They were not considered to be threats.

I watched as an Air Force captain reviewed the tapes and then went to a nearby house where they set up a command post report to what happened. The order was given to scramble bombers from nearby Ellington Field and destroy the entire surrounding area. Just wipe the entire block off the face of the earth. While most B29 bombers had been taken out of service or converted to utility vehicles some were available. With the Vietnam War raging overseas and most modern equipment devoted to overseas action and patrolling the countries shores one hundred of these magnificent machines were kept in pristine condition. Maintained by those who knew them best, they stood ready for service as if they were new. Veterans hardened by World War II and the Korean War quickly had a squadron of B29s in the air and on their way to destroy us all. As they passed over for the bomb run, the planes fell into dust and there was nothing more than a dark spot in the air to mark their passing. I felt a pang of regret as I watched the brave men pass into non-existence, but was comforted by the fact that it had not happened... yet.

I knew that the army would not stop until something was done and that something would mean death for all of us inside the building, so something had to be done. On the future screen, they realized too late that we needed power and shut it off at the main transmission line. The diesel-powered generators began to scream with the load now thrust upon them. A sniper was dispatched; he put holes in the radiators that cooled the engines from a distance that went undetected until too late. It was ordered by word of mouth instead of by radio, so it was not detected. With power reserves depleted, the next bomb run was a success and we were gone.

A sense of urgency swept over me, looking at the crater on one screen and the army outside on the other. I heard the pitch of the diesels change and saw the soldiers outside take notice. The smell of burning insulation started to drift into the room, and then there was a small cloud-like disc in the center of the room. It grew oval in shape and began to fill the lab with a pale blue light. It grew until it was large enough to step through and had miniature lightning bolts flickering all around its edge. I looked through and it was the lab, but it was dark. I could see myself in the chair, but I was little more than dust. I stepped through and could smell scorched flesh and burned insulation. I looked in the control room and everyone was dead. All burned as if in an intense fire, just flesh, not any part of the building. I stepped back through the portal. It closed and all the electrical power strain ceased. A new screen opened up and I watched as we set up the lab. Everything was the same as where I had come from, until we powered up and there was a leak in the transformer (a logical name for the huge bell-shaped object that magnified the power output). The first time we put a large amount of power into the system, the transformer ruptured and leaked fatal radiation that killed all of us, but everything up until that point was exactly the same.

It was a different dimension and we had to move. On the future screen, they were preparing to cut our power. The future had changed. I quickly opened the glass doors, even though I was not supposed to be able to, and called out to the others. They were around me within seconds, and when they were, there the entire room took on a blue tint. I maxed out the power to the control room breakers so we would have that power too. The generators outside were instantly pushed to their limits, and the lack of draw from local households greatly increased our ability to draw power from the service lines.

They too were at their limits now. My mom reached out and hugged me, tears welling up in her eyes.

"I have been so worried about you," she said with a slight sob.

"We have no time and a gruesome task ahead," I said, squeezing her gently.

The portal started to open behind me.

"We must move our bodies from the other side of the portal into this lab. I would suggest that you do not move yourselves. There may be ill effects other than the obvious mental aspects. Take someone else. Hurry! They plan to cut our power soon," I told them.

Without hesitation, everyone stepped into the other lab and dragged a body back through. Ned threw up, and the women all sobbed as they worked.

"I can't stand the smell." Ned coughed out.

When the transfer had been made, all the bodies were laid out as to look like they had been in the lab at the time of death. Everyone was a bit aghast as the real me got up from the chair and switched the transformer, then slowly lay in the chair in the new dimension.

"Go through," the artificial me urged. They did.

There was a flash of blue light that knocked everyone outside off their feet. At that, the order was given to cut the power and repeated rifle rounds disabled the generators. After the soldiers entered the building, all they found was a group of badly burned bodies, which were quickly gathered along with the equipment and taken back to New Mexico. It would be decades before anyone could access any of the technology again.

With the power level at a bare minimum and only able to sustain my image, it was able to communicate directly with my parents and friends.

"What happened?" Dad asked.

"We are now in another dimension, one that is an exact copy of our own until we powered the transformer. It had a microscopic crack in the outer casing that ruptured under stress, killing us all. We have assumed their place here. The device in me decided to reproduce me, so last night it took me out and did so, and in our old reality I am now the father of every child that could have been conceived at that time. The use of power needed to accomplish that feat caused our detection and discovery. It would have also led to our deaths at the hand of the military. We are here now and must try to make the best of it. We must be aware that there may be some subtle differences I am not aware of. We must adapt and try not to be detected again. You must leave now. I require more power, and radiation levels will be deadly for you inside this room."

With that, they all slowly filed outside, sealing the doors behind them.

38

EVERYONE SPENT THE NEXT FEW days repairing the damaged equipment, or in some cases, making a parts-needed list. They were able to get almost everything repaired. It was fortunate that overloads were expected, and spare parts had been stored for that possibility, but nothing of this magnitude. I remained in low power status, observing the progress and trying to gather more information about the new dimension we had moved into. I was hoping that it had not been a mistake. There was little time to choose, and I was not even sure how I had.

After three days of naps and long hours, there was agreement that all that could be done had been done. I was safe, and a night at home was called for. I told them to all go and relax, and that it appeared that I could take care of myself. It was late and always quiet in the area, so reluctantly everyone planned to leave for a hot meal and real rest. As usual, Floyd was last one out the door. There was a hush that greeted him as he closed the door.

Everyone stood looking at Floyd and Edna's car. It was in the exact same place it had been parked, but instead of turquoise and white, it was navy blue with a white top. The emblem on the rear of the front fender stated 427 not 390 and it had only two doors.

"I thought about buying this exact car, but couldn't get it," Floyd said slowly.

"Looks like you did this time. Did you lock the doors?" Ned shot back quickly.

"No," Floyd returned, still staring at the car.

Ned pulled out his keys and checked his door key to make sure it worked. It did. It put the rest on alert. There were inquiring glances of the surroundings, but all seemed to be as they recalled. Floyd tried his keys on the car. The door key worked, but the trunk key did not.

"I wonder if we still live in the same house," Mom asked.

"Let's go find out," Dad shot back, opening the right door and climbing into the back seat.

Nothing seemed out of place on the short trip home. There was tension in all as they wondered if they had a place to call home, if someone else lived there, or if it even existed. It would be only a guess until they were there. Floyd could feel the raw power under the hood, and had a hard time controlling the urge to use all of it. Instead, the dark car throbbed its way the few short blocks to the house that was their home.

"Everything looks okay," Edna said from the front seat beside Floyd.

"It's a different color too," Ned observed from his position by the right door. Everyone strained their eyes in the headlights to confirm Ned's statement. It was true. The house was light gray, not light green, in this reality.

As they exited the car, everyone looked at each other with great concern, not knowing what to expect next. It became an everyday thing to see something that would drive others to hysterics, but the added stress and exhaustion put them on edge. Inside the house, nothing seemed out of place and a quick plate of fried hamburger mixed with diced potatoes satisfied both hunger and the need for speedy retirement. Within an hour, the lights were out and none were left awake. They slept a restless sleep.

From back at the lab I could see them—all asleep, resting in their beds, unaware that I could watch over them as I was, also unaware of the blue glow that I could see emanating from each of them as a result of exposure to the energy I emitted. Ned had little contamination, so his energy signature was low, but the others glowed like a streetlight on a dark night. All their lives, as well as mine, had been drastically altered forever, theirs in ways I could not imagine. The energy somehow made us connected.

With the electrical input at a minimum, I could do very little. The real me was, of course, locked to the chair, and the other me sat on a stool looking at me in the chair. Kind of confusing, isn't it? I'm not sure how long I sat there looking, then checking on the others, but after a while I became curious about myself. I stood, walked over to the chair, and touched my cheek. I could feel it. I jabbed my cheek and it hurt. My left side was facing me, and my left hand was on the arm of the chair. I touched it and looked at my other left hand. As I touched my real hand, a dimple appeared on my reproduction. We were definitely physically and mentally connected.

A screen that popped up in front of my face interrupted my amazement. It was about the size of a small television around twelve inches across. It just sat there in midair, blank for a while, and then filled with the information about the Dane. My life came next. It played over and over again. The wall to my left would occasionally sparkle, like it was trying to come to life, but never could. I could feel the power drain as it tried, and I would begin to feel tired. The screen was finally reduced to a small square over my left eye. I wore it like a monocle and could not shut it off. It did not matter if I closed my eye. I could still see the images. I was irritated for a while, but settled into going about doing what little I could, trying to ignore the repetitious annoyance.

It stopped. The small screen was gone. I had not noticed it before, but when the screen disappeared it was like walking into a quiet room. The silence was staggering, *again*. There was some kind of stimulation in my brain that created a sort of a background noise that I had ignored until it was gone. My mind became sharper. I was thinking more clearly, although I had not noticed a problem before.

I reviewed the last twenty-four hours with staggering clarity. I established that when I left the glass containment of the lab, the intact ship in Arizona detected the energy signature. The only possible way to prevent that from happening again was to sever the link between the two ships. In order to do that, I would have to go there and consult the onboard systems. Somehow I knew that there was an open channel of some sort left on from the crash. It was something like a locator beacon, but it would take a lot of power to shut it down. I would have to wait until I could start to store the energy I needed.

39

FLOYD AWOKE THE NEXT MORNING feeling quite refreshed. He lay still for some time trying not to disturb Edna. She was sound asleep and showed no signs of rousing anytime soon, as far as Floyd could tell. At last he gave in, slid silently from under the covers and dressed as quietly as he could. Carrying his shoes to stem the loud clank of their hard soles on the hardwood floors, he walked sock footed to the front door, passed through, pulled the front door to, and sat down on the steps. He slipped into his shoes and started across the lawn to his car, the one he had really wanted.

He stopped at the right side of the front bumper and put each foot in turn on top of it to tie his shoes, making sure to be careful not to scratch the chrome finish. For a long moment, he stood back and admired the lines of the car. It was his favorite of all he had owned. Thinking that he would not likely be able to purchase many, if any, more, he wanted to get the one he wanted, so he could live with it for years to come. Now, with the likelihood of purchasing more, it made him appreciate the options he had been unable to obtain with his initial purchase even more. The deep blue capped with vivid white stood out in the early light and seemed to glow in the rising sun. The hand-polished chrome proved that both he and his counterpart had been proud to own it.

He tugged at the lever located to the left of the front and center of the hood. While he pulled with his right index finger, he gave a quick push down with the heel of his left hand, the mechanism clicked, and the massive hood was free. When opened fully, it gave a jolt of pleasure revealed by his wide eyes. Not only had he been able to get the larger engine, he had landed the best they had to offer. The chrome valve covers reflected everything. There was not a spot to be found on them. They reflected the morning light and the care it took to keep them in pristine condition. The large open air cleaner sat on top of two massive Motorcraft four-barrel carburetors, which in turn sat on a "high-rise" intake manifold. Floyd had fallen in love with the 425 horse, 427 cubic inch when it came out as an option in the sixty-three and a half Ford Galaxy. However, he had managed to get this one, it was truly a dream come true.

"You got a spare belt?" Ned asked, snapping Floyd back from dreamland.

"Uh… what?" Floyd stammered out.

"Hey, look, I can see myself in that thing. Is it supposed to shine like that?" Ned said, looking at his distorted image in the valve cover.

"Not… usually. What did you say about a belt?"

"It would seem that I liked to eat a little more on this side than I did on the other. None of his clothes fit. I was fat here, although I didn't look all that big."

"You and all the rest of us were burned to a crisp, dolt. How would you expect to be able to tell? Besides, you could use some meat on your bones. You look like you're sick, thin like that. Keep hanging around Bea and you'll be looking right as rain in no time," Floyd said, barely shifting his eyes from the engine.

"Well?" They looked at each other for a short time before Floyd realized the question again.

"Nope, no belt. Sam has a few, or he did anyway. If we can't find one, I'll fix you up," he said, pulling the engine oil dipstick from its tube and admiring the crystal clean oil on its tip.

"Good! I'm tired of this already," Ned stated, tugging upward on the handful of extra pants he was holding in his left hand.

They entered the first door to the lab and could not help but look at the gray, fog-filled glass container I now called home. There was nothing to see but the slow swirling cloud that filled every ounce of space inside. They still stared, as if it were a window with a beautiful landscape outside. It was an unreal sight; in reality, a swirling smoke filled room that never stopped showing movement.

"Good morning, all," my voice boomed like it was on a loudspeaker.

Everyone answered as if I had just come into the room. There was a mixture of greetings and lots of puzzled looks. This was something new... again.

"I wish to explain a few things to you all, if I could."

"Are you all right, dear?" Mom asked, still unable to let go of her deep concern.

"Yes, Mom, I'm as good as I will be for the rest of my life. Things will get better for me as I learn to use this thing that has attached itself to me, but I will not ever be better or different. I can only get worse from here. In our original reality, we got a chance to see what can happen, and unfortunately, it could be worse," I boomed in.

"Worse than being blown to bits or burned like bad toast? I'll pass on that one, but tell me how," Dad fired back.

"We are all saturated with the form of energy that this device uses to do all these fantastic things. It binds us together. Haven't any of you wondered why none of us go crazy because of all the weird things we have seen and done? We are in a different reality, living out our lives here for the moment. We could be in another by nightfall. No one seems to be shocked or afraid," I said.

"I did wonder why we were handling all this so well," Floyd said. "We just seemed to take it all on the chin."

I continued.

"This device provides its user with a tranquilizer of sorts. It calms the nerves, and actually makes you think faster and with more reason. The design was extraordinary. In critical situations, you could do your job with all emotions reduced to mere warnings. No panic, fear, or indecision.

It ties us all together by simple exposure. It is a form of radiation, and I cannot say how harmful it will be over an extended length of time, but so far it has not seemed to have too many harmful side effects. It has made changes in us all, but most seem to be for the better, however odd and difficult they appear. I paused for a second.

"I can see you all at any time or place, and with time and patience we will be able to have limited communication over quite some distance. That will take time and practice, but we will make it happen. I checked in on all of you after you went to sleep, just to make sure you were safe. Had it not been for the calming effects of the energy, I doubt that any of you would have been able to sleep at all. I will not invade your privacy, but I will ensure your safety, regardless of whether we have to move again or not, provided you all agree."

There were no refusals, only silence.

"The thing that is worse than death is capture. Looking at all of you, I can see a blue energy emanating that, if discovered, would only lead to misery for the rest of your lives. I suspect for some of you that would not be very long. Knowing the people involved in the administration of my former employer's lab, some, if not all of you, would be killed in some fashion for study. I will not let that happen. As I gain control of my new abilities, I become more formidable. I feel that we will be able to avoid confrontation in the future and defend ourselves if necessary. That remains to be seen, but I believe it to be possible.

"In order to hide ourselves and remain safe, we will have to cover our tracks with legitimate business dealings. For that, we will of course need a business. Three miles north of here on Old Humble Road, there is a two-story house, and Mr. Schwartz will be able to secure it for us. We will need to have him do that as soon as we can. We will start a company. It will be very diverse. It will be used to cover what we are doing and make us able to hide the fortune we will soon acquire. We will call the company TNT. The paperwork can be filed at the courthouse in downtown Houston.

"We must buy property in specific places for future use. I will lead you to it when the time comes. Once the new offices are set up, we will begin in earnest, but for now we must lay the groundwork. Start to establish yourselves in local social circles. Get to know the people you need to know to make connections. Try to stay low key. You will all soon be very rich, and it will help you hide if you are in the proper circles. It will also help to explain away any number of questions about your past if proper answers are created now. I cannot stress the need for secrecy enough. It should be obvious from my last mistake.

"Mom and Dad will lead on this venture, and I will require that Floyd and Ned help me here. I think it would be best that Bea and Edna help Mom and Dad on a daily basis. If you wish to have separate houses, there is another close by that we could acquire. It is entirely up to you."

"Do you want to use the gold at the house to buy all this?" Dad asked.

"No. We still have several coins to sell that will give us the capital to get started. Paying for too much in cash may attract unwanted attention for the moment. Mr. Schwartz should be able to get us help with credit locally. It may make appearances better. You will need to move the gold here from the house. Soon it will be too valuable to lose."

40

AT THE THREE-HOUR MARK, FLOYD pressed the power control levers all the way to their stops and rechecked each one to be sure they were at full output. A faint whisper filled the air. It was a low moaning tone as if a ghost had invaded the control room.

"Start the auxiliary generators at one hour intervals. Set all power output levels to maximum prior to starting the next one." Without further comment the process continued. Each engine was started from the control room, warmed to operating temperature, then loaded slowly to its peak. When all four engines were loaded and had been stressed to their breaking points, it was time.

"I will leave now." My voice boomed inside the control room. "Reduce all power output to zero. Now."

The remote throttles on the external engines were pushed to idle, and the generators were unloaded. The power levels from normal transmission lines were pushed to zero, and the output breakers were thrown. The cloud inside the lab became a torrent of boiling angry gray, turning ever darker. Flashes of brilliant blue light pierced the turmoil, giving the appearance of an indoor thunderstorm. The flashes grew more and more frequent until it was more like a strobe light, then just a blinding brilliant beam.

Inside the lab I could see the goal and understood exactly what I had to do. I examined the possibilities and proceeded. The oval disc that formed in the center of the lab was a bit different than the one that had brought us here earlier. This one was more compact. It had a blue line that encircled its outer edge, and the jagged bolts of energy around it were smaller and more focused.

I arose from the chair and immediately stepped through. All activity in the lab ceased, and the room was empty except for the chair and a fading gray mist.

Ned and Floyd strained their eyes through the large window in the control room looking for a sign of me. There was nothing to see. I was gone.

I stepped from the lab directly onto the ramp leading into the intact ship back at the agency warehouse. This was a more focused form of transportation than I had used on my earlier trips here. It was essentially the same, but I had a better understanding of the process, not to mention more control. The aperture actually took on a physical appearance now instead of simply pushing me through the eye of a needle. It was a much more comfortable trip.

The entire warehouse was filled with a blue light. It seemed odd because all of the facilities had used a brilliant white light before. I quickly realized that it was not coming from the lights in the room. It was the field around me. I was inside a pocket of energy that separated me from my surroundings. From the reactions of the people around me, I could gauge that I was not visible to them, but I had apparently set off some kind of alarm. Activity increased the instant I arrived. It would change nothing. The task ahead had to be completed if my family and friends were to survive in this new reality.

I focused my thoughts and felt the power levels inside me increase. I had focused the power field around me to fit like a second skin. There was a great hiss and the ship in front of me trembled and panels lit up internally. It had, as I thought, reacted to the energy concentrated inside me. It was the link I had come here to sever.

Everywhere around me was now chaos. Soldiers with massive M1 Garand rifles poured down stairs and out of doorways and positioned themselves in a shoulder-to-shoulder perimeter around the ship. Standing at the ready, they searched for any sign of what called them to alert. They would never see me or know what this was all about.

I calmly walked up the gangplank into the ship, which had activated and was now hovering. Soldiers passed right through me as if I were a ghost. My mind seemed to process even more new data as my amazement increased. It seemed that I was in a bubble of time outside the normal time-space that surrounded me. This allowed me to be in two dimensions at once, unseen by those around me, but visible to myself because of the focused energy field I was creating.

I made my way to the control panel designated H333. The components inside me originally came from this area on the wrecked ship. When I approached the station, a section of the floor fell away and a chair rose and locked into place. Once it did, spotlights activated and focused on the chair.

In the distance I heard a voice shout, "Got him on camera, but I can't see him otherwise."

I looked to my left as I approached the chair to see a huge camera on wheels headed my way. Several people were gathered around it, and I could see the barrels of several weapons pointed in my direction. Ignoring them, I sat in the chair and the panel lit up.

I started to feel faint, weak. I looked at my arms and they seemed to be flashing, maybe flickering. They were changing color from normal flesh tone to gray to blue. It was the worst I had felt since this ordeal had started, and again my thoughts turned to death. In the reflection of the polished panel, I could see my face as it flashed from mine to the one of the Dane who had operated the station. A fleeting thought passed through my mind, and I tried my best to relax and let the transformation take place.

I was adapting to the requirements of the H333 station. It was changing me at the molecular level, as the technology had been doing from the start. This was just another step in the process. The small black pellets that had formed before now pressed out of every pore in my skin. Like a million grains of sand they fell onto the floor around the chair and I started to feel better immediately. The change was almost instantaneous. While still far from recovered, I could function. A small panel opened at the base of the console and a shelf with two small round balls shot out. Without understanding why, I quickly grabbed them and put them in my mouth. At that moment I realized what had started this whole tragedy. The same vile taste spread through my mouth and filled me with the urge to wretch.

"Hey, Captain. He's eating something the ship gave him. It shot out a drawer or something and he put what was in it in his mouth."

There was too much activity around me. I had to silence these people and proceed before I lost total control of the situation. I looked up into the steel gray eyes of an army captain looking down at me. He stood at the side of the chair looking at it as if he could see me there. He reached out his right hand and waved the 1911 Colt Government pistol through the area where I was sitting.

"You're sure he's there?" he questioned the cameraman.

"See for yourself, sir. You just put your hand right through him," the cameraman said, fixated on the screen at the rear. The young captain moved skeptically toward the display at the rear of the massive apparatus only to see a fleeting image rise from the chair and grab the camera lens that protruded from the front. If he had blinked, he would have missed the image. The camera erupted in a cascade of sparks and began to burn in several places. Everyone in the area jumped back as the fireworks continued. Then training took over. Two soldiers shoved the flaming monstrosity toward the doorway, and it fell on the gangway, tangled in its own cables.

"Get that fire out. Sergeant, get the general on the phone!" the captain barked. "Get another camera in here! *Now!* We need to see what this guy is doing. Did we get any tape?" Everyone snapped to action and, within an instant, the activity in the immediate area was at a minimum.

"We can't stop him or even see him, but maybe we can get some idea of what he is doing. Report," the captain ordered.

"He looked like a normal guy at first. Then he kind of jumped back and forth between a human and one of the aliens. He seemed to be in control of what was going on because the chair came up just before he got to it. We were still moving into position, but I could see that much through the monitor. He seemed to get sick or something until he ate that stuff, then he grabbed the camera and that was it," the corporal reported, standing somewhere close to attention.

"How long before the other camera is up and running?" the captain shot back.

"We'll have to see how much damage was done to the rest of the equipment once the other camera is hooked up."

Their attention turned back the console where I had retaken my seat. It began to flash and chirp.

"Get that camera in here!" the captain shouted.

A pale blue panel of light began to form over the console, and I leaned over until it engulfed my entire head. Warmth filled every fiber of my being. It was a like being bathed in knowledge with no hint of fear, a joyous feeling of enlightenment. More and more knowledge flowed through the connection and into my mind. It was unlike the partial and incomplete machine that I had been dealing with. This system functioned properly. The pounding of combat boots pulled me back to the mission at hand. The corporal was bringing in another camera. I realized also that my head was outlined and quite visible as I interfaced with the console. The orientation was over. I had to shut down the device that tracked us. It was a sensor that was designed to locate the lost ship that had been left on during the recovery attempt. The sensor pinpointed any sign of the alien power and would display that location once the power output became detectable.

In my mind I probed the systems, gaining knowledge of each as I progressed. Suddenly I was there. I could see the entire system. It was as clear as daybreak in the desert. I somehow shut it down and isolated that particular system from the others. I felt the relief of that moment and knew it was time to go. My reserve power was fading. I would soon be trapped here and captured. In my mind I watched the consequences of that scenario. It would be quite unpleasant—long hours of torture and attempts to extract information that I would not know, and the eventual capture of my friends and family, whose fates would be far worse.

I stood and, after a thought, returned to the console. It was the control for navigation, speed, and a sensor array to help guide the ship. It also had a link to the larger arrays on the ship so the crewmen could analyze data while in orbit. It explained much of what I had not understood before and why the images I had seen were so varied in scope and so unrelated. I was only getting a partial view of what had flowed through the station. I reentered the control field and set a power spike in the conduit running closest to the door. I was becoming visible as my power reserves ran out, and that I could not afford.

I felt weak and energized at the same time. My mind was full of new, fresh images of worlds I could not have imagined, and I could feel my power reserves falling to nothing. I was trying to make it to the door in the hope that the power I requested was available when I stumbled, feeling as if I was going to pass out. It would be a fatal mistake for us all. My hand slapped the wall as I steadied myself and someone shouted, "There he is!"

Guns and attention all turned my way. All the efforts to make the new camera work stopped as faces turned to my silhouette leaning on the wall near the door. Luck was with me that day, for I had already programmed the proper sequence into the computer. I tapped directly into what seemed to be a power outlet. The energy that flowed into my body felt like the power of the sun itself, and in a brilliant flash I became a glowing outline. The blue light caused all in the entire warehouse to stagger from the flash. In that instant of contact with the real energy that drove this technology, I had reached an energy level unobtainable with our primitive means of generating power.

I looked around at the fear and amazement on the faces that surrounded me and knew I had to leave. It was time for a portal and one started to form. This time it was not small and man-sized. It formed and engulfed the entire wall of the massive hangar. It was like pasting a living photo of our lab on the wall. I could see Ned and Floyd in the control room looking directly at me. I could see the flashes of light I emanated dancing in their shadows. Men on the floor tried to enter the field but passed through as if it was not even there, though they could see it clearly. I calmly walked down the gangway toward the aperture. A single shot rang out. The captain had to take the chance that it may stop me. It had no effect. The bullet was simply absorbed into the field and was gone. I walked through the portal and we vanished as if never there. With the wall-sized opening gone, there was momentary silence, then all efforts were concentrated on recovering and retaining all the knowledge possible.

On the other side, Ned and Floyd had relaxed a bit, but were still kind of anxious. There were a few flashes from the lab and then it was flooded with light. An image of a brilliant man-shaped light took form, and then they were looking a spacecraft sitting in what looked like a warehouse. There were soldiers swarming everywhere in pursuit of some unknown duty. It made Ned and Floyd want to hide, because they knew all too well what had happened when the military discovered them in the other dimension. The thump of the captain's pistol made them jump as they observed the events unfolding in front of them. They regained their composure and watched as the captain looked at his pistol in disbelief and then placed it in his holster. The man-shaped form of light approached the area where the wall of the lab should have been. Then the ship and everything with it was gone, and the wall, complete with clouds, instantly returned.

"I am relatively all right," my voice quietly reported to Ned and Floyd.

"What was that?" Floyd stumbled out.

"It was the warehouse where the complete spacecraft is stored. I had to turn off the equipment that has been detecting our presence. That ship was searching for the other that crashed, and the system was never deactivated. It would have been a threat to us until we were eventually caught or it was shut down. I chose the latter."

"Will they be able to find us now?" Ned asked.

"Not for some time to come. Now we have the advantage, thanks to all the knowledge I have gained through this venture. I now know how all of this started. It was part of the H333 console that I had in my briefcase. It held a compound that enhanced the mental link between the crewman at the station and computer control. My genetic makeup is somehow close enough to the people who used it that it released a control nodule into my briefcase and I ate it. That linked me to the equipment, and it spiraled out of control from there. The race of people who created the ships is called the Dane. They live millions of light years from here. Their home world looks like ours from space except they originally lived on their moon. It had an atmosphere and the planet, our Earth, did not. They have reached out to millions of worlds in the search for knowledge and for the good of their race. They somehow devoted themselves to the benefit of their people and avoided the costly wars and self-destruction we have in our history.

Their technology is based on living tissue, and through their stored records I have seen the brave souls on their world that sacrificed their lives and lived as brain tissue donors for the experiments that gave them the ability to achieve those wonders. They sat in chairs for years with their brains exposed in a sterile field while bits of tissue were harvested and used to perfect the bio-based computer systems. The packs that you allowed to enter into my body back at home were parts of people who died thousands of years ago, but live on in the systems they helped design. The system modified me at a genetic level so it could survive inside me, so we could both co-exist and function. This was part of the programming to help ensure the survival of the entire system. Once I have had time to assimilate what I have learned this day, we will be safe for some time to come."

"Are you sure you're all right?" Ned asked once again.

"Do not turn on the power feed until I ask. My reserve power levels will now take some time to deplete. You both may do as you wish. I will meditate for some time. Security is no longer a problem. I will contact you when it is time to proceed."

None of their other questions were answered. Eventually, and reluctantly, they went on their way.

41

EVERYTHING PROGRESSED OUTSIDE THE LAB as I had instructed. Mr. Schwartz had found the proper connections, and there was an established sand and gravel business on the San Jacinto River in the proper place. It was the proper cover and would give us security for what was to come. We were fortunate enough to have local people well-versed in the business, and we paid them well for their knowledge and experience. In turn, the business would thrive, and all were well-rewarded.

I sat, feeding off the energy I took from the ship, for months to come. I rummaged through the information I had stored and filed away what I did not understand. I made a game of it to preserve my sanity. Each bit of information was filed in a cabinet, like it was on paper. It gave me a familiar sense of organization in the beginning. Once sorted, I looked through all of them one by one, and once I thought I had a grasp on what it was and what it meant, I moved on.

One day, the loop started again. It was the same one as before, a brief history of the Dane, but now it stopped with an image of me. It would not stop. I am not sure how long I stayed in that loop, but I eventually interpreted its meaning. The living part of the Dane technology wanted to review *my* history. I was lacking in knowledge of my own world's history, and at this point knew more about the Dane's than mine. I reviewed what little I could remember. It played out around me, as if the brief visions from prehistory until today were happening inside the lab. It was incredibly insufficient. I stumbled around in my mind, looking for more, but there was nothing else to show.

"Books," my voice croaked as a low whisper in the control room.

"What kind?" Ned asked as I was sitting in the room. "Physics?"

"It would take the world decades to decipher the level of physics I comprehend. I must have history. As much United States history as you can find. I need thousands of books. Buy them, get them any way you can, as many as you can, quickly," came the haunting reply.

Floyd looked at Ned. "There is an old bookstore in Humble. There has to be a few stores in Houston that sell new books. We'll just have to find them."

"We can check them out of the library downtown again. They were helpful last time. We will just have to get everybody to go again if we want to get as many books as we can," Ned replied.

"Get started. I'll call the house and get everybody ready," Floyd said, picking up the massive black phone receiver.

"You may go as well, Floyd. I will be safe until your return. Dad is not available. He is out finalizing the lease for the sand pit. Schwartz has a truck. It may prove useful," I told them.

Floyd unfroze and continued the call by dialing the five digits it took to connect to the new office, gave a brief description of the plan, hung up, and locked the doors as they left.

42

I SAT, BOTHERED THAT I had no real information to share. I quickly
reviewed the limited resources in my mind. Even with all the books
I had read since arriving in Texas, and before, it seemed to be little more than a handful of facts. I thought of every angle and then
thought of my grandmother, my mother's mother. She had passed
away when I was very young, but made an impression the few times
I had seen her, she was a dynamic presence.

I could see her, sitting in her rocking chair, knitting. At the
time, the things she said made no sense, but now, watching myself
play in the next room, the words were clear and concise. Her voice
was scratchy but clear and full of fire.

"I can remember them 'Yanks' comin' in the house lookin' for
my daddy. He was gone off to the war, but they wouldn't believe
us. They tore up everything and just left us sittin' there in the dark.
They took the lamps and the oil. Said they needed it. Heard they got
theirs later that week. Some of our boys found 'em. Yeah, gave them
theirs all right."

Around me formed the visions of what she had said. It was
eerie to see my grandmother, knowing she was now dead. Stranger
than that was to see her narrate a story that sprung to life around us:
union soldiers forcing their way into the small farmhouse looking in
every space large enough to hold a man, without regard for anything
or anyone; frightened women and children huddled in one corner,
watching in horror.

"No one here, sir," the soldier reported to his sergeant.

"I am sorry, but we had to look for the men who escaped. We
will have to take a lamp and some oil."

"Take what you will and *get out!*" shouted the oldest of the women as she took a step toward the intruders. The soldiers seemed unaffected and stood there for a long second and turned to leave.

My grandmother stood and stepped toward me.

"Scooter, you have grown into a fine young man," she said, rubbing my cheek with her hand. I should have been racked with fear, and for an instant, I felt the shock of what happened.

"That's me there, the little one. That's my older sister Mattie. She died a few years later of the fever. I don't think my mother ever recovered. She was sick for a while with it too." Her eyes passed over the frozen image of her past time and time again. The pain in both her faces, young and old, was clearly evident. She waved her hand in the air as if to dismiss everything, the images and emotions.

"Never did understand all this. You were too young to ask back then, but I knew you were doing this. Knew it couldn't be the work of the devil 'cause I ain't scared. So how you doin' this, boy? Well, come along, don't doddle."

"Well, Grandma, it's sort of a machine that I found. It does things like this," I said, trying to explain simply.

"Machine? Well, whatever it is, you be careful with it, ya hear?" She turned and walked back to her chair. "Must be going out of my mind. Seeing things these days." She sat and resumed knitting. "Must be losing what little mind I have left," she said quietly, and then she was gone.

43

THERE WAS JUST NOTHING FOR a while. I'm not sure how long I waited.

Next, I tried to recreate the interior of the complete ship. That part was relatively easy. I had a basic understanding of the internal workings of the ship. While I had an overview of the working process, a total understanding was out of the question. It was like looking at a car and understanding that it was transportation, and then being asked to disassemble it, reassemble it, and make it work. I even decided to put a crew of Dane on the working model.

After several tours and pushing a few "*buttons*," I tried to interact with one of the Dane. I was hoping that it would somehow talk to me like my grandmother did. It did not. It just sat at its station and worked, or at least that's what it looked like.

"It took us a week, but I think we have all the books we are going to find locally," Ned spoke into the air, looking in my supposed direction. His voice broke the silence of the vacant deck of the alien ship. The lab reformed around me.

"Stack them between the lab and office. All of them," I replied.

The stacks had already been started from a week's worth of looking all over Houston. The rows were recreated and arranged from the inside wall outward. Stacked eye-level to Ned and packed as tightly as possible, they filled almost the entire space when the last had been unloaded.

"What now?" Ned asked, looking at the others, all drenched in sweat.

The room filled with a brilliant blue light, growing in intensity. It became an overpowering blue wall of light above the stacks, and then slowly moved through all of them to the floor. Then it was gone.

"Find more. I am done with these."

All four people in the room looked at each other with a touch of wonder and disappointment over the anti-climactic end to their task. Their clothes were soaked with sweat from their efforts.

"Tomorrow," Floyd said, wiping sweat from his forehead. "We'll start tomorrow."

They stood gazing at the stacks of books for a moment, as if still looking for something more after all the work, but it was over and they left.

Inside, I started to sort and file the information I had gained. When I absorbed the books, it was as if I sat and read every one. I could recall every word at will. It was as if I could feel every page as each individual letter became bright and clear.

After each subject was arranged by date, I started to run each line in each book like a ticker tape and formed a loop that repeated. When the last page of the last book had finished, the first started again. I am not sure how many times it repeated, but it was only interrupted by the addition of new material.

With the futility of the task realized and the amount of resources limited, enthusiasm had fallen off a bit. The subject matter was limited and each load of books was harder to find, but my friends were faithful to the task.

Floyd had wisely purchased a new 1968 Ford F-100 pickup to make everything easier and faster. He had never been one to rely on others, much like most of his generation. He had gratefully returned Schwartz's older truck with a full tank of gas, a fresh wash job, and a generous offer of cash as payment. His money was steadfastly refused. Schwartz felt he owed too much to our little group, becoming wealthier each day because of our financial relationship. Floyd eventually accepted the situation and returned to the search.

As the information slowly lengthened the ticker tape of letters, images were generated to represent the events. Soon the words would stop being a simple string of letters and start to swirl around me, ever growing, and end with a brief three-dimensional representation of the events described. I now understood the process, and I knew what it would take to make it work.

With the fifth load of books in the entryway, I estimated that we had amassed twelve thousand and three books. They had taken over the garage at the new house and started spilling over into the nearest rooms.

"That will do for now," I told Ned and Floyd as they recovered from their efforts. "The power levels will have to run near maximum for the next seventy-three hours unless otherwise instructed. I must run an experiment. All data and parameters must be monitored." My voice sounded disconnected and mechanical, even to me.

Floyd was sitting on the steps to the office with his hands on his knees. He threw them in the air in a faint show of hopelessness. He had counted on a quiet evening at home after the long effort to fill the last of the required space.

Ned slapped him on the shoulder as he started the climb to the office.

"Go home. I slept all the way back. Send Bea. I'll see you in the morning."

Floyd shook his head and chuckled. Never in ten lifetimes would he have imagined his life being like this. It was then that he really began to realize how fortunate he had become. Without any known reason he had been granted a second, unbelievable life, a life no one would be able to grasp or learn about. In fact, it was hard for even him to understand, let alone explain. As he left, he marveled at the strength he felt after a fourteen-hour day. Only a few months earlier it would have been hard for him to stay awake that long.

"Not so bad," he said with a smile and closed the outer door.

As the power increased, I felt the new energy and knowledge surge through me. There were several flashes that made me think of lightning. I felt Ned's concern.

"Everything is becoming… *better*." My voice boomed in the control room.

"My god!" Ned screamed, clasping the sides of his head to cover his ears.

"*Turn it down!*"

I did not respond.

44

ALONG THE BOTTOM OF EACH wall, there was a row of what looked like photos. I stood in the exact center of the room, and each was precisely the same distance from me. I stood there not really knowing what of make of the small, clear images that surrounded me. After due consideration, I thought that I would take a closer look, so I picked out one and moved closer. I seemed to be walking down a long hall toward an open door. While I knew it was only a few feet away, it seemed like I covered hundreds of yards.

As I approached my target, it grew and appeared as a huge opening in the wall. The other images seemed to move into the distance as I approached this one, and faded away, all growing smaller as the one expanded. What had looked like a photo of a rolling field twenty feet away was now life-sized. I stood there looking at the grass swirling under a light wind. Then I felt the breeze touch my face. I stepped out of the lab and into the field. I could feel the grass crunch under my feet and smell the sweet fragrance flowers, fresh trampled grass, and the nearby pond. The odors were pleasing, but so intense it was almost painful.

I felt a pang of momentary panic. It passed in an instant, but the realization of what it meant took less time. I turned to look for the exit back to the lab, but there was none. I did not feel fear, just the realization that I could once again be in for more surprises. I did not have to wonder for long. Distant voices started to grow near.

To my right, I saw a wide row of men dressed in colonial-type clothing coming over the distant hill. Behind the first row was another, then another, each with long rifles pointing in the air. My best guess was that they were one hundred wide, shoulder-to-shoul-

238

der, marching steadily forward. They were too far away for me to make out their faces clearly, but their determination was clear in their deliberate step. Like ants out of an angry mound, they continued to pour over the hill, one row behind the next.

There was metallic clanking to my left, and as I turned to look, there were men in brilliant red uniforms on horseback, surveying the situation. They did not take long with their assessment. Orders were shouted, and shortly there were rows and rows of red uniformed men marching toward the others. It was a battle from the Revolutionary War. I was not sure which one.

The colonials marched past me without notice and directly into the oncoming British troops. At point blank range, both sides fired again and again. Cannon fire erupted, and bodies were torn into shreds. Men on both sides fell in heaps as they were mowed down by opposing gunfire. The battle line passed back and forth in front of me. Hand to hand combat broke out shortly after the first volley, and that only produced more bodies on the ground. Men dead and dying were in piles, producing rivers of red that stained the bright green grass. The smell of gunpowder and blood filled the air, along with the cries and moans of those willing to fight and die for their cause. For hours, the fighting raged. It was hard to tell who had won the battle as medics from both sides raced around the field, looking for those not beyond their help. I should have been sick, but I was not. I was only fascinated with the cruelty man could wreak on his fellow man. I felt as if one of the Dane were looking over my shoulder asking, "Why and how could you do this?"

As the light faded to darkness and the medics called for torches, the doorway opened back into the lab. I stepped through without feeling anything.

I was back in the lab, looking at the row of photos surrounding me as if I had never moved. I was processing the information. I relived each sound, each smell, each scream. It did not affect me emotionally. It just seemed like... *information*. As I stood there, the lights brightened a little, just enough for me to see the bloody footprints that I had made on the way back to the center of the room. I began to form a hypothesis.

Once I had committed every single bit of information to memory, I began to wonder about the next photo I would pick and what would be inside. As I approached the line of photos, I chose the one to the right of the last. It seemed it would be the next in progression. A habit I suppose as I learned to read left to right. I could see the last, and it still held an image of the bloody field, frozen as I had left it, covered with the dead and dying. The one I was about to enter was mostly covered in concrete, and that did not make sense. I was expecting something closer to the time period before, perhaps the signing of the Declaration of Independence or the westward expansion. This was far from either, far into the future.

45

I STEPPED INTO THE PORTHOLE and spun when I heard the sound of a vehicle coming my way. It was close. It was an Army Jeep. Willis. It stopped dangerously close to me, and the young airman dressed in a World War II flight suit, behind the wheel shut off the engine. It sputtered into silence.

"There you are. We thought we were going to have to report you *AWOL*."

He sat there for a second, then quickly exited the driver's seat, grabbing my arm and pulling me over to the rear of the open vehicle.

"Still *drunk*. I know you think so, but *is* she really worth a few years in the stockade? The captain won't let you miss another mission, and *we* won't either. We almost got shot down last time. Now get in!"

He punctuated the last statement by shoving me into the rear of the Jeep, then grabbing my legs at the knees and rolling me into the rear section behind the two front seats. I had given no resistance and fell in between the bench-type seats with a low thud. The driver cranked the Jeep, and it lurched away, generating its unique sound, a combination of gear whine and engine noise.

"You had better *try* to look like you can walk anyway. You'll get a few days in the stockade if the captain sees you lying there like that," the driver shouted over his shoulder, but only loud enough for me to hear.

I stirred and tried to sit. I was disoriented. The word *drunk* came to mind, but it seemed wrong. After I was seated, I looked down at myself. I was clothed in a brown leather jacket and pants with sheepskin showing at the ends of the sleeves. It did not seem like me, but there was a familiar faint blue glow around me.

The Jeep was proceeding at its top speed of about forty-five miles per hour down a long concrete strip. Green shapes started to come into focus as we passed them. Some were very noisy, others seemed to be coughing and whining. None of my senses seemed to be working right. I could see with limited clarity up close, but my vision past a few feet was only a blur. I could hear what was said around me and seemed to understand what was said, but could not act on anything. I seemed to be here, wherever here was, and the driver knew me even though I had never seen him before.

Finally, my vision had cleared enough to see that the green coughing blobs were B-17 bombers. The loud noises were those already running, and the coughing was the Pratt and Whitney radial engines sputtering to life. The images were familiar. The letters on the pages of a book that I had absorbed began to flow and float in front of me. It was a description of what I was experiencing. When a photo in the book came into view, the Jeep skidded to a stop. The page in the book slowly lowered out of view, and I was looking at the same image in front of me, but for real this time.

"Come on, Dan. Don't you have enough pictures yet? All you do is take those things," someone was shouting from beside the plane.

Several men gathered around the Jeep, looking at me.

"You're gonna kill yourself, Will. It just ain't worth it. Not every night, it ain't." A childlike face came closer. The blue eyes and a mop of blond hair sticking out from under a baseball cap added to his young appearance.

"Get him in the plane. Where is the captain?" the man who had been driving asked.

"He went to see the colonel. Something about the map being wrong. Where did you find him this time?" a disembodied voice returned.

"He was just standing out near the gate, still too drunk to move. That girl must have the constitution of an elephant. She meets him at the gate every night, and he comes back like this every morning," the driver replied.

"How does he get by with it? How does he get off base every night?" another asked.

"Not sure about that, but it will be it for all of us if we get caught," the driver shot back.

By this time, the small group had ushered me into the rear of the plane and dumped me on a seat just inside the doorway.

"Load the ammo. Everything you can get. This is gonna be a bad one. I'll start the pre-flight," the driver said, looking down at me and shaking his head.

"Dan, stow the camera and pour some coffee down him," he added.

"Yes, sir. Coffee may not help, but a few 109s and firing his fifty will sober him right up. Always does. Haven't seen him this bad this late, though. Must have been quite a night," Dan said.

My vision had failed again, so I could not see Dan. He calmly moved around near me, shuffling things, and eventually started pouring a vile liquid into my mouth. It resembled coffee, but barely.

"Yup," he said, as he tried to poison me time and time again. "When this war is over, I'm gonna write a book about it all and make myself a fortune. I'll get married and get elected president. Yup, that's it, president."

There was a jolt. I was standing up beside Dan looking at the hapless body I had been inside of. He was a short man with curly hair and a dark completion. His dark brown eyes were bloodshot, and he looked very unkempt.

He sat up quickly and looked around. He looked directly at me, startled.

"Who are you?" he shouted, pointing at me.

Dan turned slightly to make sure no one had slipped up behind him and shook the man in front of him slightly. This turned his attention back to Dan.

"You had too much hooch again last night. Nobody's there. That Limey moonshine is gonna kill you if you don't stop. What's her name, Linda, will finish you off, if that nitro her dad makes don't first. That is if the Jerrys or the captain don't beat them to it, Tim. Drink some more."

Tim looked directly at me. His eyes told me that he could not see me this time. His eyes seemed to clear quickly, but there was a slight blue glow that surrounded him now. It was as if he had been exposed to the energy field from the ship. It was a soft glow, meaning that his exposure had been light, but it was definitely there. The possibility of exposure to me or some other unknown source occurred to me, but I would probably never know how he was exposed. I accepted that and continued to observe, since I had no real choice.

"There was someone there. Just a minute ago. A guy in a white coat. Like a doctor or something," he said, dodging the rank cup of liquid. He stood up and looked around, waving his hand through me. "I swear he was right there."

"Sit down," Dan said, pushing Tim in the stomach and causing him to flop back to his seat. "Drink! We'll be taking off soon."

"No! I'm fine! You know I don't like coffee. Especially that strong," Tim insisted.

The other three men entered, carrying boxes of ammo, and interrupted them. In the boxes were belts of fifty-caliber cartridges for the weapons on board the plane.

"You weren't fine five minutes ago. You were out of your mind, drunk," Dan continued, as he started to help stow the boxes that were entering in a steady flow.

"Couldn't have been. Drunk, I mean. I only had a few beers. Linda and I were going to call it an early night. We sat at the pub and talked for a while and decided that we would have a shindig this weekend or next time I got leave. I think I'm gonna ask her to marry me," Tim said, getting clearer with every word he spoke.

"Marriage now," Dan spouted. "I knew she had you when you started sneaking off base. Have to be in 'love' when you want to get shot to see her," Dan said in a fanciful tone.

Everyone laughed but Tim.

"No! Really, you guys. I did not get drunk. We went outside to where the bikes were at, and I kissed her goodnight. I got on the bicycle to head back to the base, and it looked like somebody hit us with a searchlight. It was dark outside, really dark, then it was brighter than daylight. The wind blew a little, and the next thing I remember was the lieutenant putting me in the Jeep," Tim said excitedly.

"Yeah, yeah, that's what they all say," the baby-faced blond said with a wave of his hand.

The conversation was interrupted by the whine of the starter of the number three engine. Everyone froze and looked forward.

"Get in position," Dan said, moving forward past the others. "The captain can't be happy if he's firing up without talking to us first. Let's go get that ammo stowed. And get strapped in." He had lost his quiet demeanor and started giving orders.

Things became a bit jumpy from there on. It seemed like I was losing connection with what was going on around me. I thought about it, and it seemed to be following the pages of the book again. At first, I was living inside Tim, then only watching him. Now it was vague at times, but after scrutiny it followed the information available. The detailed portions were areas where the books I had read overlapped in description. The more information I had on the subject, the more detailed simulation I was afforded. It did not explain why I assumed Tim's identity, why he seemed to recover after I stopped, or why I felt as if I was him during that time. There was a connection there I would have to look into.

The planes were lined up on the runway, and one by one they took flight into the foggy skies. The sinking feeling of when the plane leaves the ground followed a long, bumpy run. The smell of fuel, paint, exhaust, and something musty overwhelmed me, but did not seem to bother the others. They sat with grim expressions on their young faces, knowing the possibilities of survival were bleak.

The plane lurched, and the sound of debris hitting the plane was loud and obvious. A rolling blast of flame boiled in through both waist gun openings. The shuddering and bouncing was short-lived, and then the captain's voice rang out into the headset Dan was wearing.

"Get everyone checked out then look us over. We can't see anything damaged from up here. We will be at altitude shortly," the metallic voice chimed.

There was no need for Dan or anyone else to ask what had happened. They had not seen it until now, but all knew that two of the planes ahead of them had a midair collision. In the fog-laden skies over Britain, it happened all too often. There was no hope for the crew of either plane, because if anyone did survive the crash and explosion that followed, they were too close to the ground for a parachute to do them any good.

Dan checked everyone, and then they all split up to look for damage. It was not normal for anyone to move around until the plane finished its initial ascent, because it was going up and turning sharply in an upward spiral. It was difficult to maintain your balance and it added to the difficulty of controlling the plane. These were not normal circumstances.

Once the plane had leveled off, the inspection was completed and there was no visible damage. Tim motioned for Dan to come back to the right waist gunner's station, looking like he was going to be sick. Dan was the medical officer on board, but his title was engineer. Tim pointed to the floor when Dan arrived. There was an arm lying on the floor, clad in the same flight jacket they all wore. There were spots and tracks of blood and smaller parts marking the walls leading to the next bulkhead, but nothing that could not wait until their return to base. After a short moment of uncertainty and nausea, Dan lifted the arm, carried it forward, and wrapped it gently in a blanket for storage until they got back. He returned to his station and hooked in his radio.

"No damage that we can find, sir. We did catch part of a crewman though. I have the arm stowed amidships." There was no immediate reply.

"We'll have someone get in close and have a look as soon as we can. If we see *anything,* we will return to base, but we have lost two planes already. If we can make it, we need to. Everybody check in. Let's make sure the com system is working. We'll be okay," the captain finally replied.

One by one, all ten men called in to assure they and their equipment were okay. Later, another bomber flew around them—top, bottom, both sides, front, and back. No problems could be found, at least from that distance. The mission was still on. Everyone moved to their stations, plugged in their heated suits, and prepared for the long day ahead of them.

Things skipped ahead to the bomb run. It was a straight, tightly bunched flight path that led to the target they planned to bomb. It was designed to promote greater accuracy in payload delivery. Large explosions began to erupt outside the plane, and the sounds of debris raining into the plane would shortly follow some of them.

"Jenny's going down," Tim yelled into the oxygen mask after activating the radio at his throat. Outside the opening, he stood in front of the plane that had Jenny (an artist's rendering of one of the crewmen's girlfriend) on the nose started to fall. The right wing folded upward at the point where the flames were shooting from it. The bomber fell downward and to the right, starting to spin as it dropped. One of the German eighty-eight millimeter "flack" shells had found its mark.

"Look for chutes. Everybody look for chutes," the captain's voice rang in their ears. They had to report any sightings of parachutes after the mission, but it was more important to see that their friends and fellow airmen had made it out. There were none. Over a major city, as they were now, escape was unlikely, but survival started with an open parachute. Today, Jenny took all her men to the ground with her. She had started to spin out of control on her plunge into the city, and the centrifugal force of that spin held the helpless crew pinned inside until the crash.

The instant the bombs were released, the plane lurched upward. It was the release of the tons of weight the bombs represented. As they fell, so did I. It was as if I had fallen through the floor, pushed out as the plane moved upward.

In an instant I was standing inside a factory of some sort. Somehow I knew it was before the bombs had been dropped. The screaming of air raid sirens became apparent to me, and the workers standing around various types of machinery became more and more anxious. Several abandoned their machines and ran for the door that was blocked by guards. Nazis armed with machine guns turned them back.

"Return to work. They are going to another part of the city. There is nothing to fear," they ordered in German, but I could understand every word. It was quite odd because I did not know German, I thought.

The workers, with constant glances and sometimes long stares upward, reluctantly returned to their jobs. They knew if they didn't, the guards would shoot them. They had seen it before. And then they were gone. In slow motion I watched everything around me erupt in flames and destruction. The guards had been wrong. The facility was the target on that day. All but one woman inside died. Most were vaporized along with everything else. Some of the larger equipment was thrown blocks away, but basically there was nothing left where the factory was now a crater. Hilda Schultz, although severely injured, would survive and relive her agony, telling Dan her story for his book. With that I stepped back into the lab.

46

I STOOD AND DIGESTED WHAT I had just witnessed. It was more realistic than the colonial battle. It appeared that with enough information, I could be wherever the porthole took me. I reviewed the book that Dan had written, letter by letter. It had no mention of the events before takeoff. I was apparently watching actual events as they unfolded. Even the fact that body parts had been recovered on that flight was omitted from the book due to respect and etiquette. Yet I knew all of what I saw was true.

The blue glow Tim had emitted was somehow connected. Without further research it would remain a mystery, but somehow he had been exposed to the alien power source that was now affecting me. I stored all the facts for later review.

I started to look into my memory for the greatest amount of information I had acquired. It was on the American Civil war. I started to access the information in an orderly fashion, putting things in a chronological framework. There were sketchy details of several battles and the surrender at Appomattox, but little real detail. There had been many books on the battle of Shiloh, several with firsthand accounts of the carnage there. As I delved through the details, the photo on the wall that held this information moved to me instead of my having to seek it out. It moved ever forward, growing to life size and crashing into me as if it were a train out of control.

I was standing in the rain and cold, looking at a line of Confederate soldiers. It was nearing dawn, and there was little else for them to do but stand and wait for the battle to begin. I could feel the cold and the rain pelting my lab coat. I was soon soaked to the bone and felt as if I would freeze. Activity started at dawn. The rain had stopped and the carnage began. Like before, I walked the battle-field and watched thousands die. The death was the same as before, but just on a grander scale. At the sunken road, hundreds died in mere seconds and the fighting raged for hours. The tactics used were much the same as the revolutionary battle I had witnessed. Frontal assault by great numbers to overrun the enemy's position was the strategy, but it failed to work. The results did not change, nor did the tactics, just the number of dead.

At the end of the first day, thousands lay dead. Medical advances had been made, but not in battlefield care. They had little knowledge of germs, or any real way to repair any injury. They could only try to save a life by stopping the bleeding, which in most cases meant amputation. When opiate pain relief ran out, they simply held down the soldier and amputated anyway. It was the only real way they had to help. Most died, some lived, but all would have perished without help.

At the end of the first day, the Confederate command had the impression that the battle had been won and relayed that to most of the troops. It was far from the truth. Much was to be learned on both sides about warfare.

At the start of the second day, the Union was reinforced and the Confederates were in disarray. Thinking the battle had been won, the Confederates were relaxed and overconfident. It was their downfall. The second day did not register as many casualties as the day before, but was a total rout of the Southern Army. They were run off the battlefield and forced to abandon the town and ground that they had held, leaving weapons and men to be taken by the advancing Union army. As I watched the Union advance stop and the Confederate retreat continue, I stepped back into the lab.

47

I AGAIN ASSIMILATED THE KNOWLEDGE I had gained. I had not experienced a representation of that battle; I had actually watched it happen. I had heard and felt every second of it, looked at the face of every soldier, and watched everyone who died pass on. It was an odd feeling knowing that much, but it seemed to have quenched the thirst for knowledge I had about war. It was horrible, and that was the only fact that stood out.

The next sufficient amount of information I had to look into the past was about George Washington. I had liked his story in school, but still had only fragments about the first part of his life. Somehow I focused in on the last days of his life. There was a photo in one of the books of his study.

I was there. A small fire crackled in the rear of the room. Everything was well-placed and in order inside. My fascination was interrupted by the sound of boots hitting the hardwood floor.

"Oh. Hello, Terrance. How are you today?" George Washington said, entering the room. His voice was deep, raspy, and very British.

"I'm well, sir, and you?" I replied, as if we were old friends.

"All is well, although I'm not feeling my best, but I have things to do. What have we come to visit about today?" he asked, placing his hat on the desk and taking a seat behind it.

"I just came to see how you were. Wanted to talk," I replied, trying to hide my nervousness.

"We have talked several times over the years, and each time you have filled my ears with information about how I will be remembered for recent happenings. I still do not understand you or why you visit, but I enjoy our conversations. You are so... insightful."

"For me, this is our first conversation, sir. I will accept your word that we have visited before, because I am not sure why or how this is really happening. I am just proud to actually get to speak to the father of our country."

"That is a new phrase you must have picked up. I assume you are referring to me. Is that how I will be remembered? Bloody historians! Never wanted all that rubbish," he said deliberately.

We talked for about an hour. We talked about how America would grow into the most powerful country in the world and about how he would be revered as the father of that nation for at least the next two hundred or more years. He was both happy and disheartened that the other founding fathers had been so overlooked in history, but had no real choice in the matter. He seemed to have a realistic take on most things. I did find it strange that he was not frightened to see me. An apparition from the future should have made him at least nervous. I asked him about it.

"The first time you showed up, you bloody well nearly scared me to death. I was much younger then and had not started my adventuresome ways. There was something calming about you after a few moments. I rather liked it and you, even if you still refuse to tell me anything of real importance. I made up my mind that I wasn't crazy and you were really here. The rest was simple. I didn't understand, but there was no harm in you, so what difference would it make? I did decide to keep you a secret, just in case I was crazy. Sorry, but I must go. Have some crops to look at. Thinking about going to Philadelphia to see that scoundrel Adams in a few days. Have to get things in order."

"Thank you for your time, sir," I said, and he left the room. I stepped back into the lab, realizing that on that night he had contracted the sickness that would cost him his life. I felt fortunate in two ways. One, for actually having seen him in person, and another, for telling him how great America had become. Unfortunately, it was shortly before he died. The thought crossed my mind that I could have given him some disease from my time, but it was hardly possible since it was not really I that was there.

48

I WAS DRAWN AWAY FROM my thoughts. Ned was saying something. It was a whisper at first, and then it slowly became clear.

"We have more books if you are ready."

I did not answer but absorbed them.

"How long have they been out there?" I asked him.

"A month since you flashed the last stack of books. We had these in here two weeks ago, but you didn't respond. Every few hours I would come down to the front here and call to you. Glad to see you finally answered. We were going to start cutting the power," he answered.

"Bring Bea to where you are. Get a large pad of drawing paper and several sharpened pencils. I have a project for all of you."

"Your dad has the sand business up and running. He met some guys that helped him get started. He hired one of them. They have sold a few loads already."

"It is a good cover. We were very fortunate to acquire the location. It will have to be maintained for an indefinite period of time to cover what we are about to do," I told him, and he left to retrieve Bea.

When they returned, I began to instruct them in what to do.

"Touch the back of your head to the glass," I instructed her, and with pencil and paper in hand she complied. She started to draw. Page after page she filled, each covered with drawings I was placing in her mind. When we were done, she leaned forward, amazed with what she held in her hands.

She had sketched eight drawings, each a time progression of the other that started with Confederate soldiers on a wagon. The next showed them struggling near a river as if the wagon was stuck in the mud. Next, they were hiding its contents, and then the wagon was gone and just the river was there. The last few showed how the river changed over the years, and the last was where the wagon had sat in relation to where the new sand business was located.

"One day soon, we will recover the remaining gold buried there. It is a local legend that the wagon was full when it was abandoned. Many have looked, and a few have been close, but none have realized two things: the soldiers took a less common trail while trying to be more discreet and that the wagon was unloaded. All that could be carried away was, and those facts were lost in the waning days of the war. There were plans to recover it at first, but only a few knew of the shipment, and so with the death of a few it soon became lost to all. It will secure our future," I told Bea.

"You seem to be able to zero in on Confederate gold pretty easy," she replied, still looking over her accomplishment.

"That's what is available. We are, and have been, in the south. There was consistent activity in this general area for a prolonged period of time. It considerably increases the odds of successfully finding relics. Also, I believe that the equipment I have joined with was in the process of making a mineral survey when the mission was interrupted. In theory, that fact makes locating precious metals far easier. Less valuable items will be forthcoming," I returned.

"So what do you want me to do with these?" she asked, finally getting her fill of looking at the drawings.

"Show them to everyone and together decide on your plan of action. Check back with me and I will approve or disprove the plan. One of the dump trucks will need to be available to haul away the gold. It would be advisable to recover it on a weekend morning at first light. There is far less activity in the area at that time. I will review the plan and dates to guarantee success."

With that, she headed upstairs where Ned and Floyd were asked to wait.

49

OVER THE NEXT FEW DAYS, several plans to recover the gold were discussed, but one problem or another appeared as I reviewed future events. There were also power problems. As I stretched the limits of my future vision, the power drain became excessive. Breakers were thrown, wires burned, and the portable generators outside failed from overload. I began to become concerned that we would be unable to recover the one thing that I could see as stability in our future.

Power was the problem. It would help to move to a more commercial area with even more voltage available. It was impractical to try to move this soon after getting established where we were. The nearest property that would fit our new needs was miles away, and that in itself was enough to look for alternatives. I found one. I shut down all activity and started to store energy again.

When the energy reserve level was high enough again, I opened a portal to the intact ship again. I knew, somehow, that there was a plasma power source there that would solve the problem I had.

The crackling oval disc formed in front of me, and the deck of the ship was only a step away. I took that step and was on the craft instantly. Once again, the military personnel onboard were frozen in time, locked in place as I moved freely around them. I had the urge to paint them green, to make them look like the toy soldiers I had been given as a child but never played with. They just seemed too simple to be any fun. The sensation passed quickly, and I returned to the task at hand. I gathered the awful tasting balls of connectivity from several stations and put them in my coat pocket. When I requested the station to dispense them, each one became active. Each seemed more familiar than the single console I had activated before. I was not sure if I knew more or if the others were just simpler.

I made my way lower into the ship. Three decks down, there seemed to be a section for storage. I located the item I was looking for. It was a yellow rectangle about four feet long, three feet high, and three feet wide. It had what looked like a layered, glass-covered opening on each end. There were no handles or handholds anywhere to be found, so I simply slid my right hand under the center and lifted it to my shoulder. I knew then that my power reserves were beginning to fade. It was time to leave. I also knew now that this generator would temporarily solve my difficulties. I felt that it was input from the systems around me that gave me the insight I had. It did not seem like fact but more like a subtle suggestion. In the storage compartment, the portal opened again and I stepped back into my lab.

I sat the portable plasma generator down about four feet from the amplifier. I pointed one of the glass bowl indentions on the generator at the large glass bell and walked away. It sprang to life and shot a six-inch beam of blue light at the amplifier. I felt the power spike inside me. Everything inside the lab became crystal clear. It was like living with a candle for light and suddenly having bright halogen lights. I felt spectacular!

"Cut the external generators. Return them. We need them no longer," I told Ned in the control room.

He complied as he should, slowly lowering the RPMs of each engine, then allowing each to cool at idle before shutting them down completely. Once at an idle, the generator to each was released from its load as remote breakers were thrown.

"Now lower the other output to fifty percent."

Ned complied once again, slowly lowering the input from the power lines to half of its maximum capacity.

"That will suffice."

There was a pause for several seconds, then it looked as if lighting struck inside the lab repeatedly. Ned stood at the ready waiting orders. None came.

Instead I merely told him, "We will recover the gold this Sunday. It will go well. Gather here Saturday afternoon and I will give all of you the details."

Ned settled in for the remainder of his time on duty for that day. Inside, I started to explore the new world that had been opened by limitless power.

50

BEA HAD ABSORBED MORE OF the plasma energy than any of the others, so she was the easiest to make contact with. With my newfound power source and the lack of tracking from the intact ship, I could afford small breaches of security. I knew it would be only a matter of time before someone figured out how to turn the console back on and relink my signature with that ship, but for now we were relatively safe.

"Dig here," Bea said in a strange voice. She stabbed the ground with the shovel she was carrying and walked on slowly. Floyd casually took the shovel and started to dig. Mom and Dad joined him, but Ned followed Bea, who was walking slowly forward. Her steps were awkward and spastic.

"Here," she said, burying her foot in the loose sand. Her eyes were glassy and her voice sounded more like two people talking in unison.

"Are you okay? Terry told me to watch you," Ned said with true concern.

"I can see it Ned," she said in her haunting voice. "The river was between us and the others. The men were here. I can hear their voices. 'The Yanks won't ever get this gold. We have to get at least some of it to the captain. Put some on each side of the *crick*. Take all you can carry. We'll be back for the rest when we can get another wagon. They went that way toward the south, toward Houston. The river moved south later after a massive flood." Her bright blue eyes twinkled as if there were tiny lights inside and turned more normal. She shuddered and stumbled as if she would fall. Ned caught her instantly, holding her gently, his love for her showing obviously. She assured him it was only the effects of not being mentally connected to me anymore, that she would be fine, and with that she took one of the shovels he had and started to dig.

"Do you think Edna is going to be all right?" Bea asked Floyd, as everyone took a short break.

"She just hasn't felt good for the last... well, sometime now. Something going around probably. I'll take her into Humble to see a doctor if she doesn't get better in the next couple of days," he said, filling a cup from the five-gallon metal water can they had placed on a small stump convenient to both digging sites.

"You don't think it could have something to do with Newton and all this nonsense we've gone through, do you?" she asked.

"I don't think so," Floyd said with doubt in his voice. "What has happened to all of us is fantastic and impossible to believe, but I can't see any of it hurting us after all the good it has done. If it has hurt us, then there's really nothing we can do anyway. Lord knows it will have made our last days much more interesting than sitting at the house, waiting to see who passes first." His voice had regained its hard tone by the time he had finished, and he started back to the dig, shovel in hand.

"Newton!" Bea yelled. "You talk to me!" she continued yelling into the air.

Everyone turned and looked at her because of the outburst.

"What's wrong with Edna? You said you would look after us! Now tell me what's making her sick! It can't be you, can it, my boy?" sounding at the end more like her real age than how she appeared now.

Suddenly, she threw her hand to her face, covering her nose and mouth and looking down as she blushed heavily. She chuckled and became even redder as she looked from Floyd to the rest of the group.

"Should I tell them?" she asked the air, still giggling. "Okay," she added and picked up her shovel to start digging again.

"Well, let's have it," Floyd said sternly, stepping close to Bea as she casually walked away from the water can.

"She will be fine," Bea said smugly. She smiled and touched her finger to Floyd's nose. "Besides, it's all your fault," she said, taking another step, keeping her eyes locked on his by turning her head as the rest of her moved on.

"My fault," Floyd half shouted indignantly. "How could I have made her sick?"

Everyone had closed ranks, gathering to hear the news as Bea continued to taunt Floyd. She threw her arms out in front of her as if carrying a large bag and puffed out her cheeks, then started to walk as she was carrying a ton of weight. Round and round she went inside the newly formed circle of her friends. In part because of their real age and her bad acting, the others just stared at her attempt at charades. When it did not work, she grabbed Floyd in a wild hug and kissed him lightly on the cheek.

"Congratulations, *Dad*!" she spat out with a loud laugh.

Floyd departed from his usual steely disposition and flopped down, having a seat on the soft sand. There was a round of congratulations from everyone, and Floyd quickly recovered to his normal self, except for the broad grin on his face.

"Well, let's get back to it. Have to provide for the family now, don't we?"

The conversation soon faded as the reality of moving large amounts of sand settled back in. It was fine and dry and ran like water. Unlike digging in dirt, much more had to be moved to get the hole opened.

Ned struck first.

"I've got something," he shouted to alert the others that he and Bea had reached their goal.

"Careful. You don't want to damage it," Tupnic said. "We could lose it easily in the sand."

"That's why we had to do this by hand instead of using that awful tractor," Bea cautioned him.

"That guy can see anything. I think he just wanted to see us work all day," Ned said, only half kidding.

The reason for caution soon became apparent as they uncovered remnants of burlap bags. There were large black lumps of metal inside their meager remains, and as the first was freed and lifted out it fell into a scattered pile of coins. Bea picked one up and looked it over carefully.

"This is a US coin. It's a double eagle. Lord, there are thousands of them here," she said in awe.

"Get the blanket. We'll lift them out of the hole and lay them there until we get them all out. If we had hit them with the front-end loader we would have scattered them all over the place. Probably would have lost plenty. Here, let's lower things here so we can put the blanket there. We won't have to lift them as far at first," Floyd said, passing out directions in his usual take-charge manner.

Everyone complied, and soon eight separate stacks had been exhumed, each about the size of a five-gallon pail. Once satisfied that everything was recovered there, the other site got everyone's attention. It was not coins they found this time, but bars. They had corroded and looked black on the outside. Without knowing, most people would pass it off as trash or decaying wood, without looking long enough to find its real value. The bars were carefully separated and stacked on the edge of the hole so they could be loaded easily.

The fortune in precious metal was soon loaded in the bucket of the front-end loader, transferred to the waiting company dump truck, and was ready for transport. Once the last bar was loaded, a feeling of relief passed over everyone and a small celebration broke out. Like little children, they ran to the river and plunged into its cool water. There was a deep spot in the edge of the curve where they entered, and for half an hour they played, enjoying their newfound freedom. At the lab, one wall displayed their actions as if I was standing on the hill above, observing.

*****

51

KELLY REALIZED, AS THE IMAGES faded, that he had been surrounded by a three-dimensional representation of what he was seeing. Now, it was just the fireplace, the two plush chairs, and dead silence.

"You are aware of the company we represent," Tupnic broke the silence.

"To a certain extent. It's one of the world's most valuable and diverse. Into everything from energy to speculation," Kelly replied.

"Most of the rewritten history over the last few decades has been ours, and most of the technology that you see that generates a blue light came from our lab, or from here to be exact. I engineer a product or improve one and have Ned's branch sell the basic idea to a larger development company. Most are worth millions. I still like the archeological finds more than the others. My mom will pick an event and do research for a proper amount of time. For appearances, she then turns it over to me and I go there, just like you and I reviewed our beginning. I can be a part of it or just observe. I like to observe most of the time. It is too easy to damage the timeline," Tupnic explained.

"I suppose you could easily think of yourself as a god with all the power you have. Is that how you see yourself?" Kelly probed, letting his reporter instincts show.

"I am far from a god, and resent that accusation," Tupnic replied flatly.

"Has this power let you see God himself?" Kelly shot back.

"With that line of thinking, if I appeared to a caveman with a butane lighter, he would probably worship me. Most likely, from my observations, he would break open my head and make a bowl from my skull. I am just a man with a machine, nothing more than the car you own. It does things that you do not understand, but that does not make it magic, Mr. Kelly. I know that good and evil is out there, especially when I am powered up. I choose to believe that the good is God, but I have no concrete proof of that, it is just my belief. I can feel both tug at me from time to time. I choose to take the side of good. I protect my family and friends, and try to simply live out the rest of my life. I try not to change anything, except in the course of those two goals. If we are located, our lives are over as we know them, and I am not sure how long any of us would survive at all. To that end, we move around from time to time, inside the state or dimensionally, and I choose very carefully where we go. It can only be a place where we are safe, and no other 'us' will be compromised."

"Fair enough. Any other amazing things you can do that you haven't told me about, like that eye thing all those people were doing before when I was freaking out on the sidewalk?" Kelly asked.

"The 'eye thing' you referred to is a side effect of someone outside this facility being in contact with me. Certain DNA profiles make it more likely that I can communicate with an individual. On a purely subconscious level of course, in most cases, other than those you know about. I risk being discovered by the government each time I communicate in that way, but after review, I take the chance at times. I felt it necessary to observe you as closely as possible for a short time. The phenomena you observed was the least likely way I am afforded to observe you without being caught. When the eyes appear to flash I am seeing through the eyes of that person.

"I have also found that at the time a fetus dies before being born, if I become aware of the pending tragedy, I can share a small jolt of the plasma energy to sustain the life. It also gives me a link to that person for their entire life. It is a great source of information."

"You can save lives with this stuff," Kelly said in disbelief.

"If I am aware of the event and there is not any significant physical damage, yes. It is not unlike the electric shock given to someone when their heart stops, except I retain limited contact with them."

"How do you know when they need help?" Kelly asked.

"I just do," Tupnic replied. "You met Carl. He is one that would not be here without the plasma spark I provided. His parents chose to come to America, and it just so happened that he came to be in my service. He is fiercely loyal, and I am not sure if the energy has anything to do with it or not. I certainly hope it doesn't. I would prefer to think it has no effect at all." Tupnic paused then continued, "The offer still stands, Mr. Kelly. I can show you anywhere and anytime you wish. You just have to report it in a way that will not lead anyone to my associates or me. Time begins to get short. The trucks have arrived."

The comfortable surroundings started to dissolve, and they moved from inside the room with a fireplace to standing in an open field.

"I like it outside. Don't get a chance to get out much," Tupnic said, clearly in awe of the scenery. Kelly stood there looking at his feet, and not the large open field that they stood in now.

"How did you get new identities for everyone?" Kelly asked without looking up.

"Before the age of electronic record keeping, it was not too complicated to switch your personal records. You simply had to find a name of someone who died early in life that had not generated any permanent records. File a request in that person's name for a birth certificate, and you became them. It was that simple. There was no cross-reference to death records, so that was about all it took. I made the search easier by checking each name prior to the application date," Tupnic explained.

"How did you turn everyone young again, and why am I not affected like that?" Kelly asked, raising his head to meet Tupnic's steel gray eyes.

"It was a mistake. All of this was a great error. I took the nodule that the ship produced to help enhance connection at the console. Its function was simply to make work easier for all involved. Once I ingested it, thinking it was a jellybean, I was connected to the ship and all its technology, especially the H333 console. That was the designation given to that panel by the ARGO Lab, and I was assigned to research its function. I had part of another device at the time of activation, and it was part of the drive control. When both components were activated without their related parts, it created the effects you saw. An envelope was created around me, and the reserve energy was released. That envelope has yet to close. My concern at the time was for Bea, and my anger was directed at the people who wanted to hurt her. The results were obvious. As I slowed in time, I had thoughts of my parents, and that is why they were affected. The bubble expanded to envelop Floyd and Edna next door, because it lay in direct line with Mom and Dad. My only conclusion is that as I resolved myself to dying at the hands of the soldiers that day, I was thinking that I was only twenty-one years old and too young to die. Everyone affected that day, that survived, ended up at roughly that age. There is some variance but not much. The communication then and still today is beyond my control. Their language and thinking process is so alien to us that it may never be possible to fully understand them. With total access to the surviving ship, and time, I could decipher and understand everything I have come to believe, but that would be impossible. I would be discovered and captured if I tried to attempt anything more than a few moments per attempt. No parts removed from the ship would function independently either. It is integrated together like a person's brain. The bio-organic nature of the systems link together, and when unlinked they function with different parameters. Much of the design came from the brains of the Dane themselves. At a molecular level, I have basically ingested reproduced brain matter from ages-dead Dane volunteers. Some spent most of their adult lives strapped to a chair with their skulls open and sections of their brains harvested for the system to be successful, all for the good of the Dane race. The lack of emotion was programmed in later. It was considered advantageous to the function of each crewmember to react thoughtfully and not emotionally. That is why in the first days of our adventures, no one lost their mind under the circumstances. That too is why you are as calm as you are now. Helpful, I always thought."

"Quite," Kelly said with an almost sincere smile, which quickly faded.

"What about finding all that gold at first? How and what was that all about? I mean, how did you just zero in it without having any real control?" he continued.

"It was like being caught in two thoughts at first. The crewman at the H333 station was searching for minerals when whatever caused the ship to crash happened. Both the added technology and I locked in on gold and protection. I still locate all sorts of precious metals. I have a long list."

The field vanished and they were standing in white, no floor or walls, just white. A list of words started to flow up the wall Kelly was facing.

"All an accident," Kelly said flatly.

"Completely. Even what progress I have made in controlling the effects are by trial and error. With the portable plasma generator, I have had only marginal success in understanding any part of what I have become," Tupnic replied.

"Have you ever used your power to influence events to flow more favorable for you and your little group?" Kelly asked.

"No," Tupnic said slowly. "My efforts have been to preserve the timeline and keep us safe. Jumps have been used for that sole purpose. I research and observe time in all forms but make all efforts to only observe. It is also useful to occupy my time. Without my observations I would have little to do.

"I have located artifacts that would have gone unclaimed for years, possibly never found. That in itself changes things, but it is not an effort to change the line but preserve our safety. Our original dimension, I will call it that, was a victim of the device and the organic matter it is made of. By bonding my DNA to all females ready to conceive, it has destroyed that world. In the beginning, there was a mix of joy and anger. It was the unexpected news that drove both, but it became much worse as the months passed. Many women lost their husbands or boyfriends when the pregnancy became obvious, and upon the births of blond-haired, blue-eyed children all over the world, the murders started. The images of sorrow filled one of the walls. Infidelity was the first accusation. The punishment continued as children orphaned or in good homes grew up, married, and started having children of their own. The gene pool was so corrupted that the infant death and deformity rate soared. Once DNA testing was available, it told a sad tale and quickly became a lawful requirement before marriage. The discovery of so many children not belonging to their presumed fathers led to more bloodshed and couples separating in every fashion imaginable. The truth that a common source of DNA was the cause was kept secret from the public, for there was no logical explanation. Only the unexplainable could account for any of it. The birth rate declined so severely that the planet was in danger of economic collapse. A worldwide voluntary donor-breeding program was started, but there is little hope that any society will survive. It will bring them back to the dark ages before they start to turn around, if ever. Since then I have been in control, relatively speaking. There has been no attempt made to take control or even communicate. I don't know if it is just suppressed, burned out, or somehow afraid. For that matter, I don't even know if any of those things are possible. It seems to be submissive or cooperating with me now. Possibly the compound has simply integrated into my molecular structure and no longer is separate from me."

"You said that my DNA was a close match to yours. Wouldn't your parents be a closer match?" Kelly asked.

"I am a combination of the two. The results make us a closer overall match than either of my parents," Tupnic replied.

"So how does it work, this moving to another dimension?" Kelly asked.

"Without my regard for preserving what seems like normality for my friends and I, it is relatively simple. I just concentrate on another portal and it appears. I move through and decide from there which timeline to occupy."

"That simple, is it?" Kelly smiled.

"A suitable analogy would be to enter the center lane of a freeway on a one-way, one-lane ramp. This freeway has an infinite number of lanes with an infinite number of cars packing the lanes. In each car, I choose to put my friends and I inside. Each auto is identical as are we traveling in the same direction at different speeds. I have to choose which one best suits our needs, which amounts to making sure that everything including every speck of dust is properly placed inside and outside. I simply enter the auto, and it exits the freeway," Tupnic explained.

"Difficult?" Kelly shot back.

"So far I have seen, but not reviewed, a quadrillion to the one thousandth power possibilities. Billions of facts must be reviewed before I will allow entry. One tiny missed fact would be disastrous for us all. One fact to take into consideration is my ability to power up in an alternate dimension. Without that single fact, all would be lost and I would probably die. That would leave my friends exposed and helpless. That is the only fact out of billions upon billions I must consider before a jump. It is why I hesitate to do so. If I miss the smallest detail, it could be the end of us all."

Kelly appeared to be mulling over the facts then asked, "What about the GI that ran into the lab wall? Whatever happened to him? Was he okay?"

"Yes, James Mayhe. I visited with him in my special way a few days later posing as an intelligence officer. I questioned him and explained that what he had experienced was a new form of weapon. I did not give credit to either side in the conflict, but told him to be prepared if he was involved with it again so he could help the others around him. He swore to keep it secret until the time arose to deal with it again. He never had to. After the war, I had my mom and dad visit with him. They were posing as government officials also. They took his statement and commend his actions in the matter. He pledged to keep silent again, stating no one would believe it anyway. I kept track of him. The visit was in 1970. Both were to try to keep his life from being destroyed by that one event that neither of us could explain."

"Just how much power does that thing have?" Kelly asked.

"It will generate more power than the entire United States power grid combined for a thousand years. If it were to go critical, it has the potential to easily produce an explosion one hundred thousand times more powerful than the explosion at Hiroshima. The equipment that I have been linked to is the propulsion system. It generates a time-space distortion field that aids in the great speeds the ships are capable of. Alone they are capable of faster than light speeds, but with the distortion field the speeds become unfathomable. It revolutionized their capabilities. I generate one of those fields. That is how I do what I do. So far I am capable of about one percent of potential. The instruments produce all capabilities, then that energy is passed to the power core, which only magnifies the signal. It requires tremendous power for this process to work, which is why I was limited at first with just electricity. While I still have to have a relatively large flow, the generator provides most of the used power. Electricity is the source of the bond that makes it all work. I only need to understand how to make more of it work."

"If you and this *thing* have that much power… then why didn't you just get all of the pieces in one trip? You could have taken the amp and generator together. Seems more practical and safer. You could have taken the entire ship and solved all your problems at one time? By now you would be flying all over the universe," Kelly said slowly.

"At first I had no idea what was happening with any of this. I ingested brain cells from creatures that have been dead for centuries. With only impressions for answers, I proceeded with the answers I could find. Too many intrusions were risky, but prolonged episodes were impossible. The energy consumption was enormous at first. As I integrated with the mechanical and organic portions, functions became easier. Even today I am gaining more control and abilities.

"Taking the entire ship then was not an option. The power consumption to transfer an object that large and complex would have been too great. I could not have absorbed that much energy. A fraction of the required amount would have destroyed me.

"If it had been possible to relocate the ship it would have been fuel for ARGO to pursue us relentlessly. Their efforts have been sporadic at best. With the majority of the technology in their possession, we were mostly an afterthought. When research had a breakthrough or hit a standstill they refocused on us until they had something to focus on back at the lab. Do not think for a second that we were ever forgotten. We were just less of a priority at times.

"I feel that under the circumstances we did very well. I have viewed other possibilities regarding our survival. You have witnessed a few. The incident with the fractured amplifier, where we were burned alive, and being bombed into oblivion to name a few prove my point. It is a gamble at best. The only difference is that I can see all the cards all of the time. It helps determine the results of the game."

There was a pause and Tupnic continued.

"In or not, I must know. I must move now," Tupnic said, looking away as if there was something unseen in the sea of white.

"I'm in. Let's go," came the reply.

52

Everything started to fade. The bright white light began to fade. It became a lab with all sorts of instruments and storage cabinets. That faded after being visible for only seconds. Then there was only a chair, a large glass bell device, and large yellow block. In the chair was a contorted figure that was gray all over—clothes and all. Kelly walked close to the petrified figure, and the Tupnic he had been talking to reappeared at his side.

"This is me. The real me. I will be able to move soon," Tupnic stated, and he was gone again.

Kelly watched as the gray started to fade and the frozen figure began to stir.

"Mr. Kelly, how do I look?" Tupnic asked as he started to rise, shaking off a layer of dust. A spot of gray ran across every part of him as if chasing something.

"Can't seem to stop that," Tupnic said before Kelly could respond. "Can't stop the dust either, no matter how I filter the air. How do I look?" he repeated with a huge smile.

"Like crap," Kelly returned, matching Tupnic's smile.

"You're right. I need a haircut. Haven't had one in forty years," Tupnic said, running a hand through his dusty but still regulation military length hair.

"Call me Brad if you don't mind. You're old enough to be my dad, even if you do look twenty-one."

"Well, Brad, I really am still twenty-one. We have to go. I am exposed without the buffer field. The layer of clouds that usually surrounds me," the real Tupnic said quickly.

271

Moving from the chair, Tupnic grabbed the glass object in one hand and the generator in the other and tucked each under an arm.

"Want me to help?" Kelly asked.

"Both weigh in excess of two tons each. I must get them moved before my reserves are depleted. This way," Tupnic fired, and he made for a door in the back of the room.

"The floor is reinforced for the weight and this is how we moved in. We came to this building in about 1975. We outgrew the capabilities of the other lab rather quickly, but stayed there until it was appropriate to leave. Now a suitable location has been prepared."

"Stupid question, but how do you survive carrying all that weight? It seems like you would break something."

"I am structurally supported by the field, as will be our transportation. In order to be discreet, I had to resort to trickery. You will soon understand," Tupnic related without slowing his steady pace.

They walked down the long, winding ramp in silence for what seemed a long time. The only sounds were the loud thuds of Tupnic's footfalls and the quiet pat of Kelly's.

"It's funny, I'm not hungry or thirsty. How long were we in there? Must have been days," Kelly broke the silence.

"3.4 seconds," Tupnic answered.

Kelly stopped, too shocked to speak, but that answered the question of why he wasn't hungry. Tupnic stopped, put down both of his burdens down with a thud, and placed his right palm to his forehead. Kelly hurried to catch up. As he reached Tupnic's side, he stopped to see if he could spot a problem. Tupnic looked in pain, and Kelly carefully reached out to touch him.

Tupnic sprang on him like a wild beast after prey, grabbing him in an unbelievably tight bear hug. Kelly started to resist, but he was struck by blue lightning. The light was so intense that it pushed him to the point of unconsciousness. It flashed again and again. He began to feel sick and thought that he had lost his battle to avoid passing out. Then it was gone. Tupnic released him, gathered up his items, and started down the ramp again.

"What was all that?" Kelly asked shakily, while trying to keep up.

"We had to jump. I had hoped not to, but there was an unexpected interruption that I could not correct in time. ARGO had progressed further than I was able to monitor. It is a delicate balance of being able to spy without being found out," came the response.

"What was the light? I thought it was going to kill me," Kelly said, steadier now.

"Without the device on your head you would be little more than dust," Tupnic said casually. Kelly touched the thin metal around his head.

"I'm glad it didn't take too long. I'm not sure I could have taken a lot more. It felt like the light was so bright it went down into my bones," Kelly said, back to normal now.

"It was not light. It was plasma energy. You perceive it as light and it did get down to your bones. It penetrated the fibers of your DNA and beyond and it took four days. I spared you the details."

"What?" Kelly spat.

"It took four days in the vortex because I had to contact and move everyone involved to this dimension after I deemed it acceptable."

"You move everyone each time you jump? Why? They are the same... aren't they?" Kelly asked excitedly.

"Yes, I do move them. They are my friends and the only ones that possess the unique memories that make them... just that. *My* friends. I moved you also."

"What happened to... us where we came from?" Kelly asked cautiously.

"An agent fired his pistol at us and struck the transformer. The damage set off a chain reaction that destroyed most of Western Louisiana, Texas, and Northern Mexico. It also poisoned a large portion of the Gulf of Mexico. Along with the catastrophic loss of life, the areas' ecosystem will start to recover after ninety-eight years."

"You moved us over and allowed the destruction of our counterparts from this dimension?" Kelly stated as a question.

"With all due respect, Mr. Kelly, I had never met them. Although they resemble us, they are not."

"How do you tell them to... die?"

"I seem to be the original. I have control even over my other selves when we meet. Can't explain that either. That's just the way it is."

"I thought we were in a hurry," Kelly stated flatly.

"We are. The point was to avoid a jump. We did not avoid it, but we cannot waste time. We do not need to damage this timeline, or we will have to abandon it as well," Tupnic replied.

The ramp flattened out and Tupnic again set down what he was carrying. He walked to the cream-colored wall and stared intensely at it. It became a view of the parking lot and service road in front of the building.

"There he is," Tupnic said.

A man was on the shoulder of the 610 Loop, pretending to change a flat, but observing the building. The scene switched to five new Peterbilt trucks and new box van trailers sitting at the rear of the building.

"They have not started loading yet, so let's give our friend out there something to think about," Tupnic said, changing views back to the front. The spy had returned to the front seat of his car to check in and prolong the pretense. There was a mild flash of the blue light, and the trucks were sitting at the service road, waiting to enter. The agent on the shoulder looked shocked at the sight and quickly reported the situation.

"He thinks he went to sleep. He has no idea that I skipped him and us ahead four hours. Let's go," Tupnic said, reclaiming his items.

They passed through a set of automatic oversized doors and walked directly to the back of an old pickup with a camper shell on the back. The back of the truck opened up just as the doors of the building had. Tupnic sat the glass object down and loaded the generator first, then the other. The back closed by itself. Tupnic produced a set of keys and handed them to Kelly.

"If you would be so kind, we need to leave post haste and I need to hide as well as I can," Tupnic stated, and as soon as Kelly took the keys, both headed for their respective doors.

It was a 1971 Ford pickup, a sort of chocolate brown in color, and looked as if it had seen better days. Inside and out it was spotlessly clean. Kelly was unsure why his impression was otherwise. It started with little more than a hint from the starter and roared to life in the closed garage.

"The field makes it look ragged. It is protected by a field that makes it able to haul the weight, but look as if it is on its last leg. I have had Carl drive it to work for the last few months so nothing would seem out of the ordinary when it left," Tupnic explained.

"Great!" Kelly said excitedly. "Where are the trucks headed? Not with us, I hope. They would be hard to hide."

"They will make a round trip to Billings, Montana, and unload here when they return. I have placed a chair that I saturated with field energy in one of them. The agents looking for me will not realize that it is not me until the return trip starts. We will be protected again soon."

"Where to?" Kelly asked.

Tupnic leaned the seat back as far as possible and slumped down to be out of sight.

"Take the loop to 59 North. We will be there in about thirty-five minutes," Tupnic said and became motionless. Kelly cut through the back streets until he wound his way to TC Jester Street, crossed under the freeway, and entered the 610 traffic. They passed under I-45 and soon exited onto US 59 North on a long exaggerated ramp. Traffic was light, and Kelly was not afraid to push the speed limit. The old truck performed flawlessly. He wondered what the extent of the modifications were, but did not ask. He figured that he wouldn't understand anyway. He was onto the greatest story this planet had ever seen and would be the one to bring it to everyone's attention. When the time was right, he would.

"Exit here," Tupnic said, almost startling Kelly.

They entered the service road at FM 1485 in New Caney and made the U-turn to take them back south. About a quarter of a mile later, they turned into the drive of a new five-story building. They circled to the back and entered the small, belowground parking garage. Kelly backed up to the oversized doors as instructed.

"There was once a truck stop nearby. It gave us the ideal cover to start construction by digging up the place. Removing fuel-tainted soil, cleanup, and that sort of stuff. With lax building codes, Reggie's construction company was able to build the building I wanted. Five stories above ground and five below. It was easy." Tupnic stared as they passed through the doors.

They went inside and into a waiting elevator. It took them down five floors into a spacious but almost empty room. The only item inside was a grand but odd chair. Kelly did not need to ask what it was for or mention the updated look. Tupnic exited and came back shortly showered and with new coveralls.

Tupnic positioned the two items he had brought with him and calmly took his seat. Lying back, he looked at Kelly and smiled, then began to contort in a frozen gray statue of pain personified. The generator sprang to life, a beam of blue light shot out and connected to the amplifier, and with that the interior of the room transformed into a lab much like the other had been. The artificial Tupnic faded in beside Kelly along with George the alien tree animal.

"Well, my imaginary friend, what do we do now?" Kelly asked, excited about the possibilities now in his future.

"The first thing is for you to go to the TNT office downtown and fill out your paperwork for employment. A formality, since you actually work for us already, but official paperwork is required, unfortunately. It will give you access to company assets. In the parking lot there are several cars. One should be to your liking. The keys are locked in a cabinet you can open with your palm print. There is several hundred dollars in cash in there also. There are also new company credit cards. Feel free to take it all," Tupnic replied.

"Here alone? Well, besides me and George, that is," Kelly asked.

"This building will be Ned's new office. They will start to move in next week. It will be good to be close to them again. We have not been within miles of each other in years. It was important to remain undetected, as you can see. With this new facility, we are safe for a while. They will learn enough, sooner or later, to detect us, unless I can find a way to hide us permanently. Would you like to take a short trip?"

"Sure, why not. Where are we going now? By the way, how is everybody these days?" Kelly asked.

"Reggie and Mr. Schwartz are doing fine for approaching ninety years of age. They have hidden their real ages well. Limited exposure over time seems to extend one's life. Another corporate perk that you now share. The rest seem not to have aged more than a couple of years. Ned should have, but we suspect that it is transference of energy from the others. None have been sick or had any ill effects from exposure. Floyd and Edna's daughter is brilliant and beautiful, and also a permanent twenty-two years old. Ned and Bea are expecting again. He will have the same benefits. I have viewed ahead to make sure. They stay out of the limelight as much as possible, and we will eventually have to acquire them new identities. It is uncertain how long any of you will live."

The walls of the lab formed a black line at one end that started to sparkle on one side, then on both, as it moved toward the other end. After it had passed, Kelly and Tupnic stood on a hill of sand looking at what looked like an anthill of activity in the distance. The Sphinx stood alone, except for the foundation of a pyramid under construction.

"Are we?" Kelly stammered out.

Tupnic only nodded.

They stood for a few hours, watching. The heat of the daytime sun became torture enough to make them return to the lab.

"Were we really there?" Kelly asked.

"Yes. All indications are that we were, but I have not thought to confirm that fact as of yet."

"We will have to try it," Kelly said, enjoying the cool temperatures inside the new lab. "Is this what it will be like from now on? Will this be my life?" he asked.

"This is our life now, such as it is. You can return to your old life at any time you wish, but I think the new is much more appealing."

"I agree, especially after what I have seen today! The old days of reporting are nothing short of boring now. I have relatives that fought in the Civil War that we could check in on. See what really happened to them. Family history just got easy," Kelly said, starting to explore the possibilities.

JOHN ALLYN

"The device has some interest in the Civil War. I think it is because we were fighting against ourselves. It is a concept that was foreign to them. War, that is, especially with yourself. They progressed far past us in a shorter time because they sacrificed for the greater good of all."

"I have always wondered what would have happened if the South would have won that war," Kelly said, with fascination in his eyes.

"We shall explore your personal history soon, but now I have a few tests to run on this new facility. You will have to leave because the power levels would be fatal, even with the device. I will have to design another, perhaps an implant, so you can enter freely. Yes, that will do," Tupnic responded.

"Well, here's to the future days of old," Kelly said, raising an imaginary glass.

"Isn't that an oxymoron?" Tupnic asked, already knowing the answer.

"Such is our life now, my friend," Kelly said and started toward the door, which was now visible.

"Indeed," was Tupnic's only reply.

Kelly left the parking lot in the old pickup. He felt at home in it, and in a way it was a symbol of his old and new life. It was old, but without the power field, it appeared new. He had to pretend to be what he wasn't to get the story. Yes, the truck would do just fine for now. He would be back in a few days, as soon as he could wrap up a few loose ends.

Tupnic watched him leave on the lab wall and was a bit amused that he had not taken one of the luxury cars or the cash provided for him. He could have seen those facts if he had wished, but letting them unfold naturally seemed more acceptable in some cases.

The generator began to increase its output, and the crackling line of change began to move across the lab's interior. Tupnic stood in the air above Fort Sumter, watching the first shots fired in anger beginning the American Civil War. He considered strongly the question Kelly had asked about manipulating the timeline. Perhaps past events were pliable. He had visited the past, seen the future, and altered current events to protect his friends, but had never considered changing the past, especially for pleasure. It had been survival only up until this point. There was much to consider as the sounds of shots rang out.

In 1855, I touched the mind of Mickelberry Lindsey.

References

WHILE NO PRECISE FACTS WERE intentionally used from the books listed below, I thought these deserved an honorable mention. I read them in search of facts about family history and as research for the second book of this series.

The facts used were taken from memory and information provided by others with personal experience of the given situation. While these statements are a bit vague, I feel they are better than a lengthy explanation.

Crosby, Harry H. 1993. *A Wing and A Prayer*. Harper Collins Publishers.

The 95th Bomb Group (H) Association. 1990. *B17s over Berlin: Personal Stories from the 95th Bomb Group (H)*.

Cooling, Benjamin Franklin. 1987. *Forts Henry & Donelson The key to the Confederate Heartland*. The University of Tennessee Press/ Knoxville.

Daniel, Larry J. 1997. *SHILOH: The Battle That Changed the Civil War*.

About the Author

JOHN ALLYN WAS BORN IN the mid-1950s on the north side of Houston, Texas. He had a normal childhood and started college. His love of music took control of his life for several years. During this time, he found the love of his life and they were soon married. With only local success in music, he entered the job market and found a career in transportation management. This enabled him to begin restoring American performance classic cars.

The idea for Time Trials: H333 and the series is one that sprang from another of his passions, science fiction. Writing was always part of his life in his music, short stories, and unpublished novels. The Time Trials novels are the result of seeking an original path to successful publishing.

John still lives in the Houston area with his family.

Printed in the USA
CPSIA information can be obtained
at www.ICGtesting.com
JSHW082100060823
46003JS00001B/29